**Praise for bestselling author
SHARON SALA:**

"Ms. Sala tugs at our heartstrings
with tender persistence, making us ache
with joy and wonder."
—*Romantic Times Magazine*

**Praise for bestselling author
MARIE FERRARELLA:**

"Marie Ferrarella is a charming storyteller
who will steal your heart away."
—*Romantic Times Magazine*

**Praise for bestselling author
LEANNE BANKS:**

"When life gets tough,
read a book by Leanne Banks."
—*New York Times* bestselling author
Janet Evanovich

**SHARON SALA** realized that she was meant to be an author when she found herself loving to read, hating her job and constantly daydreaming. "I joined the Romance Writers of America and never looked back." Born and raised in Prague, Oklahoma, Sharon still lives in the state she has always called home, with her two grown daughters nearby. She describes her writing style as "instinctive. I rarely have to sit down and think of a plot or character for a new book. They are always floating around inside my head, waiting to come to life."

**MARIE FERRARELLA** swears she was born writing, "which must have made the delivery especially hard for my mother." Born in West Germany of Polish parents, she came to America when she was four years of age and settled with her family in New York. Marie wrote her first romance novel when she was eleven years old. After receiving her English degree, Marie and her family moved to Southern California, where she still resides today. Marie, who has written over 100 novels with Silhouette Books, has one goal: to entertain, to make people laugh and feel good. "That's what makes me happy," she confesses. "That and a really good romantic evening with my husband."

**LEANNE BANKS** is a national number-one-bestselling author of romance. She lives in her native Virginia with her husband, son and daughter. Recognized for both her sensual and her humorous writing with two Career Achievement Awards from *Romantic Times Magazine*, Leanne likes creating a story with a few grins, a generous kick of sensuality and characters that hang around after the book is finished. Leanne believes romance readers are the best readers in the world because they understand that love is the greatest miracle of all. You can write to her at P.O. Box 1442, Midlothian, VA 23113. A SASE for a reply would be greatly appreciated.

# Sharon Sala
## Marie Ferrarella
## Leanne Banks

# Labor of
# Love

**Published by Silhouette Books**
**America's Publisher of Contemporary Romance**

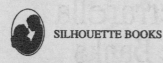

**SILHOUETTE BOOKS**

LABOR OF LOVE

Copyright © 2001 by Harlequin Books S.A.

ISBN 0-373-48450-X

The publisher acknowledges the copyright holders of the individual works as follows:

SYMPATHY PAINS
Copyright © 2001 by Sharon Sala

THE BABY IN THE CABBAGE PATCH
Copyright © 2001 by Marie Rydzynski-Ferrarella

THE MONARCH AND THE MOM
Copyright © 2001 by Leanne Banks

This edition published by arrangement with Harlequin Books S.A.

® and TM are trademarks of Harlequin Books S.A., used under license. Trademarks indicated with ® are registered in the United States Patent and Trademark Office, the Canadian Trade Marks Office and in other countries.

Visit Silhouette at www.eHarlequin.com

Printed in U.S.A.

# CONTENTS

Dear Reader,

When asked to write a story for the *Labor of Love* anthology, I of course jumped at the chance. Being a mother was, for me, the greatest accomplishment of my life. Family is the warmest security blanket a person should have, knowing as you grow that, however stupid or wrong your decisions may be, you will be forgiven first by the people who love you.

I adored my babies. They grew up far too fast. But then we are given grandchildren, and that's when fate gives us all a second chance—to do the little things with them that we didn't take time to do with our own children.

In writing "Sympathy Pains," I relived the highs and lows of being pregnant and the fear of giving birth. But there is that afterglow, much stronger and sweeter than any pain, when you look into the eyes of your child and remember the love with which they were made.

I hope as you enjoy our stories that you have had such a childhood in which you can remember the safety of a mother's unconditional love.

I love to hear from my readers and can be reached at P.O. Box 127, Henryetta, OK, 74437, or online care of eHarlequin.com.

Sharon Sala

# SYMPATHY PAINS
## Sharon Sala

This book is for my mother, Iris,
who not only gave her own children
unconditional love, but gave thirty-one years
of her life to teaching other children, as well.

Thank you, Mother, for all the nights you crept
into my room to make sure I was covered against
the cold and for the things you did for me
that I took for granted.

I love you most.

# Chapter 1

It had been snowing since daybreak. The flakes, some the size of small feathers, were falling so thick and fast that it was difficult for Marilee Cash to see the Texaco sign at the gas station across the street. The city streets in Amarillo were becoming impassable and the traffic on Interstate 27 was almost nonexistent. Interstate 40, which intersected with Interstate 27 a couple of miles north of the Roadrunner Truck Stop, where she worked, was already closed due to drifting snow. One trucker, who'd just made it through as they were closing the roads, had come into the Roadrunner talking about the six-foot-high drifts and the abandoned cars that were being buried under the snow at the sides of the road.

"Hey, honey! How about a refill?"

Marilee turned away from the window. It was the trucker who'd come in from the storm.

"Coming up," she said, and went to get the coffeepot to refill her customer's cup.

An hour came and went and still the storm showed no signs of abating. Except for Calvin, the man who owned and cooked for the Roadrunner, and three waitresses, including Marilee, the diner was empty.

Calvin came out of the kitchen, scratching his balding head as he looked out the window.

"You girls might as well go on home while you can still make it."

Marilee hesitated. "Are you sure? What if you get a diner full of stranded travelers?"

"Living in this danged old panhandle, it sure wouldn't be the first time, would it?" Then he grinned. "If I do, we'll have ourselves a party. Now, you girls go on. I mean it."

The other two waitresses didn't need any more urging. They were anxious to get home to their husbands and children. Marilee, on the other hand, had no one but herself.

No one in Amarillo knew anything about her

background except that she'd grown up in East Texas and that her parents were dead. There was no need for them to know that her mother was dead because her father had killed her, and that her father had been executed by the state of Texas for the murder. It wasn't something she often dwelled on anymore, but it was part of her past, whether she liked it or not.

She'd been almost nineteen when it happened and twenty-three when her father had been put to death. She'd gone to her mother's funeral and her father's trial. After that, she had considered herself an orphan, even though it had taken four more years for that to be a fact. So, being snowbound in the diner would not have posed a hardship for Marilee, and she would have rather stayed on the job.

The other two waitresses were already gone before Marilee had her snow boots on. By the time she came out of the break room, Calvin had turned the television channel to his favorite soap opera and was settled in the corner booth with a bottle of beer.

"Guess I'll be seeing you," she said. She had started out the door when a black extend-a-cab pickup truck pulled off the highway and into the parking lot.

She didn't have to look twice to know who it was. It was Justin Wheeler, the man of her dreams. For six months this man had been a weekly regular at the Roadrunner. And every time he came, he sat at one of Marilee's tables, laughing and teasing with her. For him, she knew it was only casual conversation, but not for her. She liked everything about him, from the way he wore his Stetson cocked a little to one side, to the set of his shoulders when he stood. And when he smiled, his eyes crinkled up at the corners and a hint of a dimple appeared in his left cheek.

Yes, Justin Wheeler had been the fodder for many a sweet dream, yet all she really knew about him was that he was the only child of a couple who'd made their money in cattle and oil, that he was single and that he loved Calvin's chicken-fried steak and Dutch apple pie.

"Looks like you've got one straggler," she said, pointing to the man getting out of the truck.

Calvin turned. "Lawsy mercy, it's that cowboy...what's his name?"

"Wheeler. Justin Wheeler," Marilee said, and then blushed when Calvin grinned and winked.

"Know his name, do you?" he asked.

She shrugged. "I've waited on him before." Then she stepped back to one side, pretending great interest in buttoning up her coat as Justin bolted through the door.

"Boy, what in hell are you doin' out on these roads?" Calvin yelled. "Don't you know it's snowin'?"

"I do now," Justin said, as he took off his Stetson and gently tapped it against his leg to knock off the snow. "If you don't mind, I need to use your phone. My cell phone's out and I need to find a room here in town for the night. There's no way I'll get home in this."

"I heard about an hour ago that all the rooms were taken," Marilee said.

Justin turned and then grinned. "Hey, honey. I didn't see you standing there."

She smiled, reminding herself that he didn't mean anything by calling her honey. It was just a Texas, good-old-boy word for girl, but it made her feel good—almost special.

"I was just leaving," she said. "But if you're hungry, I can get you something before I leave."

He shook his head. "Thanks, but all I want is a room for the night."

"I don't know about that," Marilee said. "The local radio station has been broadcasting that every motel is full up between here and Lubbock."

"She's right," Calvin said. "I doubt there's any rooms to be had, but you're welcome to the phone just the same."

Marilee showed him the phone, handed him a local phone book and then lingered near Calvin's booth. Both watched as Justin made one call after another, and listened as he struck out.

When he hung the phone up for the last time, he was frowning. "Well, you were right. They are all full. I don't suppose you happen to know anyone who might rent me a room for the night?"

Calvin frowned. "No, can't say as I do," he said. "'Course, you're more than welcome to stay in the Roadrunner with me. I reckon I'll be spending the night right here in this booth."

"You could come to my house," Marilee said, and then couldn't believe she'd said it.

The moment it was out of her mouth, she was wishing she could take it back. Just because he'd been in her dreams, didn't mean he would want to be in her life.

Justin was as surprised by her invitation as she was. For the first time, he caught himself thinking of her as more than the tall, lanky waitress with that bun of brown hair who worked the north end of the room.

A little embarrassed, Marilee tried to be casual

about the invitation, hoping that he would turn her down.

"I don't have an extra bedroom, just a really big couch. And it's sure nothing fancy. You probably don't want to—"

"I'll take it," he said, and then wondered if he looked as surprised as he felt.

"You will?"

He waved his hand toward the snow.

"Honey, your invitation is the best news I've had all day. Do you need a ride or—"

"No. I have my car in the parking lot out back. Just follow me, okay?"

He glanced outside, eyeing the condition of the streets.

"The streets are getting pretty slick. Maybe it would be better if I—"

"I've been taking care of myself for nine years," she said quietly. "I got myself here. I can get myself home." Then she turned to Calvin. "If you get in a bind, you've got my number."

Calvin nodded, a little unsure of what he thought about the offer she'd made. But she was a grown woman, and from the little he knew about her, a good woman. He figured she knew what she was doing.

"You be careful," he said.

She smiled, aware that he meant more than careful driving.

"I will. See you tomorrow."

"Don't bother coming in until they plow the roads, okay?"

She nodded and waved a goodbye, then glanced at Justin before going out the door.

"Ready?"

"Yep. I'm right behind you."

As he followed her outside and into the storm, it occurred to him that he probably should have called home just to let his family know he was all right. He decided he'd do it later, after he got settled.

To his surprise, Marilee navigated the snowy streets with skill, maneuvering her Oldsmobile around corners as if she'd been driving in snow all her life. Once, she started to slide toward a stranded car and Justin found himself holding his breath, expecting her to crash into it. Instead, she calmly steered into the skid and then straightened the wheels before driving on past with room to spare.

He found himself smiling an approval. "Way to go," he muttered, and then followed her around another curve in the road. All of a sudden, he saw her left turn signal blinking. He began to slow down, hoping to take the turn without skidding. Moments later they were pulling into a driveway. The house beside it was tiny—a white clapboard house almost invisible against the snowfall, with a long, narrow porch that ran the length of the front.

As Marilee got out of the car, he saw her clutch at the collar of her coat, then lower her head against the snow. As Justin followed, it occurred to him that he should have offered to carry her through the snow or at least break a path, but she was already on the porch before he could stop her.

She stomped her feet to remove excess snow, and he did the same. When she fumbled with her keys, dropping them on the porch, he assumed it was because her bare fingers were cold. He didn't know that she was starting to panic.

As he followed her inside, the warmth of the small house enveloped him. He gazed around the living room, comparing it to his ranch house, and felt a brief shaft of guilt regarding the luxuries of life he took for granted. It wasn't as though she was sitting on crates and eating from the floor, but the furniture was old and worn-out, and the rugs, clean though they were, were threadbare.

Marilee saw him looking at her home and knew that he was used to much better, but she refused to apologize for what she lacked. She glanced sideways at him, hoping her nervousness didn't show, and then pointed toward a small closet.

"You can hang your coat in there," she said. "I'm going to change out of my uniform and then fix us something to eat, okay?"

Justin was feeling just as awkward as she looked. He smiled and nodded as she left the room, then looked around for her phone. It was on a table near the couch. That, he supposed, was going to be his bed. It was about a cushion too short for his length, but it still beat sleeping in his truck in the cold.

"Mind if I use your phone?" he called out. "I need to let my folks know I'm all right."

"Help yourself," he heard her answer, then settled down near the phone to make his call. A few moments later, the phone at his home began to ring.

"Hello?"

"Dad, it's me, Justin."

"Justin! Thank God you called. Your mother and I have been worried sick. Are you all right? Where are you?"

"Yes, Dad, I'm fine. I knew you'd be worried. I got as far as Amarillo before they closed the roads. I'm in for the night and as soon as they get the snowplows out tomorrow, I'll be heading on home.''

"That's just fine. You stay until it's safe to drive." Then he added, "I figured the motels would be full of stranded travelers. You're lucky you found one.''

He glanced around the room, eyeing the cheery flames in the gas-heating stove.

"Yeah, Dad, you're right. I am pretty lucky. Tell the hands to put out extra hay for the cattle and make sure they have my horse in the barn.''

"Already done.''

Justin grinned. "Sounds like you have everything under control. Tell Mother I said hello and I'll see you tomorrow.''

He hung up just as Marilee came back into the room, and it was just as well he was through with his call, because he wasn't so sure he would have been able to talk. Somewhere between the front door and now, Marilee the waitress had turned into a walking, talking centerfold. That appalling bun was now a cascade of chocolate-brown hair, hanging long and loose past her shoulders in abundant waves. She had on a pair of old moccasins and some Levi's that had been washed so many times, they clung to her hips as if they'd been knit to fit. The ancient Texas A&M sweat-shirt she was wearing should have disguised the fullness of her breasts but did not.

"Did your call go through?" she asked.

He nodded.

"Good thing you called now. If this storm doesn't let up, we're going to wind up in the dark."

Justin nodded, but he was already wondering what would happen if the house did go dark.

"Are you hungry?" Marilee asked.

He nodded again.

She arched an eyebrow, telling herself that his noncommittal state surely had nothing to do with his brainpower. She'd talked to him plenty of times before and he'd never seemed slow or dull-witted. Maybe he was just cold.

"The bathroom is down the hall...first door on your left. When you're ready, come on into the kitchen. There's fresh coffee brewing and the remote for the TV is over there on the shelf below the set. Knock yourself out, okay?"

He nodded again and then finally found his voice enough to squeak out an answer. "Okay."

He watched her walk out of the room and knew that he'd just accepted and moved into a higher level of faith. Only God could have made something as structurally perfect as Marilee.

A few minutes later he wandered into the kitchen and then stopped in his tracks. The radio was on and turned down low, but he could still hear enough of the music to know that the slight but constant sway of her lower body was moving to the rhythm. He closed his eyes and then shook his head, making himself focus on something besides her hips. The aroma of the coffee she'd promised settled somewhere between his brain and his lust, reminding him of why he'd come in.

"That coffee does smell good," he said.

Marilee turned, a half-peeled potato in one hand, a paring knife in the other. She pointed the potato toward a cabinet.

"Cups are in there," she said. "Help yourself."

Justin poured the coffee and then stepped aside as she began to wash the vegetables she'd been peeling.

"I'd be glad to help," he said.

"Can you cook?" she asked.

He took a sip of the coffee and then grinned. "Uh...I can pour milk over cereal."

She rolled her eyes. "Typical male. Offers to do something he knows good and well he can't do to insure himself against having to do anything at all.''

He laughed. "You have a pretty poor opinion of men.''

She thought of her father. "So far I haven't met any that would give me a reason to change it, either." Then she grinned. "Except maybe for Calvin. He's a good boss. Best I've ever had.''

Justin leaned against the counter, drinking the coffee as he watched her work. With little wasted motion, she chopped and stirred, sliced and steamed, and the scents of down-home cooking filled the tiny little room. As he watched, it occurred to him that, although he'd seen her plenty off and on during the last six months, he didn't know a thing about her but her first name.

"Marilee?''

"Hmmm?''

The fact that she hadn't bothered even to look up struck him somewhere between amused and piqued. He wasn't used to being ignored, especially by pretty women.

"It has occurred to me that I do not know your last name, and since you have been kind enough to offer me shelter from the storm...''

She paused in her stirring, and he thought he saw her flinch, as if bracing herself for something, but when she looked up and smiled, he decided he'd been imagining things.

"Cash. My last name is Cash, and before you ask, no, I'm not related to Johnny."

"Had a lot of that, have you?"

"More than you can imagine."

He refilled his coffee cup and then moved to the kitchen table to get out of her way. Pulling a chair from the table, he turned it around backward and then straddled it as if he was mounting a horse, leaning his forearms on the chair's back.

"Did you grow up here in Amarillo?" he asked.

Again he thought he saw a hesitation before she answered.

"No. I grew up in East Texas. I fried up some ham slices. Would you prefer cream, or red-eye gravy?"

She'd changed the subject. He let it slide.

"Since you're asking, honey, then I'd say cream."

She strode to the refrigerator and took out a gallon of milk. He watched her as she dropped a large dollop of flour into the skillet where she'd cooked the ham, then started to stir.

"That's a gift, you know."

"What's a gift?" Marilee muttered as she

poured some of the milk into the roux she'd just made and then resumed her stirring.

"Making good gravy."

She looked at him and then grinned.

"How do you know it's going to be good?"

He leaned forward, resting his chin on his forearms and fixing her with a devilish, green stare.

"I may not know how to cook, but I think I know a good cook when I see one."

She smiled briefly, then turned back to her task, unwilling to admit, even to herself, how inordinately pleased she was with his comment. A few minutes later the last dish was prepared. When she handed him some plates and cutlery, he took them readily and began setting the table, realizing that he was suddenly starving.

Marilee carried the food to the table, and as she did, it hit her that in the years since she'd lived in Amarillo, he was the first guest she'd ever had to dinner.

"Please sit," she said.

"After you, honey. My mother didn't teach me how to cook, but she did knock a few manners into my head."

Looking at his smile had been deadly. She was lost, no matter what life had taught her about good-looking men who lived without promises.

She sat, trying to ignore the heat of his hands against her back as he scooted her chair toward the table.

"I can't believe you cooked all of this in such a short time," Justin said, admiring the ham steaks, mashed potatoes and gravy and the small bowl of green peas.

Pleased with his praise, Marilee smiled as she passed him the ham. After that, the meal went smoothly. They talked as they ate, like old friends with a lot of catching up to do.

About halfway through the meal, it occurred to Justin that he'd never been so at ease or had this much fun with a woman and not been in bed. Not in his entire life. The women he dated were all about what he could do for them and how much he was willing to spend on them.

"Want some more coffee?" Marilee asked as she got up to refill her cup.

"Please," Justin said, holding out his cup as she lifted the carafe from the coffeemaker. As she began to pour, he looked up and grinned. "You know something, Marilee? You're real good at pouring coffee. Ever think about becoming a waitress?"

She laughed as she spun around, replacing the carafe without wasted motion.

"Do you think?" she said, and then returned to her seat. "It's weird, you know...how people come to the jobs they have. It's not like I grew up wanting to be a waitress."

Justin had just finished the last of his food. Curious, he pushed his plate aside and leaned forward, bracing his elbows on the table.

"What did you want to be...when you were a kid, I mean?"

Marilee thought about the chaos of her childhood and then shrugged.

"I just wanted to grow up and get out," she said. "Obviously I didn't think my choices through very well, did I?"

Suddenly Justin wished he hadn't asked. He didn't want her to think he looked down on her choice of occupation.

"I didn't mean anything by that," he said quickly. "I was just curious, that's all."

She nodded, then made herself smile. "I know. No offense taken. What did you want to be?"

"Anything but an only child."

The conversation had taken a serious tone that neither had expected, but the ease with which they confided was comfortable.

"Pressure?" she asked.

He nodded.

"I figured as much. Knew a girl back in high school who had everything money could buy...except the freedom to make her own choices. Her mother and father had run her life as competently as they ran their real-estate business. Then one day I guess she had enough. She ran away with the town bad boy. I never did think she really loved him. Always had the feeling she'd done it out of spite."

"Yeah, I can understand that," Justin said.

"So...are there any revolts in your past, or have you been a good boy?"

Justin shrugged. "A few revolts, but nothing drastic, and I have to admit I like what I do."

"Which is?"

"Run my ranch, raise my cattle and ride my horse."

"So that hat and those boots you wear aren't all for show after all. You not only talk the talk, you really walk the walk."

He grinned. "You are a sassy thing, aren't you?"

She arched an eyebrow. "I just call 'em like I see 'em." Then she stood abruptly and began clearing the dishes. To her surprise, he began to help, carrying plates and bowls to the counter as she began to put away the leftover food. Within minutes the dishes were done and the table was clean.

Marilee reached in front of Justin's chest to hang up the dish towel and felt the warmth of his breath against her cheek. Although her heartbeat skittered once, she didn't let on.

Dusting her hands against her pants, she turned and found him staring at her.

"What?"

"You."

"What about me?"

"I don't know yet," he said cryptically, and then frowned and shoved his hands in his pockets as if he'd suddenly said more than he should.

The lights flickered briefly and then everything went dark.

"Well, poop," Marilee muttered. "Don't move. I'll get some candles."

Justin grinned. *Poop?* He chuckled softly.

"Nothing is funny," he heard her say.

"I'm not laughing."

He heard a soft snort of disbelief and then another word, much stronger, that sounded nothing like *poop*.

"I heard that, too," he said.

"Don't suppose it's the first time you've ever heard it."

"No."

"Good. Then I won't have to sleep with the guilt of your moral downfall on my conscience tonight."

He laughed aloud. There was no getting around the fact that Marilee Cash was fun.

Suddenly a match was struck and the first bit of light began to burn at the end of a big, red candle.

"I was saving it for Christmas," she muttered as she carried it to the kitchen table, and then she rummaged in a drawer for others.

Soon the kitchen was bathed in the soft, warm glow of candles that she'd set about the room.

"I don't know about you, but it's too early to go to bed, and watching television is out. So...how about playing a game?"

He grinned. Game? "I think the last game I played was Spin the Bottle."

She rolled her eyes and pointed toward the table.

"Sit. I'll be right back."

She picked up a flashlight and walked out of the room. Outside, he could hear the wind whistling beneath the eaves of the little house, yet he felt a sense of safety and comfort, the likes of which he'd never known. Before he could decipher the feeling, she was back.

"Monopoly," she said, and then slammed the game box in the middle of the table and lifted the lid.

## Chapter 2

Candlelight flickered, casting shadows on Marilee's face as she grabbed the dice and rolled.

"Four!" she crowed. "I got a four!"

"You also have every danged piece of property but Boardwalk," Justin muttered as he watched her count off the spaces.

"I won! I won!" she shrieked, and jumped up from her chair, her arms over her head in a jubilant gesture as she danced a little jig.

Justin grinned. He didn't like losing at anything, but the unabashed joy on her face was too great to ignore.

"Yeah, so you did."

Marilee turned, her delight still evident as she then leaned forward, palms down on the middle of the table.

"I wiped you out," she said.

Justin found himself looking up at her lips, only inches away from his face, and acted on an impulse that had been with him all night. Within seconds he was on his feet. With the table between them and their fingertips touching, he slanted his mouth across her lips and kissed her hard and fast—before she could move.

Marilee inhaled sharply beneath his mouth and moaned. Every dream he'd been in, every fantasy she'd ever had about this man was nothing compared to this searing kiss. When he thrust a hand through her hair and cupped the back of her neck, tugging her forward, she followed. Monopoly pieces went flying as she shoved them aside and crawled across the table to meet him. Justin groaned beneath his breath and took her by the shoulders. Within seconds she was flat on her back on the kitchen table and he was on top of her. Brief moments of sanity came and went. Enough to know that his hands were tracing every curve that she had and his mouth was ravaging every bare inch of her skin. After that, she discarded all caution.

There was one moment when Justin knew he

was losing control and seriously thought about stopping, and then Marilee moaned. The knowledge that she was as moved by what was happening as he was, was an aphrodisiac he wasn't prepared to fight. Instead of stripping her bare and taking her there on the kitchen table, he slid off the table then picked her up in his arms.

"Bed," he mumbled as her fingers tugged at the buttons on his shirt.

"Go left," she whispered, and then groaned when he nipped the curve of her neck just below her chin.

Within moments he had her flat on her back in the middle of her bed, stripping her clothes as he went. Hers came off first, then his followed. Outside, a gust of wind rattled the old panes in the windows beside her bed, but neither of them heard it. The storm outside was nothing compared to what was going on within. When Justin began ravaging her body with his lips, she gasped. She wasn't a virgin, but no one had ever touched her this intimately, and in so many places.

"Oh, Justin, I—"

He hushed her words with another searing kiss. By the time he lifted his head, she was past help and so was he. Never in his adult life had he so completely lost control. There was nothing on his mind but getting inside this woman's body and seeking that soul-shattering pleasure of physical release. Then, because Justin Wheeler always got what he wanted, he plunged himself into Marilee and took them both into sexual bliss.

They turned to each other over and over throughout the night, sometimes tenderly, sometimes ravenous for the body-to-body connection. It never occurred to Justin that Marilee was giving him more than just a bed and a tumble. He didn't know that she'd given her heart.

It was the absence of sound that first awakened Justin to the new day. Then he heard Marilee's gentle breathing. He raised up on one elbow to look down at the woman beside him. There was a part of him registering the fact that she was as beautiful now as she had been last night while bathed in candlelight. But there was that other part of him that was thinking what in hell had he done? He'd not only gone to bed with a woman who was a virtual stranger, but he'd said and done things to her that he'd never said or done to another woman.

Ever.

And it scared him.

Without wasting another second, he slipped out of bed and began putting on his clothes. When he was down to his boots, he picked them up and started out of the room, then paused in the doorway and looked back.

Marilee was still asleep, one arm hanging off the edge of the bed, the other pillowing her cheek. The covers had slipped off one of her shoulders and the slim, creamy curve reminded him of the beauty of her body, still hidden beneath. Twice he started to go back to kiss her awake and tell her he would never forget her or the shelter she'd offered from the storm. But he was afraid if he did, he would not be able to leave. So he wrote a quick note, leaving it in the middle of the kitchen table among the scattered Monopoly money. Then he put on his boots, grabbed his coat and his keys and let himself out of the house.

To his relief, a snowplow had already made a path down the street, although he had to wade through a good foot of snow to get to his truck. The engine started easily. Thankful for four-wheel drive and a three-quarter-ton rig, he backed out of Marilee's driveway and drove away without looking back.

He was already at the outskirts of Lubbock when Marilee woke up. Even before she opened her eyes, she knew he was gone. The bed was cold and so was she—all the way to her soul. With a muffled sob, she rolled onto her belly.

*Six months later*

It was five minutes to 6:00 p.m. and the main dining room of the Roadrunner was bustling with locals as well as the first wave of vacationing tourists. The day had been unseasonably warm for May with no signs of cooling off. Marilee reached above an empty booth on the west side of the room to lower the window shades and winced as her belly bumped into the back of the booth.

"Sorry, baby," she muttered as she gave her belly a pat.

Even though she'd had six months to get used to the idea that she was going to be a mother, she sometimes still forgot to accommodate her new shape to old habits.

"Marilee, I'll get those shades," Dellie said, giving Marilee a quick pat on the back.

"I'm not crippled," Marilee grumbled.

"And we'd like to keep you that way," Dellie said with a wink.

Marilee smiled and went to fill water glasses instead. It wasn't the first time the other waitresses had jumped in and taken a job off her hands that they considered too strenuous for her. She appreciated their thoughtfulness, but didn't want Calvin to think she couldn't handle the work. If she lost her job, she didn't know what she would do.

"Order up," Calvin yelled, and rang the small bell at the pick-up window.

Marilee saw the four plates were hers and began loading the tray to carry them to the table.

"That's gonna be pretty heavy," Calvin warned.

"Not you, too," Marilee said.

"It's just 'cause we care, honey."

Marilee smiled her thanks, but loaded the tray the same way she always did and took off across the room with it shoulder-high.

Calvin frowned as he watched. She'd never said one word about her condition or about the man who was responsible. One day she'd just shown up in a maternity top, her eyes brimming with unshed tears and her head held high. No one had asked and she hadn't offered an explanation. After a few days it became a matter of course. They now knew the baby was due around the last of July or the first part of August and that Marilee was saving every penny of her tip money to pay for the upcoming hospitalization. Beyond that it was all a mystery.

And while Calvin was keeping his personal thoughts to himself, he had a real good idea who the father might be. Justin Wheeler had been a weekly regular until the night of the snowstorm when he'd gone home with Marilee. They hadn't seen hide nor hair of him since.

"Worthless cowboy," he muttered, and went back to his grill as Marilee carried the orders to her customers.

"Chicken-fried steaks all around," she said as she laid the plates in front of four hungry men.

"Thanks, honey," one of them said, and then smiled. "I can see you're packin'. Is it a boy or a girl?"

She sighed. "Best guess is a boy."

"You mean you ain't had one of them pictures took of your belly? My wife did with every kid we got. She don't like surprises."

*Yes, surprises can be a bitch,* Marilee thought, and then said, "Had one, but they couldn't be sure. How many children *do* you have?"

"Four," he said, and then grinned a little wider. "All boys. She wants a girl—but not enough to take another chance."

"I sympathize with her decision," Marilee said. "Will there be anything else?"

"Got any Tabasco sauce?"

"Coming right up," Marilee said, and turned away, glancing toward the entrance as she headed for the kitchen.

At that moment, she knew the rest of her day wasn't going to go as smoothly as it had started, because Justin Wheeler was walking in the door. Her thoughts went from shock, to panic, to anger and then numb. But it was the anger that finally resurfaced. She lifted her chin, snatched a bottle of Tabasco sauce from beneath the counter and put it on the table.

"Enjoy your meal," she said, and then hissed at her friend Dellie as she passed her by.

"Dellie, do me a favor, please?"

"Name it, honey," the waitress said.

"Take that man's order."

Dellie turned, looking in the direction that Marilee was pointing, and then frowned.

"But he's sitting at your table, honey. Are you sure you—"

"If he came in here to eat, then someone else is going to have to serve him," Marilee snapped. "I'll catch this couple for you instead," and went to get menus for a couple who'd just sat down.

Realization hit as Dellie turned to stare. She didn't know his name, but she would bet a week's worth of tips that he was the man who'd put that baby in Marilee's belly. She snatched up a menu from the end of the bar and then stomped across the room.

Justin Wheeler was a little antsy. It had been a long time since he'd been to the Roadrunner.

Long enough that whatever panic or embarrassment he might have felt at seeing Marilee again
had been replaced by pure shame. He'd known
within minutes of leaving her house that morning
that he should have awakened her first. And all
the way to Lubbock he'd told himself he would
call. Only, he hadn't. Then, when Christmas drew
near, he'd started to send her flowers, just as a
thank-you, of course, for the shelter from the
storm, but that good thought had come and gone
without any action, either.

One thing had led to another and the weeks had
turned into months. The excuses he'd made to
himself as to why he was circumventing Amarillo
on his way home from Dallas had begun sounding
lame, even to him. Finally, on this fine spring day,
he'd made up his mind that he was going to stop
in and say hello, if for no other reason than to
prove to himself that she didn't matter—that the
dreams he'd had of her every night since he'd left
were nothing more than just flights of fancy.

When he walked into the restaurant, he realized
that he'd actually missed coming here. The food
was good—well above average—and the people
were always friendly. The fact that he'd chosen
to sit at one of Marilee's tables was simply because all—well, most…uh, some—of the other
places were taken.

He took off his Stetson, laid it brimside up on the seat beside him and was combing his hair with his fingers when someone slapped a menu in front of him.

"Can I get you something to drink?"

He looked up. It wasn't Marilee who was asking, but whoever she was, she looked pissed.

"How about some iced tea?" he asked, and flashed her a grin.

She glared.

It was the first time he'd ever gotten that kind of a reaction from something as simple as a smile.

"What's good today?" he asked without opening the menu.

"I'll take your order when I bring your tea."

Justin was taken aback. Whoever this woman was, she needed an attitude adjustment. It wasn't until she stomped away that a thought occurred. What if Marilee didn't work here anymore? What if she'd moved? What if he never saw her again?

A sheen of cold sweat suddenly beaded across his forehead. It was panic, pure and simple.

God. He'd waited too long.

He glanced around the room, his stomach in knots, and then immediately the panic receded. There she was, on the other side of the room! He'd recognize those long legs and that topknot of chocolate-brown hair anywhere. He stared at her back, willing her to turn, and then when she did, every thought in his head just stopped. Everything about her was the same—just as he'd remembered, just as he'd dreamed—except for the fact that she was obviously pregnant.

"Lord Almighty," he muttered as his bones turned to mush.

He thought back to that night and of the countless times they'd made love. He hadn't used protection, which was careless, of course. But it wasn't as if he'd planned on having sex. And he'd just assumed that she was protected. Women her age knew the score. It wasn't as if she'd been a virgin, and she'd been damned willing.

Then reason surfaced. What the hell was he thinking? Just because he'd spent the night in her bed didn't mean he was the only one who had. For all he knew, he was just one of many. But the moment he thought it, he knew that he was wrong. He'd known plenty of easy women, and Marilee Cash just hadn't come across that way.

All of a sudden another thought hit. What the hell was wrong with him? Six months had come and gone. Hell, she was probably married. And the moment he thought it, he groaned. He didn't want her married. He didn't want her coming apart in someone else's arms.

*So, since when does what you want matter in*

*her life? You had your chance, buddy. You walked out without so much as a "thank you, ma'am." She doesn't owe you anything, especially allegiance.*

But the pep talk he gave himself didn't help. He watched her from across the room, trying to see if she was wearing a wedding ring, but he couldn't tell.

And then his waitress came back. He actually found himself wanting to duck when she swung the glass of iced tea through the air before plunking it down at his place.

"Know what you want yet?" she asked.

"Yeah. Some consideration would be nice," he muttered.

"You have to give it before you receive it, buddy."

His eyes narrowed as he studied her face. Something told him that there was more than a bad attitude under the little waitress's behavior.

"I want to talk to Marilee," he said. "Will you tell her I'm here?"

"Oh, she already knows."

The answer hit like a fist to the gut. For a moment he couldn't think what to do. Then reality surfaced. By God, he wasn't going to be ignored. He shoved the menu aside and picked up his hat, jamming it on his head as he got up from the booth.

"Leaving so soon?" Dellie asked.

Justin glared. "I'm not going anywhere until I talk to Marilee," he muttered, and pushed past her.

Dellie frowned. This wasn't what she'd expected him to do. In her experience, men who got women in trouble didn't go looking for conversation. She tried to get Marilee's attention, but it was too late. Justin got there first.

Marilee was in the midst of taking an order when Justin appeared at her side.

"Do you want fries with that?" she asked.

"Marilee, I need to talk to you," Justin said.

The couple at the table looked a bit startled, and the man she was talking to hesitated to answer. Heat was spreading up her neck to her cheeks, but she stood with her pen to the order pad, looking directly at her customer as if Justin hadn't said a word.

"Uh, yes, I believe I do," the man said.

"Fries, it is," she said, then smiled at his wife. "And how about you, ma'am? Do you want fries, too?"

"Marilee! I'm talking to you," Justin muttered.

Marilee took a deep breath and kept looking at the woman.

"Do you have those yummy curly fries?" the wife asked.

"Yes, ma'am."

"Then I'll have those," she said, eyeing the big cowboy who was standing between their waitress and the kitchen.

"Great choice," Marilee said. "I'll bring you some more iced tea."

She pivoted sharply, sidestepping Justin as if he was nothing more aggravating than a chair that had been moved out of place, sashayed to the pass-through, handed in her order and picked up a pitcher of iced tea on her way back to the tables. Justin was right behind her.

"More tea, sir?" she asked, calmly refilling a glass here and a glass there as she made her way back to the couple's table. She was pouring tea in their glasses when Justin grabbed her by the arm.

"Damn it to hell, Marilee. Look at me."

She topped off the glass, ignoring the couple and their curious stares as she looked up.

"What?"

Reeling from her anger and scared spitless that he already knew the reason for it, he still had to ask.

"Have you forgotten how to talk?"

"No more than you," she drawled.

It was a slap-in-the-face reference to the fact that he left her without saying goodbye, and truth be told, he knew he deserved it.

"Look, we need to talk."

"I'm busy."

He glanced down at her belly then up at her face.

"You're also pregnant."

"Yes. That sometimes happens when you have sex."

The woman at the table snickered. Her husband frowned at her and shook his head, but it was too late. Justin had already heard. He glared at her and then back at Marilee.

"You know what I'm saying, damn it. Are you going to talk about it or not?"

In the background of the noisy room, Marilee heard Calvin ring the order-up bell and she started to push past Justin, but he wasn't going through this all over again. He grabbed her arm, his voice just shy of a shout.

"Is this baby mine, or not?"

"Excuse me," Marilee said, smiling at the couple as she set the tea pitcher down. Then she drew back her hand and slapped Justin's face. The sound ricocheted above the melee of conversations like a gunshot.

Suddenly the room was silent as Marilee picked up her pitcher and headed for the kitchen. Without breaking stride, she picked up three plates of chicken-fried steak with all the trimmings and headed for one of her other tables, well aware that Justin was on her heels. The room was dead silent. People were staring, their food forgotten as they watched the unfolding drama.

"Damn it to hell, Marilee! I want an answer!" Justin yelled.

Marilee served the food to a man and his two teenage sons.

"Can I get you anything else?"

They looked a bit nervous and quickly shook their heads.

"Enjoy your food," Marilee said, and then started toward the kitchen again.

In his whole pampered life, Justin Wheeler had never been thwarted like this. When Marilee turned her back on him again, he suddenly yelled.

"Marilee, if you don't stop and talk to me now, you're going to be sorry."

She stopped, and even as she was turning around, knew she wasn't going to be able to hide her anger any longer.

"Sorry?" she shrieked. "I'm going to be sorry? What more could you possibly do to me than you've already done?"

Scalded by her fury, he still needed to hear it said.

"Then that baby you're carrying *is* mine!"

She walked toward him, and when she was only inches away from his face, she took off his hat and handed it to him, then calmly poured the rest of the tea in the pitcher down on his head.

There was a collective gasp from the customers as Justin stood there in shock, cold liquid running from his hair into his eyes. He should have been angry, but he'd seen the hurt on her face and it had shamed him instead. He'd questioned her morality in front of dozens of strangers. What the hell had he been thinking? Then he sighed. That was the trouble. He hadn't had a rational thought since six months ago when she'd jumped up from that Monopoly game, crowing that she'd won.

"Marilee, I—"

She turned and walked away, passing Calvin who was on his way out of the kitchen.

"What the hell is going on?" Calvin asked.

Marilee kept on walking.

Suddenly Justin realized that his actions had not only embarrassed her, but they could have gotten her in trouble with her boss. He couldn't let that happen.

"It's nothing," Justin said quickly. "We had a little spill, and it's all my fault."

"Well, he finally said something that's beginning to make sense," the woman said.

"Loretta, hush your mouth," the man said, and then looked at Justin and shrugged, as if to say it was out of his hands.

"I'll get a mop," one of the other waitresses said as Dellie bolted into the kitchen after Marilee.

Marilee felt as if her heart was in shreds. By the time she reached the kitchen, she was choking back sobs. Splaying her hands across her belly in a protective manner, she staggered into the break room and then started to cry. It was the tears she should have shed six months ago when Justin left her to wake up alone. They burned like acid, blinding her to everything but the pain. Frantic that Justin would find her like this, she tore off her apron and began gathering her things. She had to get out of here now, before it was too late.

Seconds later Dellie rushed into the break room.

"It's him, isn't it?" she hissed.

Marilee nodded as she opened her locker and reached for her purse.

"Well, I'll have to admit, he didn't tuck tail and run like I thought he would," Dellie said. And then she added, "But I'm still on your side, girl. You get yourself on home. We'll cover for you here and Calvin won't care."

Marilee turned and impulsively hugged Dellie. "Thank you," she mumbled.

"That's what friends are for," Dellie said. "Now get, before he storms back here and tears up what's left of the place."

With her car keys in one hand and her purse slung over her shoulder, Marilee exited the Roadrunner and headed for her car. Even though she knew Justin Wheeler wasn't through with her, she needed to be on home ground when their showdown ended.

Justin was still apologizing to Calvin and helping the waitress mop up the tea that Marilee had poured on his head when he happened to look out the window. He'd only seen it once, but he recognized her old car, and it was sailing out of the parking lot in high gear.

He handed the mop to Calvin.

"I've got to go," he said as he bolted for the front door.

Halfway across the room, someone suddenly yelled out, "It'll be the biggest mistake of your life if you don't go after her."

He kept on running. They didn't have to tell him something he already knew.

# Chapter 3

Justin came out of the parking lot just as Marilee's old car disappeared around the corner of the block up ahead. He hit the accelerator and swerved into the turning lane, desperate not to lose her. Although he'd been at her house, they'd driven there in a snowstorm and he'd left the next morning in a mental fog. Finding it again without an address would have been next to impossible.

Two turns and five blocks later, he saw her take another sharp right. When he turned the corner, she was nowhere in sight. His heart dropped. Driving slowly down the street, he passed three brick homes, one green and white ranch-style bungalow and a large, yellow house. But when he saw the tiny, white frame house on the corner, it struck a familiar chord. And then he saw her car in the drive, hit the brakes and made a quick left turn. He killed the engine, breathing a sigh of relief.

As he started to get out, he hesitated, desperate to collect his thoughts. His gut was in knots and his hands were shaking. He'd never been so scared or as uncertain about what to say. He'd done the unthinkable and made a baby with a woman he hardly knew, but he wasn't the kind of man who could walk away from that. Settling his hat a little more firmly on his head, he got out of the pickup and started toward the door.

Marilee was in the bathroom, washing her face with cold water when she heard the knock on the door. She looked up at herself in the mirror as she grabbed a towel. Her eyes were red and swollen from crying and her makeup was a mess.

*Good. Maybe he'll take one look at me and get the hell out of my life. It's already complicated enough.*

She heard him knock again. This time more forcefully. She sighed. There was no use delaying the inevitable. Lifting her chin, she pivoted sharply and headed for the door.

"What?" she said, yanking it inward.

Justin flinched. She's been crying. Then he sighed. Well, hell, of course she's been crying. He yelled at her for a good five minutes in front of God and everybody.

"Marilee, I'm sorry."

"For what? Making a scene at my job, or because I'm pregnant?"

"For yelling at you."

"Apology accepted," she muttered, and started to close the door.

He grabbed it before she could shut it in his face, and then he stepped inside, taking off his Stetson and hanging it on a hook by the door. As he did, it hit him that he'd done this once before, on the night she'd given him shelter from the storm. Then he faced her, determination heavy in his voice.

"We need to talk."

"About what? I thought you'd pretty much said it all."

He shut the door behind him and frowned as she stalked toward the kitchen. Refusing to be put off, he followed her.

"Don't patronize me, lady. I had a right to know about this."

She spun, her anger alive and growing.

"Well said. I couldn't agree more. However...since you snuck out of my bed without so much as a goodbye and disappeared from my life, I assumed you'd had all of me you wanted."

He flushed, but held his ground.

"And there hasn't been a day since that I have not regretted that."

She frowned as if she didn't believe him, and truth be told, he couldn't blame her.

"Okay, so you're sorry you were a coward and you're sorry you embarrassed me at my work, and I have accepted your apology. Now if you don't mind, I've had just about all of your apologies I can take for one day."

"Please...honey, I—"

"The last thing I am is your honey."

The wintry look she gave him was startling. It looked too much like hate.

"Marilee?"

She waited, arms folded across her chest in anger, unaware that it only accentuated the swell of her belly and how thin she'd become.

"Please," he begged. "Will you sit down so we can talk?"

She stomped into the living room and plopped down on the sofa. When he started to sit by her, she glared. He opted for the chair instead, leaving a coffee table between them to mark a boundary.

He looked at her then until her anger wavered, and she chose to stare at the floor instead.

"Now I'm going to ask this again, but please don't take it wrong."

She looked up.

"Why didn't you let me know?"

"I don't know where you live. In fact, I don't know anything about you except your name, the little you've mentioned about your parents and the fact that you have a dimple in your left cheek when you smile. Besides, I blame myself. I let it happen. It's my problem. I take care of myself."

"Does your family know?" he asked.

"I don't have any family. Remember?"

He felt his face redden. It shamed him to admit he didn't remember a damned thing she'd told him about her personal life. All he remembered was the way she'd felt in his arms and the way she'd made him feel inside, as if he had conquered the world.

"Yes, I'm sorry. I guess I forgot."

She didn't answer. There was no need. He knew she'd seen through his feeble excuses. He'd taken her to bed. End of story for him. Unfortunately it had been only the beginning for her. He took a deep breath. It wasn't exactly the way he'd ever planned this moment, but he had never walked away from a fight in his life and he wasn't going to start now. Not when the life of his first-born depended on it.

"Marilee, I'm sorry for everything you've suffered, and if I could, I would take it all away right now. However, you and I both know that's impossible. But I can do something to relieve some of your burden and it would honor me if you would permit this to happen."

She shrugged. "Short of giving birth for me, which we both know can't happen, I don't see what you think you can do."

"You could marry me."

It was the last thing she'd expected to hear. Her eyes widened and her lips parted in shock. She knew it to be so, because the room suddenly became brighter and her lips went dry. Overwhelmed, she started to cry—spilling huge, quiet tears that rolled down her cheeks.

"Marilee…don't," he begged as he got up from his chair. But when he tried to sit beside her, she wouldn't be held.

"Don't," she said, then started to shake. It was shock. She knew it because the same thing had happened the day she'd realized she was pregnant. The shock would pass, unlike the baby who was real and growing within her belly.

Then she turned sideways, piercing him with a look that made him want to bawl along with her.

"Why?" she asked. "Why are you willing to marry a woman you don't know and quite obviously don't give a damn about?"

He flinched under her accusations, although there was a part of him that had already admitted what she said wasn't true. He did care about her, but he'd waited too long to prove it. Now, no matter what he said, she was going to take it as nothing but charity. He didn't know what else to say but the truth.

"It's true we don't know each other well," he said. "But people have certainly married with less reason than we have. There are two things I do know that aren't refutable. You are carrying my child and you're not going to raise it alone."

In that moment, the wall of fear behind which Marilee had been living began to crack. He'd just given her a way to cope with her worst anxiety— that of raising the baby alone, of not being financially able to provide a decent home. But to make that happen, she had to set aside the only thing she had left that she could call her own. Her pride.

Justin was starting to get nervous. The look on her face told him nothing, and she'd been silent so long. Just when he thought he was in for the fight of his life, she took a deep breath. He found himself holding his own, awaiting her verdict.

"If at all possible, I believe it is in a child's

best interest to be raised by two loving parents,"
she said, but when he started to speak, she held
up her hand. "I'm not through."

Staying silent was difficult. He was torn between the urge to laugh and the urge to cry. Instead he waited, giving her all the time she needed
to have her say.

"Justin, when I say, 'by two loving parents,'
I'm not assuming that you will ever love me, but
I expect—no, I demand—that our child never hear
a word of disrespect from you regarding me or
my background. Also, I don't know your family
situation, but if I become your wife, I will not
stand for being judged lacking by anyone—not
you, not your father or mother or anyone else. I
will not be looked upon as less just because of
the circumstances of our marriage. Do you hear
me?"

In that moment, a strange feeling that Justin
would later recognize as pride began to fill him.
Damn his hide, but this woman might just prove
to be his match after all.

He nodded. "Yes, ma'am, and I totally agree.
I pledge to you now—and I never go back on my
word—that on the day you are my wife, you will
have the honor of my name and the safety of my
protection in every way."

"Do you have a girlfriend?" she asked.

"Uh, no."

"You'd better not be lying to me," she warned. "I will not tolerate being lied to or cheated on. We may not have a marriage made in heaven, but I better have more than face value out of you or I will be gone."

He paled. "There's no one like that."

"Then yes, I will marry you."

Limp with what felt like relief, he started to hug her, but once again she moved away.

"That's not happening again—unless you mean it. I don't want sex just for the act or out of duty."

Taken aback, Justin frowned. "What's so different now from what we had before? You weren't exactly offended by my hugs and kisses then."

Marilee lifted her chin, her eyes blazing through tears.

"But that's just it, Justin. Before, I mistakenly believed that you had feelings for me, similar to those I had for you."

Then she stood, and he could only follow, afraid that she was going to bolt once again. Instead she pointed a finger at his chest, nailing him with a truth he had to accept.

"I've never—not in my whole life—had sex. I have, on a few rare occasions, *made love* to someone for whom I cared a great deal. Unfortunately this time I made an error in judgment. Trust me, it won't happen again.''

She turned away, and as she did, he panicked. Even though she said she would marry him, he felt as if they were on different sides of the world.

''Where are you going?'' he asked.

She paused, then turned, fixing him with a cool, studied stare.

''I have a headache and my feet are swollen. I'm going to take something for the headache and then lie down for a while. I've had all the fun I can stand for one day.''

''Wait,'' he begged.

''What?''

''The baby?''

''What about it?''

''Have you had one of those...uh... Do you know what it is? I mean, girl or boy?''

''Does it matter?'' she asked.

''No.''

She relented, but just enough for decency's sake. ''Yes, I had an ultrasound and they're not sure of the sex.''

''Oh. Okay, I just thought I'd ask.''

''But their best guess was a boy.''

She walked away; a too-slender girl with a burgeoning belly, who was going to be his wife. He sat down with a thump and then took a deep breath.

A son. What if it was a boy? He had sudden visions of teaching him to ride and showing him how to catch lizards and fly kites.

God in heaven. He'd left Dallas this morning with vague plans of nothing more serious than saying hello, only to find himself at nightfall, pledged to marry the woman who was carrying his child. And in the midst of all his confusion he felt shame. Shame because a part of him had known from the start that she liked him. Shame that he'd taken advantage of her in spite of her kindness on the night of that storm. Shame that she'd cared for him more than he'd cared for her.

He sighed in frustration as he combed his hands through his hair. Well, if it was any consolation, he was suffering for it now. He didn't want this awful bridge of antagonism between them. He wanted that joy back on her face—to see laughter in her eyes. He didn't know how, but he was going to make that happen, no matter how long it took. Then he realized that his parents weren't going to take this news lightly. They'd been at him for years to settle down, but not like this.

And just as suddenly as he thought it, he realized he didn't give a damn. Marilee was where his allegiance would lie. If they didn't like it, they could take themselves back to Austin, where their home was. He was thirty-two years old. The only approval he wanted or needed was from a woman who could no longer bear the sight of his face.

Marilee dug a stack of folded underwear from her dresser drawer and carried it to the suitcase on the bed, stuffing it between clean T-shirts and some athletic socks.

"I set your bags by the front door," Justin said as he entered the bedroom. "I'll load them in the morning."

Marilee turned, looking at the man who'd just come into the room. As of eleven o'clock this morning, she'd become his wife, and it had yet to sink in. She kept expecting him to tell her he'd see her around and disappear out the door.

"All right," she said, and went back to get the rest of her things from the drawer.

"We can send for the rest of your things," Justin said, although in truth, he didn't know what they would do with the furniture.

"I'm taking everything that matters," Marilee said. "Dellie is going to move into my house. We've already settled it with the landlord so I'm leaving her the furniture. She's been living with her mother ever since her divorce and is excited about the move." *I wish I could say the same.*

"That's really generous of you," Justin said.

Marilee stopped packing long enough to look up.

"Not really," she said. "Just practical. I don't need it. She does." Then she added. "Besides, something tells me that my lifestyle and yours are poles apart. I doubt my yard-sale furniture would blend any better with your stuff than I will."

It wasn't the first time she'd insinuated that she wasn't good enough for him, and it was beginning to tick him off.

"That's the last time I ever want to hear you put yourself down. Do you hear me?"

Marilee looked startled. His anger was real and surprising—and in an odd sort of way, quite touching. She sighed then nodded.

"Yes, but I can't help but wonder if you're going to be this supportive when the fur starts to fly."

His eyes narrowed and his lips thinned. He wanted to shake her.

"I guess we'll just have to wait and see, won't we?" he snapped, and left her alone in the room.

"I think that went well," she mumbled, and tossed her hair dryer in on top of the lingerie. "I wonder if this qualifies as our first fight?"

The rest of the day passed in virtual silence. It wasn't until Marilee was getting ready for bed that Justin realized she was running on nothing but nerves.

Marilee came out of the bathroom dressed in her nightgown to find Justin digging through his suitcase. Startled, she started to reach for her robe then realized she'd already packed it. Well aware that her gown was old and thin and revealed far more of her body than she would have liked, she resisted the urge to turn and run. Damn him. Even if she didn't trust him—even if he didn't matter to her anymore except as a father for her child— she didn't want him to see her like this.

But Justin's opinion of Marilee's body was the complete opposite of what she would have expected. Although he knew her belly was round, actually seeing the faint, but unmistakable, outline beneath her gown was so personal—and so touching. He knew he was staring, but he couldn't stop. His child—no, their child—was in there. And then he looked at her face and knew she was remembering them in each other's arms, making love—and making a baby.

"My body—it's not exactly what you remembered, is it?" Marilee said, using sarcasm to mask her embarrassment.

"You're so beautiful," he whispered, and then shocked that he'd said that aloud, spun around and resumed searching through his luggage, although he'd forgotten what he'd been looking for.

Marilee was stunned, then secretly pleased. She didn't believe him, but it felt good to hear it just the same.

"I'm through in the bathroom," she said. "It's all yours."

Justin straightened and turned, watching her again as she sat down on the side of the bed then leaned back against the pillows. Seconds later she shifted position then shifted again, visibly wincing.

Her grimace startled him as he moved to her side.

"What's wrong? Are you in pain? Can I get you anything?"

She smiled before she thought, and as she did, Justin knew that at that moment he would have given everything he owned to know that her smile was sincere.

"I'm fine," she said. "It's just hard to get comfortable when the baby is kicking."

Justin's face lost all expression as he stared down at her belly, and then Marilee saw something in his eyes that gave her a small ray of hope.

"Here," she said, and took hold of his hand, pulling him down on the bed beside her. "Feel."

His hand splayed across the swell of her belly

and he caught himself holding his breath—waiting for that first moment of contact. And when it came, he gasped and then jerked, stunned by the strength of the kick.

"Does that hurt?" he asked.

She smiled. "No."

"My God," he whispered, and then centered his hand there again, holding his breath for the second moment of contact. When it came, he bowed his head and closed his eyes, too moved to speak.

Life.

They'd made a whole new person.

Impulsively he laid his cheek on the place where his hand had been, wanting to see if there was any remarkable sound that accompanied such a gift.

Marilee's heart twisted with regret as she felt the weight of his face upon her stomach. If only the circumstances of this union had been different. If only they'd made this baby on purpose and not by accident. Even though her heart was heavy, she couldn't deny the tenderness she felt for this man. It wasn't going to be easy to keep him at arm's length if he persisted in being involved. And the longer he lay there, the more tempted she was to touch him, as well. Finally she could stand it no longer and laid her hand on the crown of his head.

It wasn't until the air conditioner kicked on that Justin finally moved, and when he lifted his head, she saw tears in his eyes. It was a telling moment for Marilee because she knew then that no matter what else happened, he wanted the baby as much as she did.

Justin couldn't speak. He wanted to hug her, to hold her, to tell her how humbled he felt by her decision not to do away with this child. He got a sick feeling in the pit of his stomach every time he thought about how close he'd come to never knowing this baby existed. But she'd set down the rules of their relationship and he could only abide by them.

He started to get up when Marilee touched his hand.

"What?" he asked.

"After your shower, you may as well sleep here with me."

Hope soared. "You mean—"

"All I'm saying is…we're married. You need a place to sleep. We will share the bed."

"What about the no-touch rules?" Justin asked.

"I wasn't offering sex, just a place to sleep."

Justin grinned. It was the first break in her hard-line approach. It wasn't much, but he would take what he could get.

"It won't take me long to shower," he said.

"Take your time. I'll probably be asleep when you come out anyway."

It had to be the fastest shower he'd ever taken, and she wasn't asleep after all.

"I'm going to make sure everything is locked up," he said. "I'll be right back."

Marilee listened to the sound of his footsteps as he went through the rooms, checking doors and windows, making sure they were locked in safely for the night, and as she did, it hit her that she was really no longer alone. She would never go to bed afraid again, or wake up lonely. And he'd assured her that her money worries were a thing of the past. She hugged the knowledge to herself and closed her eyes, trying to sleep.

But Justin was back too soon, and when he sat on the side of the bed and then turned out the light, she caught herself holding her breath. The mattress gave as he stretched out beside her, and when he pulled the covers over himself, she realized he was tucking her back in, as well. Again, the simple act of tenderness was unnerving. How was she going to guard her heart against a man like this?

Justin felt her nervousness as if it were a living, breathing thing and it made him even more regretful. Impulsively he rolled over on his side and put his arm across her body then gave her a gentle tug.

"What are you doing?" Marilee hissed.

"Relax, darlin'. I just don't want you to roll off the bed."

When he spooned himself against the curve of her backside and then began to breathe easy, she willed herself not to cry. It wasn't the way she'd dreamed her wedding night would be.

A minute passed and then another and another. Marilee had almost convinced herself that nothing mattered except getting some rest, when a horrible thought occurred. Without thinking she blurted out a question.

"Justin?"

"Hmmm?"

"In the morning..."

"Yes?"

"Will you be here when I wake up?"

It was the fear in her voice that was his undoing. He buried his face against the nape of her neck and pulled her close against his body, his hand cradling the swell of her belly.

"Yes, darlin', I'll be here. You're my wife, remember? You're never going to wake up alone again."

She didn't answer because words were beyond her. Long after he'd drifted off to sleep, she was still awake, holding on to him and his promise for dear life.

By noon the next day, they were on their way to Lubbock. Marilee rode with her chin up and her hands curled into fists, braced for the troubles that still lay ahead.

# Chapter 4

All the way to the ranch, Marilee kept thinking that this was just a dream and that any minute she would wake up back in her little house in Amarillo, late for work. But the farther they drove, the more real it became. Twice Justin stopped so she could use the bathroom and stretch her legs, and she hadn't even had to ask. His thoughtfulness and understanding was unexpected. As they entered the outskirts of Lubbock, the traffic became more congested. She saw him glance nervously at her.

"What's wrong?" she asked.

"Just checking to make sure you're buckled up."

"Oh."

Another long stretch of silence came and went as they passed through the city on their way to the ranch. Finally Marilee could stand it no more.

"Justin."

"What?"

"I'm not looking forward to this."

He sighed. "I know."

"You should have called your parents. I don't think it's fair to just show up with me in tow."

He shook his head. "I know them better than you do. Trust me, okay? Besides, calling them just seems to be a coward's way out. I'd rather tell them face-to-face."

Her shoulders slumped and she tried not to sigh. Her whole childhood had existed within her parents' battle zone of a marriage. She hated confrontations more than anything else.

Justin frowned. He wished there was an easier way to do this, but at this late date in her pregnancy, it was impossible. As he glanced at Marilee again, a wave of protectiveness washed over him. The last thing he wanted was for her to be hurt.

"Marilee?"

"Yes?"

"Stop worrying so much. I'm well past grown and my parents don't run my life. I do not answer to either of them anymore. I inherited the ranch from my grandfather and the place is all mine. The fact that they are living with me is partially due to the fact that it gives my mother pleasure to let her friends think she and Dad have two homes and, selfishly, it gives me more time to tend to the ranch if I'm not dealing with the house, as well. But there's something you need to know. If you let her, my mother will run over you, especially when I'm not around. You're going to have to stick up for yourself or she'll make your life miserable."

"Oh, great," Marilee muttered.

As they stopped for a red light, Justin reached over and squeezed her hand.

"It won't be so bad," he said softly. "Just remember that I'm on your side. Stand your ground, darlin'. I know you can do it. If it doesn't work out, they'll be the ones leaving, not you, understand?"

*I'm on your side.* The words were still ringing in Marilee's ears when Justin accelerated through the intersection. Within a few short minutes, he was turning off the main highway onto a black-topped, two-lane road.

Marilee tensed. As the miles passed, she began to fidget.

"So...this is the way to the ranch?"

He looked at her and then smiled.

"Darlin', we've been on the ranch ever since we turned off the highway."

Her eyes widened. She turned around, looking back at where they'd been and then faced the windshield and the land beyond it. It seemed to go on forever without any sign of housing in sight. The longer she sat, the stiffer she got. Justin expected her to be nervous but wasn't prepared for what appeared to be anger.

"What's wrong?" he asked.

Her chin tilted, but she wouldn't look at him.

"You didn't tell me about this."

He frowned. "About what?"

"All this," she said, waving her hand toward the land through which they were passing. Then she turned to face him, her eyes blazing with fury. "You're not just well-off, are you, Justin Wheeler? You're stinking rich."

He wanted to laugh, but knew it would probably get his face slapped. He'd never met a woman who was insulted by his money before.

"Well...sort of," he said.

She rolled her eyes, her nostrils flaring in anger.

"Oh, perfect! That just takes the cake."

"I don't get it," Justin said. "Why does this matter?"

"Your parents. They're going to think I got

pregnant on purpose, you dolt! They're going to think I'm after your money.''

He frowned. She was right. They would think it. The odd thing was it had never occurred to him until she'd said it, and he didn't know why. It should have. He'd had it drummed into his head from the time he'd started to date. He looked at her again. She had withdrawn from him even more and was sitting in silence, staring out the window. Hating that she was even more troubled than before, he reached for her hand.

''Honey?''

''What?'' she muttered.

''I never thought it, and that's all that should matter.''

Marilee exhaled on a sigh as she turned to look at Justin. He was big and gorgeous, and right now was wearing an expression that could only be called earnest.

''Really?''

He nodded.

She sat up a little straighter and managed a small smile. ''Thank you, Justin. I think that's about the nicest thing you've ever said.''

He grinned. ''You're welcome. Now, let's get this over with. What do you say?''

She nodded.

He winked and then hit the accelerator. Minutes

later a large, sprawling ranch house appeared on the horizon. The closer they came, the tighter the knot in Marilee's belly grew. When he pulled into the yard and parked, she felt faint. There were at least a dozen cars parked in front of the house. She looked at Justin.

"I knew you should have called. They have company."

He wasn't in the mood to admit that Marilee was right. "Probably just one of Mother's groups," he said. "She's on the board of several charities."

"How absolutely perfect," she muttered.

Justin grinned. "Now, darlin', I know you can handle this. Where's that spitfire who nailed my ass to the floor of the Roadrunner?"

She thought about it a minute and then sat up straight.

"I'm right here," she muttered, and proceeded to get out of the vehicle before Justin could open the door for her. All he could do was follow.

"Leave the bags," he said. "I'll get them later. I want to get you inside and to our room so you can rest. I'll get the cook to bring you a snack."

Marilee almost stumbled. *Cook? They have a cook? Lord...please don't let there be a butler, too. I'm not cut out for this life.*

But then Justin slid his arm around her shoulder

to steady her, and gave her a quick, comforting hug. After that, everything settled into place. Whatever was going to happen would just have to happen. She'd married the man and it was too late to turn back.

A few moments later they entered the foyer. Marilee took one look at the wide hallway and the red Spanish tiles on the floor and tried not to roll her eyes in dismay. The hall was bigger than her kitchen back home. Then she sighed. That small frame house in Amarillo was no longer home, nor was it hers. This was going to be home, but it remained to be seen just how sweet it would be.

Up ahead, she could hear a murmur of voices. That must be where the women were gathered in their meeting. She glanced at Justin. He seemed oblivious to the tension she was feeling, but when he saw her looking at him, he gave her a wink and squeezed her hand. A little more of her nervousness faded. He didn't love her, but he was certainly standing by his promises.

"Come on, honey. I'll take you to my—our—bedroom so you can stretch out. We can do the tour of the place later after everyone leaves."

"Okay, but—"

"Justin?"

They both turned. Marilee took one look at the

cool questioning look on Judith Wheeler's face and braced herself for the worst.

"Darling! I didn't think you were ever coming home," Judith said, gliding across the floor and then lifting her cheek for her son to kiss. She glanced at Marilee and then looked quickly away as she grasped Justin's arms.

To the observer, it might appear that her actions were a form of an embrace, but to Marilee it looked more like an effort to control.

"Justin, darling, is there something I can help you with?" Judith asked while staring pointedly at Marilee. "Has this woman had car trouble? Is she ill? Have Maria call for a mechanic or a tow truck—whatever is needed. There's no reason for you to bother yourself any further. I'm sure you're exhausted from your trip."

A muscle jerked along Justin's jaw. His mother's thinly veiled insult about not bothering himself with Marilee had not gone unnoticed.

"No thanks, Mother. Marilee is with me and we don't need any help. As soon as your guests are gone, we'll talk."

Judith's eyebrows arched and her mouth settled into a moue of disapproval.

"Do you really think that's wise...? I mean...putting a stranger within our private quarters?"

"Mother, let it go for now." Then he looked at Marilee, silently begging her for patience. "Come on, honey. You're the one who's exhausted. You'll feel better once you've had some rest."

It was the word *honey* that set Judith off.

"Justin! I want to know who this woman is, and I demand an explanation now!"

Marilee held her breath as Justin turned on his mother, his voice low and angry.

"Fine. Mother, I'd like you to meet my wife, Marilee." Then he looked at Marilee. "Marilee...my mother, Judith Wheeler."

Judith's lips went slack as her cheeks turned red. The look she gave Marilee would have finished a lesser woman. But Marilee had lived through much worse things than an angry woman. She smiled and extended her hand.

"Mrs. Wheeler, it's a pleasure to meet you. I can see where Justin gets his looks."

Torn between vanity and hysterics, Judith was just vain enough to hesitate, giving Justin the opening he'd been waiting for.

"Marilee has had a long, tiring ride. As I'm sure you remember, Mother, at this point in a pregnancy a woman needs plenty of rest."

The mention of the word *pregnancy* was all the nudge Judith needed. Lowering her voice so that her guests would not hear her, she pointed at Marilee's stomach as if it were something foul.

"This is disgraceful and you know it. I can't believe you've done this to us! Marrying a—a—nothing like her. My God, Justin Wade! She's a virtual stranger!"

Marilee was tired of being talked about as if she wasn't even there. Her back was starting to ache and her feet were throbbing as she threw back her head and laughed.

Judith froze. Laughter was the last thing she'd expected to hear.

"You think this is funny?" she hissed, glaring at Marilee.

"Well…yes…a little. Especially the part about us being strangers." She patted her stomach to emphasize her point. "We got to know each other pretty well after being snowed in together last year, and if you think an insult is going to make me turn tail and run, then you better rethink your options."

Without looking to see if Justin was following, Marilee strode up the hall, hoping she was going the right way. Justin quickly caught up with her, slipping an arm around her shoulder and whispering a quiet "well done," leaving Judith with no other option except to get back to her guests before they caught on to the unfolding drama. The news would spread soon enough unless she could think of a way to get rid of this woman.

Later that evening, Marilee found that meeting Justin's father, Gavin, wasn't nearly as traumatic. By the time they sat down to dinner, he'd obviously been briefed on the situation and was wise enough to hold his tongue. He was congenial, even charming at times, and she was beginning to think this wasn't going to be so bad after all. Just as the meal was coming to an end, Justin got a call. Excusing himself from the table, he left them alone. Judith glared mutely at Marilee and then muttered something about a headache, leaving Marilee alone with her new father-in-law.

He stood with a smile. "Are you interested in first editions?" he asked. "I have some fine ones in my library if you'd care to look."

Marilee got up, thankful for normal conversation. "I'd love to see them," she said. "Reading is one of my favorite pastimes."

"Oh, I don't read these," Gavin said as he cupped her elbow and led her into the library.

Marilee frowned. "Really? Why on earth not?"

Gavin smiled, although his gut was in knots. He didn't want his son tied down to some nobody and was appalled that they were already married.

If only Justin had come to him first, he could have advised him to deal with this differently.

"Because they're worth a lot of money, you know, and some of them are very rare. Using them might damage them."

But Marilee was still frowning. "Yes, of course, I understood that. But they aren't like fine paintings, are they? One can admire a Degas or a Van Gogh without touching it, but what good is a book—rare or not—if it can't be read?"

Gavin was stumped for an answer. As they entered the library, he glanced toward the shelves holding his prize collection. Row upon row of leather-bound books were there for all to see, but as he stared, it occurred to him that she had a point. From where he was standing, all there was to see were the spines of the books. It was what was inside them that mattered after all.

"Do you have a favorite?" Marilee asked.

Gavin blinked, suddenly remembering where he was, and then moved toward the shelves.

"It would be hard to pick a favorite, but I'll show you the one I owned first." He took down a copy of *Huckleberry Finn* and handed it to her. "My daddy gave this to me for my tenth birthday."

When Marilee saw the title, she smiled and nodded as she gently ran her hands over the book.

"Samuel Clemens was an interesting man, don't you think? And yet, in spite of his fame, his personal life was so tragic. It's amazing that a man who suffered so badly from depression could be so creative."

Amazed by her knowledge, Gavin did nothing but nod. To his surprise, Marilee kept talking.

"He and his wife had four children, didn't they? Or was it three? No, four, because the son died early on, and then his favorite daughter, Susy, died when she was young. It nearly killed him. Soon after, I think his wife passed away and then another daughter sometime after that. I believe he had one daughter who survived him." Marilee handed the book back to Gavin with a sigh and then unconsciously laid the flat of her hand across her belly. "I can't think of anything sadder than for a parent to outlive his children."

Gavin felt shame as he put the book back on the shelf. So he'd misjudged her education. That still didn't mean she wasn't a gold digger. Without giving himself time to rethink his options, he strode to his desk and took out another book, only this one was black and flat and contained a pad of blank checks. He opened the cover, making sure that Marilee saw what was inside, and then he picked up a pen.

"How much?" he asked.

She frowned. "I'm sorry?"

Her innocence seemed genuine, but he wouldn't let himself be swayed. Judith was livid and he'd promised to fix this the same way he fixed everything that went wrong.

"Don't play innocent with me, lady. I've been around too long. How much do you want to disappear from my son's life?"

Marilee recoiled as if she'd been slapped. This had taken her by surprise, and try as she might, she knew her eyes were tearing. But she wasn't going to cry—not in front of him. She lifted her chin, her eyes flashing.

"Oh...I don't know," she drawled. "Exactly how much do you think your grandchild's life is worth?"

Gavin stifled a smile, convinced that he'd read her right after all.

"How does fifty thousand sound?" he asked.

"Like you don't think much of your own bloodline," she snapped, and then turned toward the door as Justin strolled through. "Justin! You're just in time!"

He smiled. "In time for what?"

Gavin's gut started to knot. This wasn't going the way he'd planned.

"Your father has just offered me fifty thousand dollars to disappear with your child, and I would appreciate it if you would tell him that this whole marriage thing was your idea, not mine." Then she turned toward Gavin and fixed him with a cold, angry stare. "As for you," she muttered, "I don't want your money any more than I want Justin's, and if you so much as offer me change for a parking meter, I will personally kick your worthless butt all the way to Sunday."

She stomped out of the library with her chin up and her eyes blazing. She made it all the way to her room before she started to cry, unaware that Justin was picking up where she'd left off.

Justin punched his forefinger against the second button of his father's white shirt. "You son of a bitch! How dare you! I'm not some randy sixteen-year-old who needs his daddy to get him out of trouble. I've known Marilee for more than a year. I care for her deeply. She's a good, honest woman and she's going to have my child."

"How can you be sure it's yours?" Gavin asked.

This time Justin didn't put his finger on his father's shirt; he put it in his face.

"Because I am," he said softly. "And if I ever hear you say otherwise again, you'll be out of my life—permanently. Do I make myself clear?"

Gavin paled. "Justin, son, you don't mean that.

You're our only child. You can't possibly be choosing a stranger over us?''

''But that's just it, Dad. She's not a stranger to me and she's going to have my baby, which leaves you with one choice. Shut up or get out.''

He pivoted angrily and strode out of the room, leaving Gavin Wheeler with the distinct impression that he'd just barely escaped intact. He frowned. Judith wasn't going to like this one bit, which meant that his life was going to become even more complicated than before.

Justin found Marilee in tears on their bed. Gathering her into his arms, he rocked her where they sat.

''I'm so sorry that happened,'' he said. ''That was unforgivable, but I promise it won't happen again.''

Marilee shuddered on a sob. ''Just forget it.''

''Can you?''

She couldn't answer and wouldn't look at him, and it shamed him that she'd had to endure such an affront.

''How about an early night?'' he asked. ''I have a big assortment of movies. I'll even let you pick.''

Knowing he was doing all he knew how to make her feel better, she nodded an okay.

''Great,'' he said. ''You get your nightgown on

and I'll turn on the TV. When you're ready, the videos are all in that cabinet.''

"Okay.''

Justin watched her as she got up from the bed. The larger her belly grew, the more fragile she appeared. It was almost as if the baby was sapping all of her strength. The thought frightened him. What would happen to her when it came time to deliver? Would she be strong enough to withstand the rigors of childbirth, or—

He shuddered and then thrust away the notion, refusing to accept any but positive thoughts.

Marilee undressed in the bathroom and then slipped on her nightgown. When she turned to wash her face and brush her teeth, she refused to look at her own reflection, afraid that the fear in her heart would be evident on her face. This situation wasn't good. All she could do was pray that it would eventually change. Living in this atmosphere wasn't going to be healthy—for her or for her child.

When she came out of the bathroom, Justin was nowhere in sight. Nervously she glanced at the door, wondering what battles were being waged beyond, then moved toward the cabinet where the videos were stored. The selection of movies was broader than she had expected. After a few minutes of browsing, she chose one and carried it with her back to the bed. Crawling in between the sheets, she propped herself up with the pillows.

The room was quiet; the muted colors of beige and blue soothing. In spite of the drama of the earlier events, she found herself beginning to relax. As the tension in her muscles began to ease, her eyelids drooped. She was hovering near sleep when the sound of approaching footsteps brought her upright. Seconds later, Justin came in with a flourish, bearing a tray of goodies.

"We can't watch movies without popcorn," he said, and set the tray down on the foot of the bed.

Marilee kicked back the covers as she inspected the tray, immediately nibbling on the popped corn as she poked through the other bowls.

"Mmm...chocolate."

"And cold pop," Justin added, lifting a napkin off two cans of soda.

"Pickles?" she asked, picking up a small jar of dills.

Justin grinned. "For my round little wife."

Marilee smiled, but she wanted to cry. He was trying so hard to do everything right.

"You don't have to eat them," Justin added. "I just brought them in case."

She laughed and the sound struck Justin all the way to his soul. His eyes raked her face, remembering the last time they'd been this happy and carefree. God, what he wouldn't give for a Monopoly game and a real good blizzard.

"What movie did you pick?" he asked.

Her mouth was full of popcorn, so she pointed instead of answering. He picked it up.

*"Dances with Wolves?"*

"It's one of my all-time favorites."

He started to smile. "Mine, too," he said. "Another thing we have in common." He started the movie and then kicked off his boots, stripped off his shirt and jeans and crawled into bed wearing nothing but a pair of briefs.

With the bowl of popcorn between them and the tray at their feet, they settled down to watch— Marilee watching the movie, Justin watching Marilee. An hour later she was asleep.

Justin removed the tray and set it on the floor beside their bed then turned off the VCR. Gently lifting all but one of the pillows from beneath her head, he smiled as she burrowed beneath the covers. He stood for a moment, watching her sleep, and then very carefully lifted a lock of hair from near her mouth and kissed the place where it had been lying. She tasted of popcorn and soda and just the faintest hint of sweet chocolate. Still smiling, he circled the bed and crawled in beside her. Spooning himself against the curve of her back, he cupped his hand upon her belly and buried his nose against the nape of her neck.

Quiet descended.

Just as he was drifting off to sleep, he felt a slight thump against his palm.

"Yes, Baby, Daddy's here," he said softly, and then took a deep breath of satisfaction.

When he opened his eyes, it was morning.

## Chapter 5

Marilee woke up hot. It took her a few moments to realize she wasn't coming down with a fever, but was wrapped in Justin's arms. Her tummy was rolling and she needed to go to the bathroom, but getting up was impossible until he turned her loose.

"Justin, I need to get up," she said, nudging him gently.

He came awake instantly. "What?" he muttered. "What's wrong?"

"Nothing. I just need to get up."

"Okay," he mumbled, and rolled over.

As she stood, she groaned softly. Lord, she

could barely remember what it felt like not to hurt somewhere.

Justin opened a sleepy eye. "Are you sure you're all right?"

"Just a little nauseated," she said. "It will pass."

She stumbled to the bathroom. A couple of minutes later, she opened the door to find Justin sitting on the side of the bed in a slump.

"What's wrong with you?" she asked, noticing the thin film of sweat on his upper lip and the pallor of his skin.

"I don't feel so good," he muttered, then bolted past her into the bathroom just in time to throw up.

Sympathy for his misery sent Marilee into the bathroom behind him where she handed him a cold washcloth to put on his face.

"This will make you feel better," she said. When he hesitated, she insisted. "Trust me. I know."

He swiped the cloth across his face as he sat down on the side of the tub. "Man, I don't know where that came from."

"I hope you're not coming down with a bug of some sort," Marilee said.

"It doesn't feel like a bug," Justin said. "In fact, I'm already beginning to feel better."

"Maybe it was all that junk we ate last night before we went to sleep."

He shrugged. "Maybe, although I've eaten worse with no ill effects."

"Do you think it's over?" she asked.

He nodded and then tossed the washcloth on the side of the tub as he stood. "Come on, honey, let's get dressed. Maria will fix breakfast as soon as we show up."

She arched an eyebrow. If he was already thinking of food, then he was definitely on the mend. "Maria is the cook, right? The woman who served dinner last night?"

"Yes, she's been here for almost thirty years. She worked for my grandfather before I inherited the place."

"Does everyone eat together at every meal?" she asked.

Justin sighed. After what she'd endured yesterday, he couldn't blame her for dreading another confrontation.

"Usually," he said, and then wrapped his arms around her and gave her a hug. "Don't worry, darlin'. Everything will be different today—I can promise you that."

"I don't see how," she said.

Justin's chin jutted mutinously. "Trust me."

She sighed and then looked up. "You have to know by now that I already do or I wouldn't be here, subjecting myself to this crap."

There was nothing he could say that would change the truth. "Give me a couple of minutes to brush my teeth and get dressed. Then we'll go, okay?"

While Justin was in the bathroom, Marilee dressed in shorts and a pink, loose-fitting top. By the time he emerged, she was pulling her hair up into a ponytail in deference to the heat.

"You look pretty," Justin said, and then realized he really meant it.

"You're kidding, right?"

"I don't make jokes about my woman," he growled, and gave her ponytail a tug. "And there's another thing you do that most women don't do."

"I'm your wife, not your woman. Remember?" Marilee said, then curiosity prompted her to ask, "What do I do that's so unusual?"

He didn't like being reminded that he was on probation, but he was willing to ignore it, at least for the time being.

"You don't dawdle. Being prompt is a good characteristic."

Marilee shrugged. "I've never had the luxury of dawdling."

Justin frowned, thinking of all those days she'd spent on her feet serving people their food—including him—and he'd never really appreciated the effort.

"Honey, you're never going to have to punch a time clock again. If you want to dawdle, then by God, dawdle. It gives me great pleasure to know I can at least give you that."

"You've already given me far more than I'd hoped for," she said.

"What's that?"

"Your name."

He frowned. "Well, it damned sure wasn't charity on my part. I wanted this, remember? I want you in my life and I want this baby. Don't forget that!"

A little embarrassed that he'd revealed too much of his heart, he grabbed his jeans and yanked them on, then put on his boots and shirt, unaware of how touched Marilee had been by his fervency.

A few minutes later they followed a bright path of sunlight into the dining room. A squat orange vase of yellow daffodils centered the table, setting off the gleam of well-polished oak from which the table and chairs were made. A pot of fresh coffee was on the sideboard beside a platter of sweet rolls.

Admiring the beauty but a little uncomfortable with the formality, Marilee felt safe with Justin's hand in the middle of her back. But what would happen in this house when he was gone? He couldn't stay inside with her forever. She knew she was going to have to find her place on her own. Then when a stately, middle-aged woman of Latino descent walked into the room, she braced herself, not knowing what to expect.

"Good morning, Maria," Justin said. "I would like for you to meet my wife, Marilee."

The woman smiled at Marilee. "Good morning, *señora*. It is a pleasure to meet you and an even greater pleasure to know that you are bringing new life to this house."

Marilee smiled and relaxed. This was her first, real welcome.

"Thank you, Maria."

"You are welcome. Now, Señor Justin, I am assuming you will want your regular breakfast?"

"Yes, please," Justin said.

Maria nodded, then looked at Marilee. "And you, *señora,* what would you like to eat?"

Marilee hesitated and Justin saw it. "Anything, honey. Maria is a whiz in the kitchen."

"First, I must ask you to just call me Marilee. As for food, have you ever heard of Spanish eggs? I've been craving them for days."

The older woman's eyes lit up and her face wreathed in smiles.

"Yes, yes, I know these Spanish eggs. Poached in a sauce of tomatoes, onions and green peppers, yes?"

Marilee nodded. "And served on dry toast, please?"

Maria laughed and then clapped her hands. "This is good. At last, a woman in this house who knows how to eat."

She disappeared into the kitchen just as Gavin and Judith appeared.

"Well, I can see you two are early risers," Gavin said, anxious to get past the ugliness of last night.

Justin looked at his father just long enough to make sure Gavin's friendliness wasn't forced, then turned his full attention to his mother. She was giving him one of her *wounded* expressions, but he'd seen them too many times in his life to be affected.

"I have a lot to catch up on today and Marilee was hungry," Justin said as he seated Marilee at the table.

Judith poured a cup of coffee and then moved toward the table, languidly draping herself in a chair beside the window. A few minutes passed during which time she took three careful sips of her coffee. Then, as if some internal clock went off, she set the cup down and turned toward Marilee, blessing her with her most brilliant smile.

"My dear, I want to apologize for yesterday. I hope you'll chalk it up to surprise and forgive me." Then she waved a hand toward Gavin, as well. "For that matter, forgive both of us for our thoughtlessness."

"You're forgiven," Marilee said, although she didn't buy a word of the apology.

"Wonderful," Judith said. "Now that we've settled that bit of business, I want you to accompany me into Lubbock today for some shopping. We'll buy you some new clothes and whatever else we can find that we can't live without. What do you say?"

Justin tensed. He didn't trust his mother, and the last thing he wanted was for her to get Marilee alone. But he needn't have worried. Marilee wasn't interested.

"No, thanks," Marilee said. "I'm still tired from traveling and, truthfully, I don't need a thing, so there's no need for me to go."

Gavin stared, unable to believe what he'd heard. There sat a woman who had not only refused a trip to go shopping, but had admitted she didn't need anything. Something told him that he was going to have to readjust his opinion of his new daughter-in-law even more.

Judith frowned. This wasn't going the way she'd planned. "Are you sure?" she asked.

"Yes, but thank you," Marilee said, and inhaled with delight as Maria came back in the room with her food and set it in front of her. "Oooh, that looks wonderful, Maria. Thank you so much."

"You are welcome," Maria said, then set Justin's plate in front of him, as well.

"Señor Gavin...Señora Judith...may I fix your breakfast now?"

Judith wrinkled her nose in disgust. "No, no, I'll just have a roll and some more coffee," she said.

But Gavin was eyeing Marilee's plate with interest. "Those look good. What are they?"

Marilee pushed her plate toward Justin's father. "Spanish eggs. Would you like a bite?"

Gavin hesitated. He hadn't eaten off anybody's plate in his entire life. He glanced at Marilee and then picked up his fork. "If you're sure you don't mind?"

She smiled. "How will you know unless you try them?"

He took a small bite and then rolled his eyes with pleasure.

"Wow. Those are damned good. Maria, fix me some of those, will you?"

Marilee hid a smile as she pulled her plate back in front of her. It figured. The way to a man's heart—any man—was quite often through his stomach. Then she glanced at Justin and grinned. If she didn't know better, she would think he was jealous.

"Do you want to taste them, too?" she asked.

He grinned. "Read my mind, didn't you?" and took a small bite, careful not to eat too much of the food she needed to be eating.

"Dang, Dad! You're right. These are really good!" Then he leaned over and kissed Marilee on the cheek. "Thanks for sharing, darlin'. Now eat up. You need that a whole lot worse than we do."

Judith was disgusted by the show of affection and kept trying to catch Gavin's eye, but it wasn't working. Gavin had already seen the proverbial writing on the wall. He wasn't about to lose the affection of his only son because his wife was in a snit. And as for the woman Justin had married, Gavin was starting to see her in a different light. Maybe—just maybe—she wasn't a gold digger, after all.

The meal passed in relative calm, but the underlying tension was giving Marilee a headache. As soon as the meal was over, she excused herself. Justin left with her, then followed her into their bathroom. When she shook a couple of painkillers from the bottle, he held out his hand.

"Give me two of those, too, will you? My head hurts like hell. I don't know what's wrong with me. I'm never sick."

Marilee stared at him as he swallowed them down and then frowned as she thought back over the morning. He was suffering every symptom she had. Could it be… Was it possible that—?

"I think I know what's wrong with you," she said.

Justin frowned. "What?"

"Sympathy pains."

His frown deepened. "Sympathy pains. What the hell are those?"

"It happens sometimes...for the expectant father, I mean. He actually suffers the same physical ailments as his wife during the pregnancy."

Justin's eyes widened. "Good Lord! If this is the case, I will not survive the delivery."

Marilee laughed out loud. "I don't think it goes quite that far."

"Thank God," he muttered, and then grinned. "Although, if I could...I would take that pain from you, as well."

"Oh, yeah right," she said, and then playfully punched him in the chest.

Before he thought, he had his arms around her and his mouth on her lips. The kiss was playful, but the moment they touched, it changed to one of need and desperation—and of a deep, abiding love.

"Oh, darlin'," Justin whispered when he finally pulled back. "Forgive me for breaking my promise, but I've been wanting to do that for days."

Marilee sighed. This was inevitable. Maybe he didn't love her, but she knew that he cared, and denying herself even this much of his affection was hurting her more than him.

"There's nothing to forgive," she said, and then cupped the side of his cheek with her hand. "Maybe I was wrong in demanding that you keep your distance. We're married, and where you're concerned, it's obvious I have no pride."

Justin shook his head and then put his arms around her, holding her close and cherishing the bulge of belly between them. This was his woman and she was carrying his child. He was the one who'd tossed pride in the dirt.

"Pride doesn't warm hearts, honey girl, but if you'll let me, my love surely will."

Marilee froze. He'd said the L word. She looked up, unaware that her own feelings for him were there on her face. But Justin saw them and smiled.

"You gonna let me love you, or am I still paying penance?"

"Do you mean—"

"Yes, I mean. You should know by now that I'm an 'all or nothing' kind of guy. I cared for you, even when I didn't want to admit it. I thought of you at least once a day ever since that blizzard, but was too bullheaded to admit to myself I cared. It wasn't until I was faced with losing you—and our baby—that I realized how much you meant to me."

Marilee's features crumpled.

"Darlin', don't cry," Justin begged, and took her in his arms.

"I have to," Marilee said as she wrapped her arms around Justin's waist.

He kissed the top of her head and held her close. "Well, hell, if it makes you feel better, then you just go ahead and bawl." Then he added, "Are you still mad at me?"

"Probably," she sobbed.

His heart sank. "What can I do? I'll do anything to prove that I really care."

She lifted her face, her cheeks streaked with tears. "I guess we *could* make love." Then she rubbed her hand across the swell of her stomach. "Unless you're too turned off by this."

He froze. "You don't turn me off and you know it, or at least you should, as close as we've been sleeping."

She almost smiled.

His eyes narrowed. "Marilee, have you been stringing me along?"

Her lips twitched. "A little."

"You knew I was falling in love with you, didn't you?"

"I was hoping that it was more than the baby that made you cuddle so close at night."

"Lord have mercy," he groaned, and took her in his arms. "How do we do this without hurting you?"

She smiled through tears. "Don't worry. There are ways."

More than two months had passed since Justin and Marilee's marriage. Day by day their relationship continued to grow stronger, much to the dismay of Justin's mother. On the outside, Judith was polite and smiling, but on the inside she was seething. This woman her son had married had come into *her* home, stole the affections of the two men in *her* life away from her and was settling in with disgusting ease. Even the hired help adored her. It was as if Marilee could do nothing wrong.

For the past two months, Judith had been on a private mission to get her life back on track. She was convinced that Marilee was hiding some heinous past, and if she could just find out what it was, Justin would finally see the woman for who she really was. A couple of phone calls and some divorce papers would solve the rest of Judith's problems. And so she waited, certain that Marilee would make a mistake and reveal her true colors.

\* \* \*

Marilee stood back, admiring the baby furniture that had just been delivered, and then opened a window to let in some fresh air. Justin had painted the walls of the nursery over the weekend and the scent of new paint was a little overwhelming. Satisfied when the air began to circulate, she reached for the hammer she'd laid on the dresser and took a nail from her pocket. The Winnie the Pooh theme that she'd chosen for the room was perfect. Now all she needed was to hang two small pictures of Pooh Bear and his friends in the Hundred Acre Woods and the room would be finished. With a few sharp thumps of the hammer, the first nail went in. She had the picture hung and was eyeballing the second location when Justin came through the door.

"Darlin', you shouldn't be doing that. Why didn't you ask for help? You know what Doc Blankenship said last week. You're supposed to be taking it easy. According to him, you're underweight and pale, and he glared at me, not you, when he said it."

Marilee grinned. The obstetrician she'd been seeing in Lubbock was in his late sixties and looked more like a veterinarian than a medical doctor, with his gray handlebar mustache and his scuffed cowboy boots, but she'd trusted him on sight.

Justin took the hammer out of her hands and then kissed her on the cheek. "I need a nail, please."

She smiled and handed him the nail.

"Where do you want it?" he asked.

"Right next to the other one, like a grouping."

"You got it," he said.

Moments later the pictures were in place.

"What do you think?" Marilee asked.

Justin grinned. "That you're cute as all get-out."

"I was talking about the room. Besides, I look like I swallowed a watermelon whole. How can I be cute?"

"Beats me, but you are," Justin said, and then swung her off her feet.

"Justin, I'm too heavy," Marilee cried, and then laughed when he began to dance her around the floor. "You're crazy—you know that?"

"Yep. Crazy for you," Justin said, and started humming the theme song from Winnie the Pooh. They made two turns around the room before Justin finally stopped. "You know what? I'm a lucky man."

"You think?"

He nodded, then suddenly serious, he cupped her face with both hands. "Oh, yes...but, darlin', I'm so sorry your parents didn't live to share this with you."

The smile froze on Marilee's face. Her parents! She nodded, while debating with herself about telling him the truth. Her parents, had they still been alive, would have been too busy hating each other's guts to enjoy anything. Then she shrugged off the thought.

"I've been on my own so long, I often forget that I ever had parents," she said, and then grabbed the hammer. "I'd better return this. I promised Maria I would put it back when I was through."

Marilee had changed the subject on purpose, because the last thing Maria would do was fuss about a hammer.

"Are you okay?" he asked gently. "I didn't mean to upset you by talking about your parents."

"Of course I'm all right, and you certainly didn't upset me." She flashed him a very big smile and suspected he could tell it was as fake as it felt. "Want some lemonade?"

Justin hesitated and then sighed. Marilee almost never talked about her past, but he was confident that one day she would feel comfortable enough to tell him anything.

"Yeah, sure, lemonade sounds great, especially if Maria has any of those oatmeal cookies left to go with it."

They headed for the kitchen, unaware that Judith had been eavesdropping on their conversation, or that she was smiling with glee as they walked away. As soon as they were gone, she bolted for the library to make a call. A few minutes later she hung up the phone, satisfied that the private investigator she'd called would dig up some condemning evidence about Marilee's past. Then she would be rid of her once and for all.

That night at dinner, Marilee noticed Judith picking at her food and mentally braced herself for a family argument. Justin thought it was funny that Marilee had picked up on so many of his mother's eccentricities, but in Marilee's case, it was a matter of self-defense. When Judith smiled without showing her teeth, it really meant disdain. When she was angry, a small tic appeared at the corner of her left eye, and when she was trying to find the perfect opportunity to introduce a subject into the conversation that she knew Gavin would dislike, she picked at her food.

To Marilee's dismay, when Judith finally laid down her fork and looked up, she was looking directly at her. And when she smiled without showing her teeth, Marilee braced herself for the worst.

"Marilee…darling…I have the most marvelous news. Some of my friends want to give you a baby shower. Of course, I told them that I would check with you first before they sent out invitations so that you could furnish them with addresses of your family and friends, too."

It was the last thing she had expected Judith to say. She glanced at Justin, who was grinning from ear to ear.

"Well…that's really sweet of them," Marilee said. "Especially since I've only met a few."

Judith's smile was simmering close to a sneer, although she didn't know it.

"I know. I was a bit surprised, myself," Judith said. "So…if you'll make out a list of names and addresses, I'll see that they get it." Her gaze slid from Marilee's face to her belly. "It will have to be soon. God only knows when the baby will be born."

Justin's smile died and his eyes narrowed sharply as he gave his mother a look.

"Oh, my...I'm sure I didn't mean that the way it sounded," she said. "I was just referring to how uncertain the arrival of a first baby could be."

Marilee refused to be led into one of Judith's famous bickering matches and laid her hand on Justin's arm, giving it a gentle squeeze as she spoke.

"As you know, my parents are deceased, and I have no other living relatives, so please tell your friends that I won't have any people to invite. I haven't lived here long enough to make those kinds of friends, and Amarillo is too far away for any of my friends to drive just to come to a baby shower. Besides, two of them don't even own cars."

Judith arched an eyebrow. "That figures," she muttered, although it didn't surprise her that Justin's wife would have friends in that sort of financial stratum.

"Mother..."

The warning tone in Justin's voice made Judith want to scream. Until this nothing came into their lives, she could do no wrong in her son's eyes. Now it seemed as if she couldn't do anything right.

"For pity's sake, Justin Wade. Stop treating me as if I was an unruly child! I'm your mother, not one of the hired help, and I will not be talked to like that."

"If you all will excuse me, I feel the need for some air," Marilee said, and got up without waiting for anyone's permission.

Both Gavin and Justin were glaring at Judith so harshly that she felt obliged to call out, "I hope you're not leaving on my account. If I've offended you, I'm sorry."

Marilee stopped, then turned, unaware of how regal she appeared in the blue, floor-length caftan with bronze-and-gold braid that Justin had given her last week.

"That's a lie, Judith, and you and I know it, but you're excused anyway. You spend your days searching for the most minute ways to offend me, but I wish you would stop, because it's not going to work. My happiness does not depend on your approval, and the sooner you get that through your head, the better off we'll all be."

Then she walked away, leaving them momentarily speechless. Justin was the first to react as he shoved his chair back and stood.

"Damn you, Mother. You never stop. You're

like a little kid with a sore, just picking and picking and never letting it heal.''

Judith's eyes flashed angrily. ''That's not true!''

''Hush, Judith,'' Gavin said sharply. ''You've already said enough for one night.''

She shoved her chair back with a jerk and stood abruptly. ''Well, I never! If that's the kind of treatment I'm going to get, then I'm going to my room. All I did was give that woman some good news, and it gets dashed in my face. I've a good mind to tell my friends to cancel the shower, after all.''

''You do what you want,'' Justin said. ''You always do. Now, if you both will excuse me, I'm going to check on my wife.''

''But Maria hasn't served dessert!'' Judith called out.

Gavin glared at his wife and then got up and left without bothering to comment, leaving her alone in the dining room.

Furious beyond words, she picked up her water glass and flung it at the wall, where it shattered into pieces. Then realizing that she'd broken a glass from her good crystal, she promptly dissolved into tears.

Justin found Marilee outside on the patio. She

was sitting in a lounge chair holding Maria's fat tomcat in her lap. She looked up with a smile as Justin emerged from the house.

"I'm running out of lap to hold Gomez," she said as she scratched the big yellow cat behind the ears.

"Gomez doesn't seem to mind," Justin said, and then pulled a chair up beside her and gave the cat an absent pat.

"I'm sorry," Marilee said. "I shouldn't have let her get to me. If I'd just kept on walking, it would have been better."

"You do not hide in your own house," Justin said, and then moved his hand from the cat to Marilee's arm. "I thought this animosity would even itself out, but I was wrong and it's not fair for you to have to put up with this. I'll speak to Dad in the morning."

Marilee's shock was evident. Even though she wished them gone, she knew Justin enjoyed their presence, especially his father's. If they left because of her, she was afraid that somewhere down the line Justin would resent her for it.

"Just let it go," she said. "It doesn't bother me...really."

"You lie," Justin said, then leaned over and

kissed her gently on the lips. "But it's a very sweet lie."

She smiled, her heart in her eyes.

"Women have always done foolish things for the men they love," she said softly.

Justin looked at her, all but lost in the blue-black shadows of dusk with that cat on her lap and the love in her eyes.

"You know what I'm wishing for right now?"

"What?" she asked.

"A blizzard."

"A blizzard? And me only weeks away from delivery? Bite your tongue," Marilee gasped.

Justin grinned. "Well, it's not going to snow in Lubbock in August, so we're safe there, but I think you know what I mean."

Marilee sighed. "Yes, I think so." She dumped the cat from her lap and stood, then moved to sit on Justin's lap instead. "That was probably the best time we've ever had together."

"Well...not the best, but certainly the most carefree."

"After the baby comes, carefree will be a thing of the past," Marilee warned.

Justin smiled. "I've had carefree and it was lonely more than not. I'll take you and a houseful of kids, rather than be alone again."

"Really?"

He grinned. "Yes, really."

"Hey, you two. Can anyone join the conversation, or is it too hot for my ears?"

Marilee waved at Gavin. "Come join us. You can have my chair. I've found a better one."

Gavin patted Marilee's head as he passed them to take a seat. He smiled at them as he sat, trying to remember a time when Judith would have sat in his lap and couldn't. It didn't say much for their thirty-five years of marriage.

"I'm sorry about Judith's rudeness," he said softly.

"It's her burden to bear, not mine," Marilee said.

Gavin nodded, then sighed. "You're a good woman, Marilee, and I will forever regret letting Judith influence me into that insulting welcome on your first day here."

Marilee surprised both men by laughing aloud. "I'm glad you didn't make that second offer, because right now I'm in no shape to kick your butt."

Justin grinned when Gavin laughed. "She's hell on wheels," Justin said. "You should have seen her take the hide off me at the Roadrunner Truck Stop."

It was the first time Justin had mentioned anything about his prior relationship with Marilee,
and Gavin was pleased that he finally trusted him
enough to let go.

"He had it coming," Marilee said.

"That I can believe," Gavin said.

"Hey, you two, no fair ganging up on me. Besides, I redeemed myself quite nicely, I believe."

Marilee leaned back in his arms, relishing the
strength and caring of the man who held her.

"Yes, you did," she said, and then winced as
the baby suddenly rolled. "Oh, Lord! Justin! Did
you feel that?"

But Justin was already scooting her out of his
lap and heading for the kitchen.

"What's wrong with him?" Gavin asked.

"Poor Justin," Marilee said. "He's suffering
sympathy pains. Everything I get, he gets two-
fold."

"You're kidding!" Gavin exclaimed.

She shook her head. "Afraid not."

Gavin looked at her anew. "He really loves
you, doesn't he?"

She looked intently at her father-in-law in the
encroaching darkness, but could only see the
vague outline of his face. She didn't have to see
him to know he was surprised by the revelation.

"At first I didn't think so, even though he kept telling me so. But I believe it now."

There was a quiet hesitation, and then Gavin asked the obvious.

"Do you love him...? I mean...really love him?"

Marilee sighed. "Sometimes it seems like I've loved him forever."

Gavin was silent for quite a while. Finally he stood and reached for her, his fingers closing around her wrist in the dark.

"Marilee...I've always considered my son to be an intelligent man, but I believe the smartest thing he ever did was marry you and bring you home."

Before she could answer, she heard a door slam and knew Justin was on his way out.

"Darlin', I don't want you sitting out here in the dark. Come on inside with Dad and me. We'll watch a movie and pop some corn."

"Can I pick the movie?" she asked.

Both men groaned loudly as she was led inside. The last time Justin had let her pick, she'd cried all the way through the show.

"I won't pick a sad one, I promise," she said.

"As long as you don't cry, we're in business," Justin said. "I can't stand to see you cry."

# Chapter 6

Several days came and went, with no further mention being made of the baby shower, which led Marilee to believe that an offer had never been made at all. She suspected it was something Judith had dreamed up just to foster a fight and had dismissed it completely. Heavy with child and complacent within the love with which Justin surrounded her, she let down her guard. It was just what Judith had been waiting for.

Judith strode through the rooms in search of Marilee with purpose in every step. The brown, manila envelope she was carrying held the key to her deliverance. She was convinced that once she confronted Justin's wife with this evidence, Marilee would slink away without a fight.

"Maria! Have you seen Justin's wife?" she demanded as she entered the kitchen.

Maria was well aware of the animosity between the two women and was thoroughly on Marilee's side, but could find no reason to withhold this information.

"She is outside by the pool."

Judith spun around without thanks and headed for the patio doors and the terrace overlooking the pool. As she exited the house, she spied Marilee sitting in a lounge chair beneath the shade of an old mimosa tree. On approach, she realized that Marilee was reading one of Gavin's first editions.

"How dare you even handle one of my husband's books?" she gasped.

Marilee frowned. She wasn't feeling well, and butting heads with this woman right now was the last thing she wanted to do.

"I'm not handling it, I'm reading it," she said. "Gavin has given me permission to read anything I want from his library, anytime I want." She held up the volume. "It's O. Henry. You should try him sometime."

For Judith, it was the ultimate betrayal. Gavin had allowed this upstart a privilege even she didn't share. The fact that she'd never asked didn't matter. It was the principle of the thing.

"Well! If you're wanting to read so badly, then read this!" she exclaimed, and dropped the manila envelope into Marilee's lap.

"What's this?" Marilee asked.

"Read it and see for yourself," Judith snapped.

Marilee laid the borrowed book aside and then opened the envelope. Several pages were inside, but it was the heading on the cover letter that first caught her eye: *Colbert Investigations.*

She looked up at Judith with disbelief. "You had me investigated?"

Judith crossed her arms over her breasts and smiled without showing her teeth.

"Yes! And I want you out of this house within the hour." To emphasize her determination, she tossed a plane ticket onto the envelope.

Marilee pushed it aside as she glanced through the papers, her anger growing with each passing moment.

"Get out!" Judith said. "You can read them on the way to the airport. And when that brat you're carrying is born, I demand a DNA test. I'll prove once and for all that you can't possibly be carrying my son's child!"

Still clutching the papers, Marilee pulled herself from the chair. Her lower back was aching and there was a sick feeling in the pit of her belly that wouldn't go away. The look of hatred on the older woman's face was unwavering, and in that moment Marilee's patience snapped. Bringing a baby into this kind of bitterness was obscene, and she wasn't going to do it. Judith didn't know it yet, but she'd pushed Marilee one step too far.

"You bitch!" Marilee muttered, and threw the papers in Judith's face. "What did you hope to gain by doing this? There isn't anything in here that I don't know, and I damn sure haven't been trying to hide it."

"You said your parents were dead," Judith said with a sneer.

Marilee resisted the urge to roll her eyes. "Well, yes, actually they are. My mother bled to death from the gunshot wound my father inflicted and the state of Texas fried his butt for the murder. How much deader can they get?"

Judith blanched. She'd expected denial, not this blatant acceptance of such sordid facts.

"But my son... We've never had such... Our family isn't accustomed to..."

"Neither were we, until it happened," Marilee said. "And you know something? You win. I'm going, but not in the way you expected. I'm not raising my baby around someone as selfish and

bitter as you. You don't deserve to be a grand-
mother.''

Without giving Judith time to react, she
grabbed the cell phone from the table and
punched in a series of numbers, knowing that Justin would answer before the second ring.

"What are you doing?" Judith cried.

"Surely you didn't think I would slink away
like some tramp in the night? I'm calling my husband," Marilee screamed. "I'm telling him what
you've done and where I'm going and if he—"

The phone in Justin's truck began to ring just
as he finished banding a newborn bull calf. Within
a few days, the tiny testicles would drop off and
the animal would continue to flourish as a steer.
It was simpler and less painful than waiting until
the animal was half-grown and then castrating it
with a knife.

Satisfied that the calf was okay, he let it go and
then took off his gloves as he headed for the truck
to answer the phone.

But his feeling of contentment died the moment
he answered the call. Before he could say hello,
he heard the sound of women screaming and his
heart dropped. Something was wrong with Marilee. He started to shout just to make himself
heard.

"Hello? Hello? Someone tell me what the hell is going on?"

Marilee had forgotten she'd made the call and stared at the phone in her hand as if it were a snake. Then she heard Justin's voice and took a deep breath.

"Justin, it's me. I can't take this anymore and I'm not raising our child in this kind of hate. If you want anything more to do with me or this baby, then you'd better get home because I'm packing."

Before he could answer, she'd hung up in his ear.

"Son of a bitch," Justin muttered. Seconds later he was flying across the pasture in the truck, leaving a rooster tail of dust in his passing.

Gavin entered the house just as Marilee was yelling into the phone. He heard just enough to know that Judith had done something bad—and from the sound of Marilee's voice, it wasn't something an apology could fix. He started running toward the noise, but was too late. All he saw of Marilee was her backside as she bolted down the hall. He turned, glaring at his wife as she came inside.

"What the hell have you done?" he asked, and then snatched the papers she was holding. Seconds later he looked up in disbelief. "You had her investigated?"

"I had to save Justin from—"

"You're the one he needs saving from!" Gavin roared. Then he flung the papers in her face as he headed for Marilee's bedroom. Someone had to stop her until Justin returned.

Judith was caught between disbelief and panic. This hadn't gone at all like she'd expected. Not only had Marilee refused to leave quietly, but she'd raised more hell than she would have believed to be possible.

"You're crazy, Gavin Wheeler! She's made all of you crazy!" Judith screamed, then stormed into the library and grabbed Gavin's cut-glass decanter of Kentucky sipping whiskey. "I need a drink!" she announced as Maria entered the room.

"I will pray for your soul," Maria muttered.

"I don't need prayers! I just need that woman out of my house!" Judith screeched.

"It is not your house, it is Señor Justin's," Maria said as she laid the morning mail down on Justin's desk.

"You're fired!" Judith screamed.

"You can't fire me because I don't work for you, I work for Señor Justin," Maria said, and then walked out of the room.

"Savages! They're all savages!" Judith muttered, and tossed back the first shot, gasping for breath as the whiskey burned all the way down her throat. Then she poured another, drinking it as if it were medicine.

Down the hall, Gavin was pulling clothes out of Marilee's suitcase as quickly as she threw them in.

"Stop it!" Marilee sobbed. "You don't understand. I've got to get out of here. This constant bickering is making me sick."

"You can't leave, honey. Justin loves you. I love you."

But Marilee was deaf to everything but the need for peace. And there was a part of her that wasn't so sure how Justin would feel about her past when he did know the truth. Her father had murdered and he'd been executed. It was a sad, but ugly, fact that Judith Wheeler would obviously hold over her head for the rest of her life. No matter how much she loved Justin, she couldn't live that way.

She stuffed another handful of her underwear into the suitcase just as Gavin pulled it out. Before she could tell him to stop, Justin burst into the room, his face pale from shock. He took one look at Marilee and took her into his arms.

"What the hell happened?"

Marilee started crying all over again. "Your mother…"

"Oh, hell, I should have known." He looked at his dad. "What has she done now?"

Gavin shrugged. "Ask Marilee. I came in on the tail end of the fight."

Marilee started to sob even harder. "She had me investigated and then threatened me with the information. She told me to get out of her house and that when the baby was born she was demanding a DNA test to prove it wasn't yours and she—"

"That does it!" Justin muttered. "She's gone too far."

"Wait," Marilee said. "There's something about my past that I didn't tell you."

"I don't give a damn about things that happened before I met you. I wasn't any angel, myself. You're my wife and that's all that matters." He took out a handkerchief and starting wiping the tears from her face. "Please, honey, you've got to stop crying like this. It can't be good for you or the baby."

"It didn't happen *to* me…. Oh, well…in a way I guess it did, but not like you think." She took a deep breath. "My mother…"

"What about her?" Justin asked.

"My father murdered her," Marilee said.

Both Justin and Gavin were momentarily speechless, but it was Justin who was the first to react.

"Good Lord, darlin'. How awful for you."

"He was executed by the state of Texas five years ago."

Justin snorted beneath his breath. "Well, at least that's one parent who won't be giving us any trouble. I'm sorry I can't say the same for myself."

Marilee almost laughed. "Then you aren't mad at me for not telling you sooner?"

Justin groaned. "Honey, there isn't anything you could do that would make me mad at you."

"Or me, either," Gavin added. "And it would seem that Judith forgot to mention that her great-great-grandfather was hanged for rustling cattle."

At that moment, Judith staggered into the bedroom with a drink in one hand and the nearly empty decanter in the other. She heard just enough of her husband's last statement to mutter something about lynch mobs, then passed out in the doorway.

Before they could react to Judith's arrival, Marilee doubled over with a groan.

"Marilee? Honey?"

"My water broke... The baby... I think it's coming."

"Oh, Lord," Justin muttered. "Are you having any pains?"

"If the ones across my back count, yes."

"How long have you been having them?" Gavin asked as Justin raced for the phone.

"Most of the afternoon," Marilee said. "I thought it was just a backache."

Gavin steadied her while Justin grabbed the little suitcase that she'd packed for the occasion over a week ago.

"Dad, help me get her into the truck."

Gavin winked at Marilee as he slipped an arm beneath her shoulder.

"It would be my pleasure," he said softly.

Marilee groaned again as a spasm of pain rippled across her lower abdomen.

"Hurry," she begged, and then almost laughed as they actually lifted her over Judith's prone body on the way out the door.

Moments later she was in the truck and Justin was buckling her inside. Just before he got in the truck, he turned to Gavin.

"Dad, don't take this the wrong way, but I need to ask you a favor."

"You don't need to ask," Gavin said. "We should have gone home to Austin the week you came home with your wife, but we didn't. However, it's not too late to fix the mess we've made.''

"Thanks," Justin said, and then Marilee groaned again. He glanced back into the truck. "I've got to go. I'll call you from the hospital when it's over."

"Use my cell phone," Gavin said. "If I can get your mother off the floor and into the car, we'll be on the road to Austin. Now get that girl to the hospital and bring home my first grandbaby, you hear?"

Six hours later, Clayton Wade Wheeler made his entry into the world, protesting greatly.

As the birthing nurse laid the child in his mother's arms, Marilee's eyes filled with tears. His hair was dark like Justin's, but it was that single dimple in the baby's left cheek that made her smile.

"Look, Justin. He has your dimple."

Justin was so entranced by the tiny male in his wife's arms that he could do little more than stare. He traced the side of the baby's cheek with his finger, lingering on the small indentation that would certainly become a dimple.

"God...he's so perfect." Then he looked at Marilee with something close to awe. "Thank you, darlin'. Thank you for loving me and for giving me a son.''

She smiled as she kissed the top of the baby's head and then began fingering the tiny hands.

"You're very welcome," she said, and then shifted the baby in her arms. "Clay boy, it's time to meet your daddy. Justin, hold your child as dearly as you hold me, and he'll never come to harm.''

With tears in his eyes, Justin picked him up.

"What do you think?" Marilee asked.

Justin looked at the baby and then back at Marilee. "I think we're pretty damned good at making babies," he said, his voice gruff with emotion.

Weary and achy, she still found enough energy to laugh. "I can't argue with that," she said, and then closed her eyes. "Lord...I'm so tired.''

The birthing nurse was still present in the room and heard Marilee's last remark.

"Your wife had a pretty hard time of it. We have to take the baby to the nursery and weigh and measure him now anyway. Why don't we let her get some rest?''

But Marilee heard them and opened her eyes. "Justin?"

"I'm right here, darlin'.''

"The baby... When they take him to be weighed...don't let him go alone."

Justin took a deep breath to keep from crying. "I won't," he said softly, and then leaned down and gave her a slow, sweet kiss. "I'll take good care of him just like I'm going to take care of you. And when you're all rested and feeling better, we're going to drink a toast."

"No alcoholic beverages if the mother is nursing," the nurse cautioned.

"We'll use juice," Justin promised.

The nurse nodded approvingly. "What are you going to toast?"

Justin grinned at Marilee. "For starters... Monopoly games and blizzards."

Marilee laughed.

# *Epilogue*

Justin stood at the window overlooking the terrace, watching his wife and son in the pool. Clay would be two in a few short weeks and Marilee was teaching him how to swim. His heart swelled with pride as he watched the ongoing lesson. Marilee's patience was unending and Clay's determination was just as strong. It made him sick to his stomach, every time he remembered how close he'd come to never knowing about Clay. And his wife—he couldn't imagine life without her.

The phone rang in the middle of his musings.

"Hello?"

"Justin, darling, how are you?"

"Fine, Mother. How are you and Dad?"

"Okay, but we'd be better if we knew when you were coming to see us again. I just know our little Clay boy is growing like a weed. Is he all right? What has he been doing?"

Justin turned back to the window, smiling to himself as Clay jumped off the side of the pool into Marilee's arms.

"He's good. Marilee is teaching him how to swim."

"Oh, Lord... Do you think—"

"Mother."

The slight warning tone in Justin's voice was enough to remind Judith of her place.

"I'm sorry, dear. I know Marilee is a wonderful mother, but don't tell me not to worry about all of you because I can't help it. It's something that comes with the territory of being a mother and, unfortunately, never goes away."

Justin grinned. The first time his mother had seen the baby and realized he was a carbon copy of her son, she'd done a complete about-face toward Marilee, even apologizing in tears and begging forgiveness. But her real test had come that first Christmas when they'd gathered together at

the ranch for dinner and Gavin had proposed the
first toast. Judith had raised her glass along with
everyone else and then turned red in the face
when Gavin toasted her great-great-grandfather's
brief career in the cattle business. She had however, taken it in good stride, knowing that it was
his subtle way of reminding her that she was the
last person who should be casting stones.

Justin chuckled beneath his breath, but when
Judith spoke, she realized he hadn't been listening
to her at all.

"I'm sorry, Mother. What were you saying?"

Judith sighed. "I asked if it would be all right
if your father and I drove up one day next week.
We can only stay one night. I have bridge club
and I'm on the planning committee for the Har-
vest Ball at your father's club, so we can't stay
any longer."

"That's fine, Mom. I'll tell Marilee you're
coming. Just give us a call before you leave."

"Wonderful," Judith said. "Give Marilee and
Clay boy our love," she said, and hung up.

Justin hung up the receiver then turned back to
the window. Suddenly the need to be with them
was stronger than updating the accounts. His
mother wanted him to give them her love.

"I believe I will," he murmured, and walked

out of his office. As he exited the house, Marilee saw him coming and waved. "Hey, darlin', how's the little fish coming?" he asked.

Clay squealed. "Daddy! I not a little fish! Look at me! Look at me! I can swim!"

Clay began flailing his arms and legs in the water, confident that his mother's hand would still be on his belly as it had been all afternoon.

Water went everywhere, dousing Marilee's face and hair, even onto the legs of Justin's jeans.

"Hey," Marilee said, as she lifted Clay out of the water, "you're getting Daddy's pants all wet."

"I don't care," Justin said, and held out his hands. "Give him to me. I'm thinking I need a big hug." Then he winked at Marilee as she lifted Clay out of the pool. "Besides, I've been at the mercy of the elements ever since the day we met."

Marilee laughed. "So the weather was your Waterloo?"

"In more ways than one," Justin said, and then grinned when Clay put both little wet hands on either side of his face and gave him a big, wet kiss.

"Mom and Dad send their love. They want to come up one day next week and spend the night."

Marilee nodded, then smiled. "I just hope they don't bring another carload of presents. Clay has too many already."

Justin looked at her then, drenched from head to toe and standing waist-deep in the pool. Her blue, two-piece swimsuit was glued to her body like skin and she had that come-hither smile on her face. His gut clenched with a wanting he couldn't deny.

"Clay boy, I'm thinking it's about time for your nap," he said.

Marilee gave Justin a Mona Lisa smile and then climbed out of the pool and took Clay out of his father's arms.

"Daddy's right, little man. You've worked very, very hard today, and it's time for all good cowboys to take a rest."

Clay's lower lip jutted out. "Daddy is a cowboy. Is Daddy gonna take a rest, too?"

Marilee looked back at her husband, acknowledging the hunger in his eyes and then nodded slowly.

"Oh, yes…I think he's more than ready for bed. Aren't you, Daddy?"

Justin's eyes glittered. "Yep, and after Mommy tucks you in bed, she's going to tuck me in, too. Aren't you, Mommy?"

Marilee laughed. "Something like that," she said, and then walked inside with their child in her arms.

Justin grinned as he followed them into the house.

Dear Reader,

I come from the generation where babies were said to be found in fields, under cabbages in cabbage patches and flown in by storks on steroids. I had a very enlightened mother who broke tradition and told me the real story, that she hadn't suddenly gained far too much weight by overindulging on chocolate (sadly, that was to come later, with the advent of designer chocolate) but that there was a baby growing in her tummy. I was seven at the time. As I waited for my first brother to be born, one of my parents' friends tried to tell me that the new addition to my family would be discovered soon in the cabbage patch, and I distinctly remember wondering why his wife hadn't told him the truth as my mother had told me. It's been many years since that happened, but the story has stayed with me.

When the opportunity to be part of this anthology came up, I decided to meld a little of that story with a few other things. There is a lovely little girl of about seven or eight in my neighborhood who can often be seen giving her little brother a ride in a little red wagon. That image, too, sticks in my mind, and it married itself to my cabbage patch memory. Taking those two fragments, adding in a recent local news item about a carjacking gone wrong and throwing in a pinch of this, a dash of that, I've managed to cook up another story that I sincerely hope you enjoy reading. I do, because I love happy endings, and if I don't find them in life, I make them up. I hope I've succeeded in entertaining you again, and from the bottom of my heart I hope you find wonderful things in the cabbage patches of your life.

Love,

Marie Ferrarella

# THE BABY IN THE CABBAGE PATCH

## Marie Ferrarella

To Nik,
In memory of the days when you were still "Nikky"
and we shared baseball games together.
Love, Mom

# Chapter 1

It amazed her how different this pregnancy was from the last.

Christina Copenhagen rinsed off her plate, having polished off the rather large club sandwich she'd made for herself. Not so much as a rumble in her stomach, she thought with a smile, patting the still-flat area with affection. With Robby, she'd all but lived in the bathroom because her so-called "morning sickness" had turned into practically an all-day event that lasted five and a half months into her pregnancy and had caused her to grow thinner instead of heavier.

It didn't look as if it was going to be like that

this time around. Tina reached into the refrigerator to gather ingredients needed to make two more sandwiches—one for her son, Robby, and one for his best friend and coconspirator, Kent. It was as if this baby she was carrying knew that life was hard enough for her without her having to deal with any additional problems. So her unborn miracle behaved well, unlike his or her big brother.

The only real indication that there was any activity going on within her body was that her size five shorts were beginning to fit too snugly. She had several size sevens waiting in the wings before she would finally give in and start wearing the maternity clothes she'd never made herself give away after her first pregnancy.

That was because she'd wanted more children. Larry, it had turned out, hadn't. Frowning, she piled each slice of bread high with ham and three kinds of cheese, just the way the boys liked their sandwiches. The dividends her ex was concerned with had absolutely nothing to do with the coupling of two people in love.

Neither had this pregnancy, Tina thought with a sigh, now that she looked back at it. Oh, she'd been in love, but Larry, Larry had been distracted. She tossed lettuce onto the mayonnaise, then topped off the ensembles with another slice of bread.

During the last couple of years, even while they made love, she could always sense that Larry's mind was elsewhere. Calculating profit margins, planning next month's travel agendas. He was everywhere, it seemed, but in bed with her—except in the most physical sense.

And now even that was gone. He'd packed up and left just before Christmas. Right after she'd told him she was pregnant again. He'd told her coldly that this kind of life just didn't suit him anymore.

Big dumb jerk, she thought, her knife coming down hard on the sandwiches, cutting each in half in quick succession.

For her part, she supposed she did miss him— but it was the man Larry used to be that she missed, the man she'd fallen in love with. It was worse for Robby. Robby missed the man he'd thought his father was, the man he'd continually tried—and most often failed—to curry favor with. But Robby was nothing if not ever hopeful that the next time he could make his dad smile.

Ever hopeful. A lot like her, she mused.

She wondered if the light of her life actually understood the ramifications of what was going on, of the divorce she and his father were getting. On the surface, very little had changed in their lives. That Larry was absent from home at night was not all that different from what had been business as usual in their house. Larry was always gone, working late, entertaining clients, away on business. He had a hundred and twelve excuses for not being a father and a husband. The only real role that fit him was CEO of his company.

"Wear it in good health, Larry. You don't know what you're missing," she murmured, wiping her hands on the dish towel.

What he was missing and would continue to miss was a wonderful kid. To Tina, there was nothing more wonderful than the enthusiastic embrace of a child who was eager to share his day with you. To Larry, that same feeling only came from fondling an envelope with blue chip stock certificates in it.

How had she missed all these signs that they were as different as night and day?

Because once upon a time they'd been the same. But, she reminded herself, "Once upon a time" was the way fairy tales began. Real life was completely different.

She had to remember that.

Tina tossed the dish towel on the back of the kitchen chair. No more procrastinating; it was time to get back to her computer and to work. Those CD-ROM business cards she'd been commissioned to do were not going to create themselves.

As she contemplated the return to her desk, Tina reminded herself how lucky she was to have a career that allowed her to do most of her work from her home. She tried not to dwell on the fact that, right now, her mind felt about as creative as a dried-up turnip. This while the Caldwell account was waiting to have new life breathed into it via a snazzy, revamped Web site and the CD-ROM business card that went hand in hand with it.

Maybe inspiration would come once she sat down in front of the computer. Like magic.

Tina smiled to herself. That was Robby's favorite term. He was young enough to still believe in magic. She only wished that she were.

The front door banged open, then slammed shut, jarring her teeth. She could just visualize that the small dent where the doorknob met the wall was getting bigger.

"Close, don't slam," she called out automatically. Not that it did any good.

"Mom, Mom, you gotta see what we found in the cabbage patch!" Robby yelled at what was almost the top of his small lungs. "Mrs. Wexler was right, she was right!"

Now what?

The cabbage patch was what he and Kent called

the over-grown vegetation that grew on the green-belt that ran just behind their cul-de-sac. She had warned him time and again not to wander too far into it. This was Bedford and hardly anything ever happened here, but that didn't mean it couldn't.

Tina shook her head. She was beginning to sound just like her mother. How did that happen?

Walking out to the living room, Tina tried to remember what Mrs. Wexler, the widowed great-grandmother down the block, might have said about the greenbelt. Nothing came to mind.

"So, what's the treasure this time?"

Robby was standing by the door, one hand on the knob, dirtier than a boy had a right to be without having gone through a sandstorm. Maybe she should have named him Pigpen, Tina mused. He attracted dust faster than a shelf of intricately carved figurines. Kent, she noted, was missing.

White teeth within the grimy face flashed at her as Robby grabbed her hand.

"Out here. Kent's guarding it so nobody takes it. We're gonna share it." As usual, he was talking a mile a minute. She had to concentrate to catch every word. "Is it okay if we share it? Kent said I can take it first because I found it."

It was a dog; she just knew it. Tina braced herself. Robby had been pleading for a dog even before his father had left. She knew she should give in, but she just wasn't up to taking in a dog, especially not a stray. Not now, not when she was still having trouble staying upbeat after this latest upheaval in her life.

"It can keep the new baby company when it gets here," Robby was telling her, giving her his very best pitch, confirming Tina's suspicions that this had to be a dog.

This was one of those times that being a mom wasn't easy, Tina thought, as Robby yanked open the front door again. "Honey, I really don't think that's a good idea. I—"

Tina stopped dead.

There, in the somewhat less than shiny red wagon that she had secretly bought for Robby last Christmas, telling him it was a gift from his dad, was a small, wailing creature that was all arms, legs and noise and every bit as dusty as her son.

Her mouth fell open as she stared at the "new treasure," before shifting her eyes to her son. Standing beside the red wagon was his ever faithful, equally dusty, somewhat silent partner in crime, Kent. Kent was beaming every bit as broadly as Robby.

"Robby, that's a baby."

"Yeah, ain't—isn't it great?" he declared.

Bending over, she quickly picked up the crying baby. Gingerly she ran one hand along the small body, testing to make sure that there were no overt injuries. The baby, a girl, if the very dirty pink romper beneath the equally dirty jacket was any indication, stopped crying and stared at her with cornflower-blue eyes that were huge.

Stunned, Tina looked from one boy to the other. Who in their right mind would entrust their child to two little boys barely old enough to cross the street on their own? "Whose baby is this?"

Jerking a thumb proudly at his chest, Robby answered, "Ours—Kent's and mine." He was careful to get his order straight. Mom hated it when he used bad grammar, though he didn't see why it mattered as long as she understood what he was saying.

"Where did you get her?" Tina didn't know how to make it any clearer than that.

"It's a her?" Robby asked in disappointment.

"I think so. Never mind that now," she said impatiently. "Where did you find the baby?"

"I told you, in the cabbage patch. Just like Mrs. Wexler said." He pointed to the wall and the greenbelt that ran right behind it. "She said babies were born in cabbage patches. Right, Kent?"

Kent, never the talkative one, possibly because Robby talked enough for both of them, nodded his head, his dark hair bobbing up and down in the late-March breeze.

Something nudged forward from the back of her mind, where all things nonessential to her immediate existence were stored. She had an uneasy feeling she knew whose baby this little girl was.

"Mrs. Wexler's wisdom notwithstanding, babies aren't born in cabbage patches." At five, Robby liked that explanation better than the one she'd tried, with the aid of a very sweet children's book, to get across to him. But that was where his preference for magic came in. "Show me exactly where you boys found her."

Throwing his shoulders back proudly, with his mom holding their new treasure and following directly behind him and Kent bringing up the rear, Robby led the expedition back to the greenbelt.

Pacing about his study, hands shoved so deeply in his trouser pockets, they threatened to tear through the imported fabric, Michael Whittaker felt hollow. As if every single thing had been gutted and carved out of him.

He'd felt this way ever since late yesterday afternoon, when his brother, Alex, had telephoned him from the police station. It was the closest to hysterical he'd ever heard Alex sound. As the rambling explanation and plea for forgiveness came out, he'd felt a wave of pure hysteria himself. Someone had yanked Alex aside as he was getting out of the Mercedes and stolen it.

It wasn't the car that was important, it was what was inside.

Unbeknownst to the carjacker, the ponytailed thrill seeker had stolen something far more precious than an expensive automobile. He'd stolen Hannah. The eighteen-month-old had been strapped into her car seat in the back, asleep.

Riding around in the car always put her to sleep, he thought with bittersweet sadness. Damn it, why hadn't Alex left Hannah with the nanny? Why had he chosen yesterday to play the doting uncle?

For that matter, why had he allowed Alex to take the car at all?

So many recriminations after the fact, none of them mattering. The only thing that mattered was that Hannah was gone. And he had to get her back, no matter what the cost.

The story was carried on all the channels, under "Just breaking news," as if this had been done solely for the entertainment of a bored March audience. Over and over again, the same scenario, the same details were repeated, yielding nothing.

Not wanting to just wait, Michael had used his clout and gone on the air to plead with the carjacker to bring Hannah back, no questions asked.

"You can keep the car," he'd said. "I won't press charges. All I want is my daughter back safe and sound." And then he'd thrown in a coda that had raised ratings and the collective police department's blood pressure. "But if one hair on her head is harmed, I swear I'll hunt you down and kill you. There won't be a corner of the world you'll be able to hide in."

Immediately afterward, he'd been chastised by the police detectives investigating the theft, but Michael hadn't cared. He'd gotten his point across. Now he had to wait.

The waiting was killing him by inches. There'd been no useful response—just a bunch of loonies, calling in. His best friend, Blaine, and his secretary, Aileen, were screening the calls that were coming in on the special line that had been set up at the house, but not a single one of the calls had turned out to be genuine.

Hannah was still missing.

After losing Rachel because of unforeseen complications due to Hannah's birth, Michael wasn't sure if he could stand this last devastating turn his life had taken.

The phone rang. He jerked up the receiver just as Blaine peered into the study, about to take the call. Michael waved him away. He wanted to take this one; it would give him something to do, someone against whom to vent his anger before he lost his mind.

"Hello?" he barked.

"Mr. Whittaker?" a soft voice asked uncertainly.

"Yes." It was all he could do to harness his impatience.

"Mr. Whittaker, this is Tina Copenhagen. I think I might have something that belongs to you."

## Chapter 2

Tina had seen the entire story on *Early Morning L.A.* Or, rather, she had seen the news bulletin that had broken into the station's regular programming. She'd been doing what she did every morning, forcing herself to do a round of mild exercises to divert her mind from the fact that, very soon, her body was going to bear a strong resemblance to a blueberry muffin.

She always kept the television on to make the time pass more quickly. The story had come on with such fanfare that she'd almost blocked it out as just more media hype. Reaching for her remote, she'd paused between sets to change channels.

Only to see the exact same story shot from the exact same angle.

Apparently the story was splashed across every station. So she'd decided to listen. By the time she finished her exercises, she could have recited the story by heart.

Michael Whittaker's younger brother, Alex, had taken Michael's eighteen-month-old daughter, Hannah, out for a ride while he ran an errand. No sooner had he stopped in a popular Newport Beach shopping center's parking lot than someone knocked him down and stole the car with Hannah in it. Since there'd been no kidnapping call made in the wake of the theft, the police were temporarily working under the assumption that kidnapping had not been the intent and that it was nothing more than a common carjacking gone awry. The thief had probably had no idea that Hannah was even in the vehicle when he'd stolen it.

Tina had stopped doing curls with her ten-pound dumbbells when Michael Whittaker came on the air to make his plea to the thief. More to the point, she'd almost dropped the weights on the floor. Wearing a baby blue pullover sweater, jeans and the aftereffects of a sleepless night, the man was so good-looking it made her teeth numb.

She'd almost turned off the TV set then. The first time she'd seen Larry in her economics class at Bedford High, her stomach had contracted so badly, she'd almost whimpered. Good-looking men now set off a warning alarm in her head. Good-looking businessmen made her want to run the other way.

But she'd left the remote alone, caught by the agony she saw in his eyes, which might or might not have been a trick of good lighting.

Now, holding what looked to be his missing daughter in her arms, Tina was glad she hadn't switched to the movie channel and had paid attention to the phone number that had been flashed across the bottom of the screen. It was the number for people with any information to call. There were promises of a reward, but she had tuned that out. Money had no place in a situation like this.

Getting through to the number had proven to be almost as much of a challenge as keeping Robby from leaping out of his skin while she tried. She'd lost count of how many times she had hit the redial button before she'd finally heard the phone on the other end ringing. One hour and forty minutes after Robby and Kent had come in to show off their latest find to her, Tina finally got through to Michael Whittaker about his missing daughter.

It had taken the woman less than three minutes to convince him that her phone call was on the level rather than just another ploy for attention and/or the reward. By now, photographs of Hannah were all over the airwaves, as was a description of what she'd been wearing at the time of her unwitting abduction.

In making his plea to the public, the police had convinced Michael to hold back one small piece of identifying information. To her nanny's horror, Hannah, in a daring leap from her swing had skinned her right knee yesterday morning.

The woman on the phone had not only been able to tell him that Hannah had scraped her right knee, but she'd given him a rather detailed description of the Band-Aid, as well. It depicted a blue-clad, dozing Sandy the Sandman, a current popular cartoon character that had found favor with the under-seven set.

"By the way, the Band-Aid was very dirty, I had to change it," the woman named Tina Copenhagen had concluded.

"Dirty?" he'd heard himself asking dumbly. "Why?"

"My son found her in the cabbage patch."

That had almost blown it until she'd gone on quickly to explain that "cabbage patch" was her son's name for the stretch of land that ran right behind their house.

Michael had run to his car in the garage less than a minute after he'd hung up, the woman's directions fresh in his mind. Alex had raced after him, asking what was wrong, but he'd been afraid to spare the time to explain. Afraid that something would happen to make the woman change her mind and disappear with his daughter.

Once out of the driveway, Michael had thought of contacting the police and asking them to come with him. He reached for his cell phone, then stopped. They'd probably tell him to go home, that they would take it from here. He wasn't about to do that. If this was on the level, and he had this feeling that it was, he didn't want anyone else retrieving his daughter. She was going to be scared and she was going to need him. Just as he needed her.

A sense of urgency accompanied him during the entire trip from his exclusive Spy Glass Hill home in Newport Beach to the small residential track in Bedford.

Holding Hannah in her arms, Tina wasn't sure just what to expect when she opened the door. Thanks to the broadcast, she knew what Michael Whittaker looked like, but there were some people whom the camera simply adored and who were less attractive in person. After seeing Hannah's father on television, Tina was sure that Michael Whittaker had to be that kind of a man. After all, nobody looked that good in person.

She was wrong.

Warning flares, set on automatic response, went off all through her. Bracing herself, she forged ahead, forcing a smile to her lips. "Hi, you must be Michael."

*Obviously,* she mocked herself in silence.

Self-mockery was the only thing going on in silence. Behind her, in their unsuppressed excitement, Robby and Kent were making enough noise for five children.

Michael had leaped from his car and nearly ran to her front door, one question on his lips. It didn't need asking. He had his answer the moment the door was opened. His daughter was here, in this effervescent-looking blonde's arms, as peaceful as if she'd just woken up from a nap.

Relief the likes of which Michael had never experienced washed over him with the force of a tidal wave. He took Hannah into his arms without asking the woman, without saying a single word to her.

Instead, he buried his face in the nape of his daughter's small neck, ignoring everything else but the feel of Hannah in his arms. It only faintly registered that she smelled of soap. "Oh, Hannah, thank God."

"No," a reedy voice coming from about hip-level piped up, "thank me. And Kent. Thank us," the voice announced proudly. "'Cause we found her."

Raising his head and shifting Hannah to a more comfortable position, Michael finally took in his surroundings and saw that the woman who had called him was not alone. She was flanked on either side by small boys, one dark-haired, one blond. Because the color was an exact match, Michael assumed that the blonde belonged to her.

His mind began to function properly again. Michael smiled down at the spokesman for the young duo. "And I can't begin to thank you enough."

Tina placed a hand on each boy's shoulder, steering them back into the house and allowing the man a little breathing space. He followed her in, taking the unspoken invitation.

For the first time in a long time, Tina found herself tongue-tied.

Robby winced. "Ouch. Mommy, you're squeezing too hard," he protested.

Tina dropped her hands from both shoulders. "Sorry," she murmured to her son and Kent, offering them a blanket apology.

Brushing one hand across the other as if to banish any dust that might be lingering there, she raised her eyes to Michael's. He was still completely absorbed with his daughter. Confronted with genuine affection, Tina found herself relaxing a little.

"I'm sorry you had to come here, rather than my coming to your house, but I don't have a car seat anymore and I didn't want to take a chance on driving with Hannah in the car with just a seat belt to hold her in place."

He was grateful for her thoughtfulness. Someone else would have been eager to collect the reward and would have taken their chances, car seat or no car seat.

"No problem. I would have gone anywhere in the world to get her back. The ten miles from my house to yours hardly seems like anything."

As he spoke, he ran his hand over his daughter's small back as if to assure himself that she was really there. That she was really whole. It had been less than twenty-four hours since she'd disappeared, but they had been the most agonizing twenty-four hours of his life and he felt as if he'd aged a century.

Gratitude shone in his eyes as he looked at Tina. "I don't know how to repay you. The reward is obviously yours—"

Tina quickly shook her head. Able to read her son like a book, she ignored the surprised and then upset look that crossed Robby's face. "There's absolutely no need for a reward, Mr. Whittaker."

"Michael, please," he insisted.

To his surprise, Hannah reached out to the woman, as if wanting to touch her. A live wire, Hannah still did not take to strangers very readily. It had taken her three days to get used to the last nanny he'd hired, and the woman had a winning way about her. Giving Hannah space, he watched as she made contact with Tina and then cooed contentedly.

"You gave me back my main reason for living," he told her. "You can call me Michael."

Now why couldn't Larry have felt that way? Why couldn't he have thought that a child was a reason for living instead of for bailing out the way he had the second she'd told him that they were going to have another baby? He'd stormed out, blaming her. As if he'd had no part in it.

"All right, *Michael*," she allowed, though she felt a little awkward about it. "There's no need to give Robby and Kent a reward."

The boys moaned in unison.

"Doing a good deed is its own reward," she told them, slipping an arm around each.

Michael noticed that she'd mentioned the boys when she spoke of a reward, not herself or her husband. He wondered if she was just egging him on to make another, better offer. It didn't matter. He could afford it. Hell, he would have given everything away if it meant keeping Hannah.

"I realize that ten thousand dollars is not all that much—"

Obviously a very rich man, she thought. Automatically she wondered if he was as married to his work as Larry was to his.

"Ten thousand dollars is a great deal more than 'not all that much,' Mr.—Michael," she corrected herself, "but this was a good deed, and I want my son and his friend to realize that the best reward is the good feeling you get inside for doing that good deed." She curled a hand under each chin, raising the boys' heads so that they were looking up at her. Affection curved her mouth. "Right, boys?"

"Right," they said with less than wholehearted enthusiasm.

Michael couldn't help smiling. He'd been a boy himself once, a hundred years or so ago before the world had weighed so heavily on his shoulders. Before life had given him great things with one hand and then taken what had mattered most to him: his wife. Blessed with a vivid memory, he remembered what it was like, wanting some-one to appreciate what he'd done.

He always paid his debts. To everyone. And he wanted these boys to have more than just his thanks. "There's got to be some way that I can repay you."

"Nope, sorry," Tina informed him. "We're just going to have to be satisfied with your thank-you and the look on your face when you took your daughter into your arms."

Robby was tugging on her sleeve hard enough to tear it in another moment. "What is it, Robby?"

Robby began to point to Michael, then dropped his hand. Mom didn't like him to point. It wasn't polite. "Can he be our coach?"

"Coach?" Michael echoed, wondering if there was a graceful way out. When he'd made his of-fer, he'd meant it in terms of money. Time was something he had very little of, and coaching took time.

Tina could see Michael wanted to beg off. She came to his rescue. Besides, the man was a stranger. Coaching was in the realm of the fathers of the team members and Robby no longer had one of those.

It would have been even more accurate, she thought ruefully, to say that he never had.

"I'm sure Mr. Whittaker has more important things to do, honey, than be your coach."

Michael didn't like the sound of that, as if it was an accusation. Though he had no time to spare, he found himself taking umbrage at her comment. "What kind of a coach—Robby, is it?"

Robby nodded his head vigorously. His eyes shone brightly. "We need a T-ball coach. Ours went away, just like my dad."

# Chapter 3

Tina saw a flash of sympathy in Michael's eyes as Robby's remark registered. She felt herself growing defensive. "Robby's father and I are divorced."

Michael automatically looked at her hand. The band had three rows of diamonds on it. "You're still wearing a wedding ring."

The words caught him off guard as much as her. He had no idea what possessed him to say that. She had every right to tell him it was none of his business.

She didn't.

She glanced down at her still-flat belly. "I'm

also going to be expanding soon due to a pending blessed event.'' She saw the surprise in his eyes. ''It keeps things simpler that way and eliminates the tendency toward reproving stares.''

It was more for Robby's sake than her own that she'd decided to retain the ring that no longer symbolized anything except Larry's ability to select fine pieces of jewelry.

He turned so that his back was to the boys. ''He left you when you were pregnant?'' Michael couldn't think of anything more reprehensible.

Because he'd displayed finesse, Tina lowered her voice and answered his question. ''Not that this has anything to do with the matter at hand, but he left me *because* I was pregnant.'' She glanced back at the boys. They could only be counted on to remain relatively quiet for so long. ''Now then, not to hurry you along, but I do have a deadline.'' Tina saw him sneaking a look at her middle. ''Not that kind of deadline.'' She laughed despite herself. ''This has to do with my job.''

He couldn't help wondering how she provided for herself and her son. ''What do you do?''

''I'm a digital graphics designer—freelance.'' Business, mercifully, had begun to pick up again after a short lull. The last two months had been very good, but she knew the dangers of becoming too complacent. "Which means I make my own hours, and to pay for that, I hustle all the time."

Unable to stand it any longer, Robby interrupted. "So is he gonna?" he asked, raising his voice to be heard amid this grown-up talk.

Her mind a momentary blank, Tina looked at her son. "'Gonna' what?"

"Be our coach, of course." Robby wedged himself between his mom and Michael. "Did you forget? She forgets a lot of things," he confided to Michael in a pseudowhisper, one man to another. "But that's 'cause she's got so much on her mind." His smile was pure innocent delight as he looked up at her. "Right, Mom?"

"Right." Taking Robby's face between her hands, Tina gave it an affectionate squeeze. And then she dropped her hands to her sides as she looked at the man whose world she had managed to right. "Well, it was very nice to meet you Mr.—Michael, but—"

There were a million things he should be seeing to. There always were. But for the life of him, he couldn't get his feet to retreat. Shifting Hannah to hold her better, he shook his head at the dismissal. "But we haven't finished our business yet."

She raised a brow, certain that they had. "We haven't?"

"No, we haven't." And he knew he wasn't going to feel right about this until they had. "There's still the matter of the reward for Hannah's safe return."

She'd thought they were all through with that. Obviously not. "Look, it was just a lucky accident that Robby and Kent were playing in the field when Hannah started crying. My personal theory is that whoever stole your car panicked when they saw Hannah in the back seat. Kidnapping carries a much higher penalty than stealing a car. They must have left her in the bushes, hoping someone would find her. The boys did and brought her back. End of story."

"No," Michael contradicted. "Beginning of story. If anything had happened to Hannah…" He couldn't bring himself to finish his sentence even in a hypothetical sense. "The point is, the boys did find her and that's tantamount to rescuing her, in my book."

"Rescuing?" Robby echoed. "You mean me and Kent—" He saw his mother raise an eyebrow. "Kent and me—I—are heroes?"

"Absolutely."

"Just like the X-Men?"

"Exactly like the X-Men." Michael couldn't resist ruffling the boy's hair. "How would you two boys like to take in an Angels game? I've got a box right over home plate.''

Both sets of eyes grew as huge as Frisbees. "Over home plate?" they echoed in unison.

He'd struck pay dirt, Michael thought. "I take it that's a yes?"

And then Robby's smile became just a shade less dazzling. "Does that mean we have to choose?"

Michael didn't understand. "Choose?"

Instead of answering immediately, Robby held up his hand for a time-out. "Just a minute." Turning toward Kent, the two conferred in hushed tones. Finished, Robby looked up. "Thank you very much, but if it's all the same to you, Mr. Whittaker, we decided that we'd rather have you as a coach."

He'd thought that a dead issue. "But I—"

Time to take him off the hook, Tina thought. There was no reason to think that he would agree to what the boys asked. After all, he had no emotional investment in either of them. Plenty of fathers who had didn't show up at the games to coach or watch.

"Mr. Whittaker never offered to be your coach, boys," she reminded them. "He has too much to do."

As her tone penetrated, Michael looked at Tina

sharply. He had absolutely no idea what possessed him to back out of the safe position he was in. Maybe it was because there was something there, in her tone, that told him he'd been charged, tried and found guilty of a crime he was entirely ignorant of.

"Now wait a minute," he heard himself protesting. "I didn't exactly say that."

Robby clapped his hands together, then pounded his best friend on the back. It was a done deal. "Then you do have time?" There was no missing the glee in the young voice.

Tina regretted allowing this to play itself out as long as it had. If she hadn't been remembering how Larry had turned a deaf ear to Robby's pleas and how much it had hurt Robby when he'd refused, she wouldn't have let this continue.

"Boys, this isn't fair. Mr. Whittaker probably doesn't know the first thing about coaching a boys' T-ball team."

She took a lot of things for granted, didn't she? "I wouldn't be too sure about that."

She looked at him in surprise. "Oh, really?"

"Really."

He thought of the trophy on the mantel in his den. The one that had absolutely no connection to his business acumen, his heritage or his position in the social structure he found himself inhabiting.

The one that he'd been proudest of for the longest time. The trophy that declared him to be the outstanding baseball player of the year in Orange County in his senior year in high school. He'd received it when his head had still been filled with impossible dreams. He'd slept with it in his room the first month.

"What happened to your original coach? Or didn't you have one?" he asked.

"We had one, all right." Though not a very good one, she thought. "He has jury duty. Some case he can't talk about," she added.

She didn't sound all that convinced of the excuse, Michael thought. He liked a woman who wasn't gullible and thought things through.

"Just when are the games?" he wanted to know, looking at Tina.

"Wednesdays at five-thirty and Saturday mornings at nine." She still thought he was putting them on for some reason. "You're serious?"

She didn't look as if she believed him. "Why, don't I look serious?"

What he looked, the thought came at her on a flaming arrow shooting out of nowhere, was incredibly handsome, but that was something she wasn't about to tell him. "Not entirely."

"Well, I am." Michael did a little mental calculation and some shuffling. He supposed it could work. He grinned at the duo looking up at him as if he was about to walk on water. "Okay, boys, looks like you've got yourself a temporary coach."

The boys sent up a cheer that roused a drowsing Hannah who whimpered, then curled up against Michael's chest. Michael felt his heart swelling and knew that whatever the boys asked for, it wasn't nearly enough.

Robby suddenly connected the dots. "Does this mean we don't get to go to the Angels game with you and sit in your box behind home plate?"

Michael had had no intention of withdrawing that from the table. He laughed, looking at Tina over the boys' heads. "This boy is going to be one heck of a negotiator when he grows up."

Tina nodded her agreement. "If he doesn't get sent away as a con artist first."

The boys were still waiting for their answer. "Yes, you get to go to the game with me and sit in the box behind home plate. Just as soon as the Angels get back in town," he promised.

Something twisted inside of Tina as she saw the look on her son's face. He was buying this, lock, stock and barrel. Setting himself up just as he had every time Larry had promised him something, only to renege at the last minute. It was going to be like that again, wasn't it? She sincerely doubted that Michael Whittaker would even remember this conversation by the time the Angels got back into town at the beginning of next month.

For that matter, she was still having a difficult time believing that he meant what he said and was going to show up Wednesday afternoon to coach a gaggle of five-year-old boys whose hand-eye coordination left a great deal to be desired.

She'd already made up her mind to pinch-hit for the coach herself. She'd grown up blessed, or cursed, depending on her mindset, with five brothers, all of whom saw her as another player in the game. She knew that five-year-old boys preferred getting their instructions about the beloved game from a male figure, but when you don't have what you want, you make do. And she was more than qualified, she thought confidentially, to make do. At least until the real coach came back from his stint on jury duty.

"And what about you?" Michael asked suddenly, turning toward her after sealing the bargain with each boy with a hearty handshake.

Tina cocked her head. "Me?"

"Yes, coaching the team is a start in repaying your son and his friend." His eyes held hers. He didn't think he'd ever seen eyes that shade of blue before. They were almost violet. "What can I do to repay you?"

She didn't think in those terms. She'd done what any normal person would have done, no more, no less. Whimsy drew the corners of her mouth up. "I'm a mother. Mothers don't get repaid. We do things for the sheer self-satisfaction of it."

Michael's eyes continued to hold hers. He hadn't gotten to where he was by taking no for an answer.

"You really don't have to do this."

Lowering his menu, Michael looked at her face as the warm candlelight played off it.

She was beautiful, he suddenly realized. Where had his eyes been when he'd picked her up earlier?

They'd just been talking about Hannah and he'd told her that the baby's pediatrician had said the little girl was none the worse for her experience. Where had this come from?

Amusement crept into his smile. "How have I given you the impression that this is penance for me? I'm enjoying myself," he informed her. "I can't remember when I've taken the time to have dinner with a beautiful woman.'' He began to raise his menu again, then stopped. ''Sorry, scratch that. I do remember. It was August 12,'' he said quietly.

She looked at him quizzically, not saying a word, and he appreciated it.

Enough to elaborate. ''I took Rachel out for one last intimate dinner as just a couple. Before we became a threesome.'' He looked down, surprised that the memory could still slam so hard into his gut. ''It was the last time we had dinner at all. She died the next day a few hours after giving birth to Hannah.''

She hadn't realized he was a widower. She'd just assumed that he was divorced, like her. ''Oh, Michael, I'm so sorry.''

He heard the genuine distress in her voice and, for some reason, it seemed to help. He didn't talk about this often. It had taken him more than a year to open up to either his brother or his best friend. The wound had run so deep that any mention of Rachel's death at all threatened to reopen it and tear him apart.

Looking at Tina over the wide, stubby candle flickering in the brandy-colored bowl, he still wasn't sure what had prompted him to make the offhand comment that led to this.

Maybe it was because she seemed so easy to talk to. Or maybe it was that she'd seen her share of problems, as well.

"Yeah," he agreed quietly, "me, too."

# Chapter 4

"So you're raising Hannah alone?"

"I wouldn't exactly say it was alone. I have a nanny for her. And my brother lives with me." Poor Alex, he thought. His brother'd been so relieved to see him walking through the door with Hannah that there had been tears in his eyes. It was probably going to take Alex longer to get over this scare than it would him. "Alex is a senior at the University of Bedford and he's a really good kid. Guy," he corrected himself.

She heard the note of affection in his voice. The man seemed genuinely to care about his family. She'd begun to think that, aside from her brothers, men like that were figments of her imagination.

"What's he majoring in?"

"Stalling," Michael told her with a laugh. "Alex isn't sure what he wants to be when he grows up."

Damn, he thought, he had to stop thinking of Alex as his little brother and face up to the fact that Alex was a man now. He supposed he was resisting because he hated things changing on him, at least within the framework of his family.

Toying with the glass of champagne Michael had insisted on buying to celebrate Hannah's safe recovery, Tina studied his face for a moment.

"But you knew what you wanted to be when you graduated," she guessed. He had that air about him, the confident, "I'm-setting-the-world-on-fire" air. The same one that Larry had had, except at the time, she'd thought it was exciting.

Michael nodded. "I was born knowing. My father wanted me to take over the company, make it expand. Take it into the next century."

And he enjoyed doing it, she guessed. It was obvious from the way he spoke. Inwardly she couldn't help drawing away from him.

To cover the awkward moment, she raised her glass to him in a silent toast. "Well, it's the next century, so I guess you did what he wanted."

The ironic smile that twisted his lips made him seem vulnerable and caught her attention. "Not quite. He always wanted more." There'd been no pleasing his father and, after a while, he'd ceased trying, feeling that it was far better just to please himself.

Tina frowned slightly. "I think I'm getting confused. Are you doing what your father wanted you to do or what you wanted to do?"

Michael chased away the serious mood that threatened to creep over him. Taking a sip of the champagne, he flashed a disarming smile at her.

"Actually, lucky for me, both. I never had the dilemma of having to choose between my dreams and my duty. Alex wants to go his own way, which I think is great," he said, switching subjects. He never felt comfortable talking about himself. "He's far more artistically inclined than I am." He stopped, realizing that he was monopolizing the conversation. That wasn't like him. "How did we get started on this topic?"

Tina shrugged noncommittally. "One word led to another."

"And what about you?" To his surprise, he realized that for the first time in over eighteen months, he wanted to reach across the table for a woman's hand. To hold it in his. He wondered if that was a good sign, or if it was merely an overdue attack of loneliness doing a job on him. He wrapped his hand around the stem of the champagne glass instead. "Are you doing what you saw yourself doing when you were a little girl?"

The question drew a self-deprecating laugh from Tina. "I don't think any little girl sees herself as the self-employed, pregnant, divorced mother of one and a third children."

There was compassion in his eyes. "Sorry, that was rather insensitive of me."

Because he was apologizing, she let the question slide. "You're new at this, I gather. I'll cut you some slack."

"New at this?"

The way he tilted his head made him seem years younger and cast him in an endearing light. *Whoa, Tina, don't get carried away. The man might have good qualities, but scratch his surface and you'll just find another Larry. Been there, done that.*

"One-on-one dinners, or was that just a line?" She pretended to busy herself with her dinner. "Because if it was, it was a very touching one."

This time, he did touch her hand. To get her to look up. Their eyes met and he could have sworn that there was a current of electricity that passed between them, marking them both. Or was that just his imagination?

"No line," he told her simply. "Life's too short for anything but honesty."

He sounded so sincere, she caught herself wondering if Michael Whittaker actually believed that. *Careful, Tina, or he'll turn you into a true believer, and you know what happens then. You get to wake up.*

She'd believed Larry when he'd promised her that they would have a wonderful life together. To her that had meant children and something other than being the consummate corporate wife, adroit at small talk and hosting formal parties that would further his career. But a wonderful life had meant exactly that to Larry. Irreconcilable differences the divorce papers had labeled it. Two sterile words that didn't begin to cover the depth of the chasm that had developed between them.

"You have a pensive look on your face." Michael's voice broke into her thoughts. "Was it something I said?"

She flushed. "I'm sorry. I didn't mean to drift off. But yes, something you said triggered some old memories." Leaning her head on her upturned hand, Tina gave him her undivided attention. After all, the man was paying for dinner at a restaurant she could have afforded to frequent once a month only if she gave up eating for the other twenty-nine to thirty days. "So, are you set for Wednesday?"

Michael found himself caught up in the way her eyes seemed to change from green to blue depending on the way she tilted her head.

"Wednesday?" he echoed.

He'd forgotten already. There was no satisfaction in being proven right, she thought. Poor Robby. "The baseball game."

"Oh, right." Chagrined, he shook his head at the mental slip. "Where is it again?"

"Brywood Park." She repeated the directions she'd given him just before he'd left her house this afternoon. As an afterthought, Tina added, "It's right opposite the fort."

He was far more familiar with Newport Beach than he was with Bedford, but he didn't recall anyone ever mentioning there being a fort within the city to him. "There's a fort in Bedford?"

Relaxing now that they were back on the topic of the children and the games, she explained, "That's what the kids call it. In a moment of indulgence, the city fathers built this towering wooden structure in the park, which looks just like an old-fashioned fort out of the 1700s. For once, they hit the nail on the head. The kids love it." Robby told her that the first thing he could ever remember was peeking at her out of one of the fort's openings.

There was a fond look in her eyes that completely captured his attention. And fired his imagination. After Rachel died, when the pain had finally become manageable, he'd still been certain that he'd become utterly hollow inside. He'd believed that the only feelings he was capable of having were for Hannah and Alex.

Now he wasn't so sure.

There was something about this woman, something he couldn't put his finger on. It stirred things within him that hadn't been disturbed in a very long time. Michael didn't know whether to run for cover, or enjoy it.

Because he'd always been the type to take a dare, he decided on the latter. At least until the evening was over.

The evening turned out to be far more enjoyable than Tina had initially thought possible when she'd accepted the invitation.

She'd given in because she'd had a feeling that Michael Whittaker would not be at peace until his "debt," as he saw it, was repaid. Since she absolutely refused to accept any sort of monetary or material compensation when he'd attempted to press them on her, dinner out had seemed the way to go. She hadn't thought it would be anything more than tolerably pleasant, if that. She certainly hadn't thought they'd have things in common, coming from different worlds as they did.

But they did have things in common, the most important of which was the way they felt about their families. She was close to her five brothers and their families and he was close to his brother. And they'd both had fathers who had incredibly high expectations of them, fathers they'd wanted to please. In Michael's case, he'd never quite succeeded, he told her philosophically.

The man was charming and, while she was leery of charming, especially when it came in a package that also included "successful" and "businessman," she'd found herself being attracted to him. More than just a little.

No amount of silent warnings seemed to dissuade her for more than a few beats at a time.

Still, she told herself, she had to be careful not to count on seeing him at the park on Wednesday. More than likely, she was going to be dealing with at least one disappointed little boy, if not two. Robby gave every indication of believing Michael's every word. Kent had been more down to earth about it, but Kent had a dad he saw every morning and every night. Robby hadn't seen his for close to four months and he was in a very vulnerable position. He actually believed that Michael was going to show and had urged her, as team mom, to call everyone to tell them the practice session was on.

So she had gone through the motions, made the calls and crossed her fingers that the substitute coach didn't have to be her, even though she was equal to the job. She knew she wasn't going to be equal to seeing Robby crestfallen.

Had she made a mistake, allowing this to get so out of hand? She didn't have a concrete answer.

Still, Michael seemed genuinely affable. Maybe he would come.

Right, and maybe there really was a Santa Claus who slid down narrow chimneys to deliver gifts to deserving children.

The air was chilly as she got out of Michael's car. She pulled her shawl tighter around her shoulders. The chill refused to leave. It became more pronounced with each step she took toward her front door.

It wasn't a chill; it was nerves, she realized. Nerves jumping around all through her. Nerves because there was a part of her that wanted to pretend that this evening hadn't been just about thanking her for her part in recovering Hannah.

That this evening had been about a man and a woman enjoying each other's company.

If it had been, she wouldn't have gone in the first place, Tina reminded herself. Her life at this junction was complicated enough without allowing something else to come into the mix.

She couldn't get her nerves to behave. They insisted on hovering around her like a tiny, edgy Greek chorus.

If she wasn't careful, she was going to get sweaty palms next.

"I had a very nice time," Tina said, putting out her hand.

He looked at the delicate hand for a second before taking it.

"Yes, me, too," he agreed. He held her hand between both of his.

"And you won't forget about Wednesday?" She was asking because she was nervous, she thought. And if he continued to hold on to her hand, her palm really *was* going to start getting sweaty, she realized in sudden panic. But pulling it away wouldn't exactly be a suave movement, either.

"And I won't forget about Wednesday," he promised, the affirmation curving his mouth slowly.

His eyes were doing very strange things to her.

She could feel an undercurrent beginning to move through her. Unsettling her.

Trying to shrug off an air of impending doom, Tina dug around in her purse, frantically searching for her keys. "Um, I'd better go. I promised the sitter I wouldn't be out too late."

He nodded, knowing he should be saying goodnight and meaning it. But he didn't seem to be going anywhere. Instead, he was remaining right where he stood. And then he wasn't. He was moving forward.

Taking her hand from her purse, he drew her into his arms. And then, as she looked up at him in wonder, he lowered his head and touched his lips to hers.

# Chapter 5

It felt as if, just for a moment, he was transported to another place, another time, when all things were possible and a man could touch the sky if he leaped up high enough.

Very slowly, his head still spinning, Michael drew his head back and looked at the woman whose lips, he suspected, were registered somewhere with the police department as a lethal weapon.

If they weren't, they should be.

Michael cleared his throat, hoping that his words would be coherent when they came out. "What just happened here?"

Was she shaking? Oh, Lord, she hoped not. Because it felt as if she was shaking. One large mass of quivering raspberry gelatin, in immediate danger of toppling over. She held on to his arms, hoping he wouldn't notice, knowing if she let go too soon, she was going to give herself away.

Tina ran the tip of her tongue over her lips to moisten them. Bad move. His taste came back to her. "I'm not sure."

Regaining his composure, egged on by the disoriented look on her face, he smiled into her eyes. "Want to do it again so we can find out? Purely for research purposes? We might be on to something new here."

She was grateful for his humor; it helped her rally. Everything within her cried "yes" in response to his question. Yes, she wanted to do it again. And again and again. She had a strong suspicion that kissing Michael would lead to a complete erasure of everything sad from her life. At least temporarily.

She hadn't realized just how much she wanted to be held by a man, to be kissed by a man and made to feel desirable until this very moment.

Which was why she said, "No," and backed away as if her toes had been in danger of hanging over a steep cliff with a sheer drop right before her.

She took a deep breath to steady her nerves and, hopefully, her voice. She succeeded marginally. "I think what just happened here was a coda to a very nice evening, and anything more might just ruin things."

She was afraid, he thought. That made two of them. But he'd learned long ago to face his fears rather than to leave them unchallenged and growing larger. "Or make them better."

Oh, she was sure he'd make them better, as sure as she was that he was a terrific lover who could make her forget her name, rank and serial number. For the night. Or several nights. But after that lay reality and the rest of her life. She was already at that point. There was no reason to go on that journey again just to wind up where she already was. Once was more than enough.

Key in her hand, she smiled at him as she inserted it into the lock and then turned it. "I guess we'll never know."

Mentally he told her not to bet on that.

Five thirty-five. Tina looked up from her wristwatch as she let her hand drop to her side. Just as she thought. There was no tall figure coming into view over Brywood Park's grassy ridge.

Hard as this was going to be for her son, word or no word, she hadn't actually expected to see

Michael today. Not when she hadn't invited him in after he'd dropped her off at her door Saturday evening.

Which is just as well, she told herself. If she were being honest with herself, she hadn't liked what she'd felt when he'd kissed her. Like the head of a match about to be struck and set on fire.

It looked as if the time she'd endured with Larry hadn't taught her anything at all because in that one moment in time at her front door, she'd felt as if she could have started that whole crazy business all over again, the one that involved getting involved.

She pressed her lips together, banishing the thought. She was as involved as she wanted to be in this life, with her son and the baby who was on the way. A man, even a great-looking man with money dripping out of his pockets, if she were to believe what the newspapers said about Michael, didn't figure into it.

She was single and she liked it just fine, thank you very much. No more heartaches for her.

Blowing the whistle she'd thought to bring with her, she called together the boys and the lone girl who aspired to make up this year's Cubs' T-ball team. Draping her arms around the two closest players, she addressed the uneven circle.

"I think we should get started. It looks like everyone's here."

Robby frowned. "No, they're not. Michael isn't here."

She wished she could break him of the habit of referring to adults by their first names. Robby was just too familiar with everyone. "I think Mr. Whittaker probably forgot."

Instead of looking disappointed, Robby's face suddenly broke out into an actual wreath of smiles. He pointed excitedly behind her. "No, he didn't! Look, he's here!"

Not waiting for his mother's response, he broke rank, along with Kent, and ran toward the man striding toward them.

Actually there were two men, Tina saw as she turned to look. Michael and another man who looked like a younger, slighter version of him. The latter was pushing a stroller. Hannah, wearing an Angels' T-shirt and clutching what looked to be a rubber bat, was fairly bouncing up and down as they joined the children who remained milling around her.

Michael was wearing jeans as if he'd been born in them and the way he filled out his T-shirt told her that he didn't just sit around at his desk. Somewhere along the line, the man found time for the gym. A lot of time. She felt her mouth grow dry.

Michael winked at her. "Hi."

Tina told herself that reacting to the wink of a good-looking man was nothing short of adolescent. Seeing as how she was surrounded by a squadron of children, she figured that maybe, just this once, it was all right.

It took her a moment to locate her mind. A moment longer to engage it to her tongue. She caught herself running her hands along her rear pockets. "I didn't think you were coming."

He nodded apologetically. "Neither did I at one point." He took out the pad he'd tucked into the rear pocket of Hannah's stroller. "Traffic on Coast Highway is murder this time of day."

Tina eyed the pad. He was going to do work. Disappointment spread over her, an overturned bottle of ink drenching her. He was only putting in an appearance for show, because he said he would.

"I told him to take MacArthur," the man next to him told her, flashing an engaging grin, "but he wouldn't listen." Leaning over the cluster of bobbing children's heads, he took her hand and shook it enthusiastically. "Hi, I'm Alex."

Tina liked him instantly.

"I brought backup," Michael explained, flipping to the first page of his pad. "I didn't know if I was equal to a gaggle of five-year-olds."

She glanced down at Hannah, who looked as if she was raring to go. "You also brought your own cheering section, I see."

He paused to stoop down and make an incoherent noise at his daughter. Hannah responded with a gleeful laugh. "Hey, never too young to learn the fine points of baseball," he told her, standing up again.

"T-ball," Tina corrected, pointing to the stationary perch she'd set up a few minutes ago where the ball would be placed, awaiting each player's best shot. "There's a big difference."

Michael found that out. For the next two hours, Tina spent almost as much time coaching him as he spent coaching twelve eager boys and one very gung-ho girl named Meghan.

"Alex is better at this than I am," he admitted as, last man down, their side prepared to take the field again. "He played this kind of ball. I didn't."

Tina found herself more interested in what Michael had done, not his brother, although she knew she shouldn't be.

"You didn't play baseball." It wasn't a question, it was an assumption.

Not that his lack of playing surprised her. Except for the time he was trying to impress a client who was a rabid Mariners fan, the only interest Larry ever displayed in the game was in betting on the outcome. She figured all businessmen were created equal. Although she had to admit this one had a great deal more heart than was usual for the species.

A smile she couldn't read played along Michael's lips. "Oh, I played baseball all right. I just didn't play T-ball." He turned away from her and to the matter at hand. "Matthew, you take over first base," he said, reading from the roster of names she'd given him at dinner on Saturday. "Robby, I need a star shortstop—"

"You bet!"

It made her heart sing to see her son so happy. Tina stood to the side, letting Michael take over. She waited until he was finished giving out the new assignments. The idea of playing each child in a new position during each of the five innings seemed a little unusual to her, but Michael had explained that he wanted to see exactly where each excelled. She found it interesting that he seemed to take it for granted that each child would excel. Obviously the man had no experience with a bunch of five-year-olds, although he and his brother seemed to be keeping them in order far better than Howard Smith, the coach they were filling in for, ever had.

The main thing, she thought, was that the kids were happy.

She came up to him as everyone scattered to their positions. "You played baseball, then."

"Played?" Alex came up behind her. "Didn't you tell her?" Not waiting for his brother to answer, Alex filled her in himself. "He won trophies."

"Trophy," Michael corrected without glancing up from the notes he was making on the leatherbound pad.

Seeing the pad, guilt pricked at Tina for her rash assumption. When she'd seen him take it out, she'd thought it was work he'd brought to do while the boys played, but it had turned out to be one of those pads used to keep score at baseball games, like the one she had. Hers, though, didn't come leather-bound.

"You have a trophy?"

He raised his eyes to her for just a second. "Just a small one," he muttered.

"Best player of the year in Orange County," Alex contradicted. He remembered how proud he'd been of his brother. "Could have gone on to get the one for the state, but our old man wouldn't let him."

Finished, Michael dropped the pad on the team bench behind him. "I had to study to get my grades up in order to get into Dartmouth."

Now she really was impressed. "You went to Dartmouth?"

Alex interrupted again, knowing Michael would just downplay the whole thing. "Our father went to Dartmouth, so Mikey had to go there, too."

"Mikey?" she echoed, turning to look at him, amusement highlighting her face. Never in a million years would she have affixed the nickname to him. But now that she did, she could almost see him as a teenager, clutching a baseball bat in his hand, stance just so as he watched the ball intently.

Hannah began to fuss. "Saved by the baby," Michael declared, relieved. "Tina, why don't you take over?"

She arched a brow. "The team or the baby?" The realization that she was enjoying herself, trading words with this man and his gregarious brother, slowly began to penetrate.

Michael told himself that staring at the team mom's cute figure was something he was going to have to leave until later. He swept his hand grandly around. The other team was getting ready to bat. "Take your pick."

She knew what she wanted was a third choice. She wanted to pick the man, and that was a very dangerous realization. She was allowing herself to get a little too comfortable.

"Well, you're doing well with the team, so I'll take the baby."

Bending over to where Hannah was sitting in her stroller, Tina began to lift her from the seat only to find that she couldn't.

"Seat belt," Alex said. Quickly he undid his niece's restraints.

"Not that it does much good when she sets her mind on getting free. Hannah's taken to crawling out the second someone stops moving the stroller." He nodded at his brother. "Mikey found that out the time he took her to the park and stopped to talk to a friend. The next thing he knew, he hears Hannah's triumphant laugh and looks up to see her scampering through the grass."

Michael's heart had stopped when he'd seen the empty stroller. "I call her Madam Houdini," he told Tina. He glanced reprovingly at his brother. "You think around the team you could find it in your heart not to call me Mikey? It sounds as if I'm five years old and waiting to test a bowl of cereal."

"I don't know about the cereal," Tina said,

lifting Hannah into her arms, "but being five would make you fit right in with the rest of the guys." Although, she added silently, he seemed to be doing a very nice job of it as it was.

Michael turned to answer her. The words melted on his tongue. Twilight was setting in, casting a dusky cloak around Tina. She looked so natural holding his daughter, he felt something press hard on his chest.

It took an effort to shake it off.

# Chapter 6

Unable to keep quiet any longer, Joyce Riley set her empty cup down on the kitchen table and fixed her youngest sister-in-law with a smug look. "So, I hear you have a new man in your life."

Picking up the two empty cups, Tina looked at her sharply before putting them into the sink.

"He's in Robby's life, not mine. The team's life, really," she added for further clarification.

Joyce joined her at the sink, leaning over so that Tina couldn't avoid seeing her smug smile. She wasn't about to let her favorite sister-in-law squirm out of this, especially since she was thrilled for her. The family knew how vulnerable

Tina was after the number Larry had done on her. They were all worried that because of Larry, Tina would stubbornly block out any genuine possibility of happiness.

She looked at Tina pointedly. "I noticed you knew exactly who I was talking about."

Doing her best to ignore the wide grin on Joyce's face, Tina stared down at the running water as she washed out the cups. "Try your lawyering out on someone else, Counselor. I just happen to be very sharp on the uptake, nothing more. No reason to make anything out of it."

Joyce picked up a cup and dried it off, then hung it up in the cupboard. "If you're so sharp, Tina, my love, why aren't you going out with him? He must have asked you." She looked at her knowingly. "If I had one of the county's richest men hanging around me—"

Tina sighed, elaborately laying out her damp towel on the rack. Joyce's husband, Rick, had come to the last game to cheer on his nephew. She should have known this was coming. Rick never could keep his mouth shut. "Michael Whittaker is *not* hanging around me, he's coaching the team."

Joyce rolled her eyes. "Oh, puh-leeze, wake up and smell the coffee, woman." Because Tina had moved away to straighten the rest of the kitchen,

Joyce moved quickly to shadow her steps. "He's not a team dad, he's doing it to be around you, the 'team mom,'" she said, reminding Tina of the title she'd taken on. Mostly because every other mother had begged off, claiming a busy schedule.

Tina would have matched her schedule against any of theirs, but because this meant so much to Robby, she knew she wouldn't have missed being there for the world. If that meant standing off to the side and making slashes on an official pad in between cheering the kids on at the top of her lungs, so be it.

She really wished Joyce would back off. If Joyce felt this way about Michael, she knew the others did, too. She had to nip this in the bud. Now. Before she was embarrassed. Before she started deluding herself and believing that Michael was interested in her, too.

"He's doing it because he's grateful we found his daughter and because Robby asked him to as his reward." She stopped. It occurred to her that maybe it hadn't been Rick who'd mentioned this to Joyce. Oh, God, she hoped no one else thought something was going on. This kind of thing could only hurt Robby, who was sensitive enough as it was. "And how do you know all this, anyway?"

"My beloved husband, your brother."

Okay, so it was still contained within the family, Tina thought; that was something.

"Rick says he's very nice," Joyce was saying. "When do I get to see for myself?"

That was easy. "Never."

Following her into the family room, Joyce chuckled, really happy for her. "Want to keep him all to yourself, eh? I understand."

That tore it. Tina swung around, the expression on her face deadly serious. This had to stop.

"Joyce, there's nothing to understand. I'm not 'keeping' him anywhere. The man comes by the field two days a week to coach until Howard Smith gets sprung from jury duty—which is beginning to look like never," she added with a hopeless air. Not that Howard really was any good at coaching the team. The team had lost most of their games last year. Not that that was supposed to count, but fifteen losses out of sixteen was pretty daunting, especially since the sixteenth had ended in a tie on account of rain.

Joyce tried a different tack, knowing that the way to Tina's heart was through Robby. "You have to admit, this is quite a boost for the kids. Rick says the guy used to be a baseball god."

Tina laughed, her serious expression fading. She knew that they all meant well and that they loved her. Family love was what had kept her going to begin with. "He's slightly lower than a deity," she confirmed. "How does my nosy big brother know all this?"

"He talked to Whittaker's brother, Alex. And you forget, my little journalist has access to many old newspaper stories at the *Times*." Something she had reminded him of when he'd come home with the news the other night. She'd sent her husband back to his office to do some digging, accusing him of being indifferent to his sister's situation. Rick had returned with a wealth of information, emphasis on "wealth." She couldn't have been happier for Tina. Now all that remained was to have Tina happy for Tina.

Tina looked at Joyce, knowing full well who'd instigated the fact-finding mission. "Maybe Rick should pay a little more attention to his job and less to a life that isn't his own."

Joyce snorted disdainfully. "What a way to talk. You need a little guidance once in a while. Look what happened the last time we let you have your own head. You brought Larry into your life." Surprised at Joyce's tone, Tina looked at her sharply. "Nobody in the family liked him, you know."

"Well, nobody told me." She'd always suspected, of course, but they all loved her and because she'd loved him, they'd gone out of their way to be friendly to Larry. It was only at times, when she'd catch looks passing between them, that she sensed the family was not crazy about the man she was about to marry.

Joyce raised a mocking brow. "And would it have done any good if we had?"

There was only one honest answer for that. She knew how headstrong she could be at times. And she had really loved Larry with all her heart.

"No," Tina conceded.

Joyce spread her hands. "I rest my case." She glanced out the window and watched Robby and Kent playing with Galaxy, Kent's golden retriever. She smiled to herself. "Anyway, this one's got looks, money and he likes kids. I say go for him."

The alternative to having a family that butted in was having one that didn't care. She knew she should be grateful that so many people cared about her. But there were times when this got a little old. Like now. "And can I say something?"

Joyce read her look correctly. "Will I have to wash your mouth out with soap?"

"Good guess." Her unscheduled break over, Tina knew she had to get back to the design on her computer. Because she was as comfortable with Joyce as she was with her brothers, she felt no awkwardness about showing her the door.

"Now if you'll excuse me, I have to get back to work."

Joyce picked up her purse from the sofa. She'd accomplished what she'd set out to do: question Tina herself. "Can't hide in that den forever, you know," she called after Tina's disappearing form.

"I can try," Tina threw over her shoulder.

Tina dragged a hand through her hair and stretched as she leaned back in her chair. Done. Finally. She'd suffered a creative setback after Joyce's impromptu visit, but had gotten back on track after she'd made Robby and Kent an early dinner—actually, sent out for an early dinner, to be accurate.

But pizza covered all the main food groups, she argued with herself, quelling her conscience. As long as she didn't make a habit of it.

The client was going to be happy, she thought, smiling to herself. The web page was a delight to the ear as well as the eye, thanks in part to the jingle she'd created.

She stopped stretching and listened. Was that the doorbell? She glanced at her watch automatically. It was almost seven. She wasn't expecting anyone.

Maybe Kent had gotten bored and returned. After all, he and Robby had been apart for all of half an hour. That was a great deal of time when you were five.

"I'll get it," she heard Robby sing out.

Her lethargic mood vanishing, Tina was on her feet immediately. She'd taught Robby to be helpful, but she'd also taught him that he was too young to answer the door by himself without having her close by. That was probably why he was so eager to do it every chance he got.

The rebellion was going to increase as he grew older. She could hardly wait.

Moving as fast as she could from the rear bedroom she'd turned into an office, she raised her voice so that Robby couldn't claim he hadn't heard her. "No, you won't."

Too late.

She reached the hall just as Robby was yanking the front door open. What if he did that while she was in the tub? She had to make him realize that not everyone in the world had his best interests at heart and, while this was considered one of the safest cities in the country, bad things still happened sometimes. Especially to unsuspecting innocents who insisted on talking to strangers.

She covered his hand with her own on the doorknob, her eyes focused on his small face, trying to seem properly displeased. "Robby, how many times have I told you not to open the door to strangers?''

"I'd hope that after nearly five weeks I wasn't a stranger anymore. Especially since I have to ask you for a huge favor.''

Tina looked up, the admonishment evaporating. Completely unexpected, Michael was standing in her doorway. Michael and Hannah, she amended, looking at the little girl he was holding in his arms. The next thing she saw were the bags that buffered him on both sides.

Had she not known it was impossible, she would have said he looked like a man moving in. What he did look like, was sheepish.

Something tugged at her heart before she could block it.

Stepping back, Tina held the door open for him, silently inviting him in. She looked at the things on her front steps. "Is anything wrong?''

He would have liked to say no, that he was handling everything himself just fine, thank you. But that would be lying. He wasn't handling anything, at least not when it came to Hannah, at the moment.

"No, and yes.''

Confused, she noticed Robby looking at her quizzically. "Which is it?''

"I need help," he confessed. "From someone I trust."

"We'll help, we'll help," Robby fairly shouted, puffing up his small chest.

She had to admit that the plea took her by surprise and had her more than a little curious.

"Help with what?" she asked, already knowing that whatever it was, she'd probably say yes. She was a walking pushover, she thought, but it was hard to turn her back on someone when they needed her. And maybe it was shallow of her, but she had to admit part of her rather liked the idea that Michael needed her, however temporarily.

"I just found out that I have to go out of town for a couple of days on business." He didn't like asking, but his back was to the wall and this wasn't about him, it was about Hannah. As a mother, he thought, Tina was bound to see the difference. "Alex is hip deep studying for quarterly midterms, and Ellen, Hannah's nanny, is down with the flu. She's at her sister's." He looked at her helplessly. "I need someone to watch Hannah." There were agencies he could call, but he didn't want to entrust his daughter to a virtual stranger, especially not after the scare he'd had that had brought him and Tina together. "I know it's a huge imposition, but she really likes you and—"

Knowing he had a flight to catch, Tina held up her hand. "You can dispense with the sales pitch—"

Did she think that was what he was doing? This was a great deal more personal than that. "It wasn't a sales pitch—"

"Yes, it was," she contradicted with a laugh. "But don't worry, I'm already sold on Hannah." She took the child out of his arms. "I'll take care of her." Looking at the little girl, she couldn't resist nuzzling her. "We'll have fun, won't we, honey?" She raised her eyes to Michael. "How long will you be gone?"

Before he could answer, Robby was suddenly at his side. "Are you gonna miss the game?" There was genuine distress in his eyes.

Tina watched Michael's face, waiting to see his reaction to the boy's concern. Compassion and understanding entered his eyes. She released the breath she hadn't been aware of holding.

"Not for the world, Robby," he promised. "The meeting's going to run late, but I'm catching the red-eye to make it back in time."

Since he was actually making the effort, she felt compelled to ease his conscience. "You don't have to do that."

Robby looked at her, horrified. What was she saying? "Yes, he does."

"Yes," Michael agreed, looking at her. "I do. I stand by my word, whether I've given it to a corporate executive, or someone important, like your son."

She saw Robby beaming as he raised himself up on his toes and rocked back and forth. Damn, but the man was getting to her, she thought, her distress not quite as intense as it might once have been.

"I've got everything Hannah needs in the car," Michael was saying before he stopped short. "Except for somewhere for her to sleep."

Tina waved away his concern. "Don't worry about it, I've still got Robby's old crib." She had stored it in the garage when Robby had gotten his "grown-up" bed, as he liked to call it. "I've been meaning to set it up again anyway." The baby would need it. "Might as well not wait for the last minute."

He looked at her in surprise, then chagrin whispered over his face. "That's right, I forgot. You're so thin that it slipped my mind."

Did that mean he was thinking about her? She bit the corner of her lip, knowing it shouldn't matter to her one way or another. But it did.

Settling Hannah in the playpen Michael had carried in, Tina left the child in the living room with Robby playing "peekaboo" between the slats with her and walked Michael to the front door.

"Don't worry about a thing," she told him.

Michael glanced over her head toward the duo. "He's very good with her."

She folded her arms against the chill as she stood on the front step with him. "Yes, he is." She was very proud of Robby. He was a great kid. "It's good practice for him for when his own brother or sister comes on the scene."

The glance toward her stomach was automatic. "Still don't know what it is?"

She shook her head. She was in the best of health and at a good age for childbearing, so there was no reason for her to submit to an amniocentesis other than idle curiosity. "I like surprises," she told him.

Michael smiled at her. "I'll try to remember that." He paused, not wanting to leave, knowing he had to get going to make his flight. "Listen, I can't thank you enough."

"Sure you can, you're doing it now. I really like taking care of Hannah."

The wind shifted and he caught the scent of something light, arousing. He felt his own stomach tighten. "You're really a very special lady, Tina."

She had no idea why Larry popped into her

mind just then. Maybe because he and Michael were both businessmen. Maybe it was for self-preservation. "Not everyone thinks so."

He slipped a hand behind her head, tilting it up to his so he could look into her eyes. "Then not everyone is bright."

Giving in to an impulse, he leaned over and kissed her. He lingered; the kiss deepened.

The next minute he was forcing himself to release her and hurried away with a goodbye in his wake. He knew if he didn't go now, the only place he was going would be back inside. The way he desperately wanted to.

# Chapter 7

Funny how long a kiss could linger on the fringes of her memory when it hadn't lasted more than ten seconds in reality, if that long.

Fringes nothing, it was there, smack dead center when she least expected it. Of course, there were reasons for that, Tina supposed. She was surrounded with reminders of Michael everywhere she turned. She relived the kiss and its effect every time she dealt with Hannah over the course of the next two days. Not to mention that Michael called several times a day just to see how Hannah was doing. And there were those calls from him, late in the evening, to ask her how she was getting along. Calls that had her stretching out on her bed, her toes curling, her imagination taking flight…

And then there was his brother, Alex. Clearing it with her first, Alex would drop in on his niece on his way to and from classes.

Being inundated with Whittakers the way she was, Tina supposed she could be forgiven if her thoughts insisted on drifting toward the man himself at almost every opportunity.

Even if she wasn't surrounded with reminders of Michael, she'd still have a difficult time not thinking about him because of Robby. Her heretofore devil-may-care son had turned into practically a cheerleader for the man who would take him aside after the games on Saturday to show him the fine points of a knuckleball and a slider.

"Isn't Mike great?" he'd ask over and over again.

She couldn't find it in her heart to disagree. She'd even ceased attempting to get Robby to call him Mr. Whittaker. There she'd been foiled by the man himself, who'd told the boys during their first practice session that they were free to call him "Mike" because he felt it was more comfortable that way. So "Mike" it was, no matter what she said to the contrary.

And it was Mike this and Mike that. Michael's

name had been finding its way into the conversation more and more often, and it seemed to Tina that during the two days he was gone, every other sentence Robby uttered had Michael's name in it. It seemed as if, now that they were inching their way toward the end of the ten-week season, the man had practically become a saint who not only walked on water but could, at will, probably take flight in the eyes of his adoring fans. Certainly in Robby's.

When Mike finally returned the evening of the second day, Tina didn't know whether to be happy to see him or leery. Robby had no such dilemma. He had suddenly appeared at the top of the stairs when the doorbell rang, hanging over the banister as she went to the door.

"You're supposed to be in bed, remember?" she told him, hand on the doorknob.

"But it might be Mike." Impatience outlined each word. "Open it, Mom, open it. Open the door."

A peek through the security hole verified the caller's identity. With a sigh, Tina braced herself as she opened the door.

"Hi," was all Michael had a chance to say to her.

The sound of pounding feet was heard behind

her as Robby sailed down the stairs, making more noise than someone twice his weight and size.

''Mike, you're back!'' he yelled, then reached the bottom step in record time, even for him. Not waiting for an invitation, Robby launched himself at Michael, wrapped his arms around the man's waist and hugged for all he was worth.

Touched, Michael smiled down at the blond head as he stroked it. ''Now that's what I call a greeting.''

He looked up at Tina and she had the distinct impression that the message was intended not just for her son.

''Welcome back,'' she murmured, not really sure what to say.

Or what to do about the funny feeling she was experiencing in the pit of her stomach. Probably just the baby, she told herself, or hormones being thrown out of whack. Most likely both.

Robby was still holding on to him. He raised his head to look up at his idol. ''I thought you weren't going to be here tomorrow, but now you are so you will be.''

There was no mistaking the enthusiasm. Robby had been moping around all day, alternating be-tween fretting that Michael would miss the game tomorrow and telling her, with false bravado, that

Michael would be here, he just *knew* he would be. Because Michael had said so.

Tina knew that in the back of the boy's mind were other promises he'd been given, promises his father hadn't bothered to keep. She knew Robby was afraid that his new hero would turn out to have feet of clay, and she'd ached for him.

For that reason she was probably happier than Robby to see Michael walk through the door. But, unlike Robby, her fears weren't set to rest so easily. Michael had come through this time, but what of the next time? After all, Robby wasn't his. The man owed him nothing.

Michael ruffled the boy's hair with what Tina could have sworn was genuine affection. Maybe there was hope after all.

*Why not? You're feeling affection for him and you've known him as long as Robby has.*

This involvement with Michael was heading down roads she hadn't wanted it to travel, she thought, disturbed. She didn't want Robby getting attached to a man who would, at season's end, disappear from his life the way his father had. If that happened again—and it would—there was no telling what that abandonment would do to Robby's self esteem.

She didn't figure into the mix, she told herself, watching the two of them talk. She could get over being forsaken and ignored, not happily, but she could come to terms with it. She knew who she was and what she was about. Robby was just a little boy. Another relationship like the one he'd endured with his father might permanently silence that laugh of his and take the sparkle out of his eyes.

She couldn't risk it. But she didn't see a way to prevent it, either.

"Brought you something," she heard Michael telling Robby once the boy had released him.

His eyes grew huge and gleeful. "You did? What is it? What is it?" Hiking up pajamas bottoms that were still a little too large for him, Robby all but danced around Michael. "Is it in your suitcase in the car?" Even before the question was out of his mouth, Robby was pulling on the doorknob, set to bolt out to the vehicle parked in their driveway.

The boy was like a Fourth of July firecracker, about to go off. "Robby," she warned.

"Hold on, partner," Michael said, catching the boy's arm and holding him steady. "No need to rush out to the car. I've got your present right here." He spared a glance at Tina, thinking how good she looked, with her hair tousled and her makeup all but faded from her face. Natural. The kind of natural men dream about when they think of having someone by their side, facing forever. "Didn't want to take a chance on it being lost on the plane," he explained.

Picking up the nondescript brown bag that Tina hadn't even noticed, Michael opened it and took out a brand-new pitcher's glove. "Pedro Martinez autographed it for me. For you, actually."

If possible, Robby's eyes grew even bigger. "For me?"

Michael looked at Tina. "Pedro Martinez is—"

She cut him off. "I know who Pedro Martinez is. He's the star pitcher for the Red Sox." She had no idea why the impressed look on Michael's face made her feel proud. She should have felt insulted that he'd treat her like a stereotypical female.

But there was nothing insulting about the way Michael treated her. Try as she might not to, it made her want to come back for more.

Robby was holding the glove to his nose, inhaling the scent of leather and oil. He looked as if he was in heaven. "He really signed it?"

"He really signed it. Look." Squatting down to the boy's level, Michael pointed to the autograph. Rather than just an impersonal signature, the autograph included Robby's name. "'To Robby Copenhagen,'" Michael read, one eye on

Robby, getting a tremendous kick out of the expression on his face. "'From his pal, Pedro Martinez.'"

Beside himself, Robby hugged the glove to him. "Oh, boy, can I go show this to Kent, Mom? Pleeeaasse?"

She knew that Kent was already in bed. The boys had recently glumly compared bedtimes. "Tomorrow," she told him, tempering her denial with a smile. "It's late."

"Okay, I'll show him at the game. I'll show everybody!" Robby declared. And then he was struck with a thought. Hesitantly he looked at his mother. "Would that be showing off?"

"Just a little." But he was so eager, she just couldn't rain on his parade. "But it's okay this once, I guess. It is a pretty special glove."

"Yeah, it sure is," Robby crowed.

Michael caught her eye above the boy's head. "I made a pit stop at the stadium and brought some things for the other boys, as well." He didn't add that his father had known the owner of the team. It seemed rather gauche to mention that.

She turned to him, hands on her hips. The man was making it damn hard for her to keep her distance from him. "What are you, perfect?"

"Pretty near," he quipped, then laughed. Robby ran up the stairs, probably to call his friend, Michael thought, if he knew little boys. "Actually, you'd be the first to ever accuse me of that," he confessed. "And you made it sound like a fault to boot. No easy trick, Tina."

She flushed. He was being nice to her son and she was being testy. *Nice going, Tina.* "Sorry, I've just spent a very difficult two days."

Michael's first thought was of Hannah. He hadn't asked to see her the moment he'd walked in because he'd assumed, given the hour, that his daughter was asleep. Besides, Robby's greeting had been a little overwhelming, and he'd paused to enjoy it.

But her comment erased all that.

"I'm sorry, was Hannah a handful?" He hoped it was nothing more. He reasoned that if anything had gone really wrong, she would have told him when he called.

The smile was rueful. "No more than Robby was at her age." She pressed her lips together, wondering if there was a way to just bow out of this now that she'd started it. "No, Hannah wasn't my problem."

She had him curious now. He'd spent the last two days thinking about her. A great deal. He'd decided that there were too many gaps in his knowledge about her. Gaps he wanted filled. "What was? If you don't mind my asking."

"Yes, I do mind you asking," she snapped, uncertain if she was angry at him or herself. "You were."

"Me?" A smile caressed his lips as he drew a little closer. "This sounds like it might be interesting."

Frustrated with herself, she gave him both barrels. "Well, it isn't. It's upsetting. You hardly kissed me when you left—"

So that was it, was it? He slipped his arm around her shoulders. "That could be remedied—"

Tina shrugged away his arm. "I don't want it remedied," she lied, putting up a hand to force him to keep his distance. She tried again, careful to keep her voice low in case Robby came back. "The point is, you hardly kissed me and I couldn't seem to stop thinking about you and it."

He cocked his head, doing his damnedest not to grin. "It?"

"It," she repeated, frustrated. "The kiss. The way you made me feel." She began to pace. "I don't want to like you, Michael."

"Why not?" He feigned innocence, hoping she meant what he thought she did. "People tell me I'm a very likable guy."

Was he being dumb on purpose? "I mean *like* you." She bit her lip. She was shouting. Tina slanted a glance toward the stairs, but Robby didn't pop up.

His smile peeled back slowly, sensuously, until it seemed to involve every fiber of his being. "Oh, that kind of 'like.'"

He *was* being dumb on purpose. "Yes, that kind of like."

He wanted to take her in his arms, but there was a head of steam she needed to work off first, he decided. He let her pace. "Well, what's wrong with that?"

"Everything." Didn't he get it yet? Did she have to spell it out for him? "I've been to hell and back. More importantly, so has Robby. I don't want to make a return trip."

Michael kept his voice even. "What makes you think you're booked?"

She closed her eyes, feeling desperate. A woman should be in control of her own destiny, shouldn't she? "I know the signs."

With the crook of his finger, he raised her chin. Tina opened her eyes. "And they are—?"

"Too numerous to mention." Trying to calm down, she drew her head back. "Would you like to look in on your daughter?"

"With all my heart." As she started to turn from him to lead the way up the stairs, he caught her hand. "But in a minute." He took her into his arms.

This time, she made no attempt to pull away. A girl could only exercise so much self-denial before she broke down. "What are you doing?"

"Finishing what I started." His mouth hovered a second above hers before it found its mark. "I don't like leaving loose ends."

# Chapter 8

Tina's head began to spin the moment he touched his lips to hers.

If there had been any loose ends, they were tied up now, she thought. Tied up good and tight in a knot the size of Milwaukee, and she hadn't a single idea on how to undo it or even where to begin.

Pleasure swirled seamlessly around her. But along with the pleasure there was fear. Fear of disappointment that was so tremendous, it was getting in the way of everything else, including her being able to draw a deep breath.

Or was that just because he was kissing her senseless?

Tina put her hands against Michael's chest, wedging them apart at the first opportunity. If she allowed him to continue kissing her, she was going to become hopelessly disoriented, possibly for all time.

She looked at him, hoping her voice was steady. "I wish you wouldn't do that."

He looked into her eyes and then slowly smiled. "No," he contradicted, brushing a strand of hair away from her face, "you don't."

He was right and they both knew it. She wanted him to kiss her like this. She wanted him to continue making her pulse race and her heart pound. But she knew where all that led. And she wasn't up for any more heartache. Not for herself, not for Robby.

Tina shook her head, praying he'd understand—understand what she wasn't all too sure she understood herself. "I'm not ready."

Suppressing a sigh, Michael dropped his arms. He backed away, though he didn't want to. "All right, I won't rush you."

He shoved his hands into his pockets, struggling for control over his own turbulent emotions. He'd just spent the last two days thinking about this very moment. Not his work, not his client, not his business, just this moment. And her. Accustomed to going full steam ahead whenever he had his mind set on something, he was stymied. Patience was something he was going to have to work at.

"Just tell me. What's the proper mourning length for a divorce?"

Was that what he thought the problem was? That she was still in love with Larry? That she was sorry their marriage hadn't worked out? All that seemed like a million years away now.

"I'm not mourning a divorce, I'm mourning promises that weren't kept and the disappointments that resulted." She searched his face, trying to see if she was making any sense to him.

He understood her fear, understood it because he'd dealt with it himself. Feeling the way he did about her had made him come to terms with his own fears. "I tell you what, I'll promise never to disappoint you if you promise never to die."

She stared at Michael, suddenly remembering that he had suffered the loss of his own dreams. "I can't do that."

Michael caught her shoulders, holding her in place, afraid she'd turn away before he could tell her. "Neither can I. But I can promise you that I will never knowingly disappoint you and that I'll do my damnedest to make you happy."

Absorbing what he was saying, Tina wondered

if she'd fallen asleep on the sofa and was dreaming. Men didn't talk like this.

Smiling into her eyes, he ran his hand along her head. "I realized something over these last two days. I didn't just miss my daughter and my knuckle-headed baby brother. I missed you and Robby." He took a deep breath, unable to say more that that for now. Not without some kind of encouragement. "I figure that's a good start. How about you?"

She could just hear Joyce telling her she was crazy. But Joyce had loved Rick since the seventh grade. She'd never had to endure finding out what a fool she'd been to give her heart to the wrong man.

She pressed her lips together. Even if she lost him, she couldn't say anything else. Not yet. "I need time."

He couldn't pretend it didn't hurt, but he wasn't going to walk out, either. Not after things had arranged themselves this way to awaken him again as a man. "All right. Time it is." He looked into her eyes. "In the meantime, think about this—"

"I have enough to think about," she began, but she made no move to turn away.

His mouth came down on hers and the lights went out in her head. Everything slipped into a velvety darkness where there was nothing left but an all-pervading warmth that bathed her body. She felt the heat of his mouth as it traveled along hers. And then there were lights, thousands of them dancing about in her head, forming a veritable light show, the likes of which she couldn't ever remember seeing or even imagining.

Tina's arms went around his neck as she leaned into the kiss.

She was doomed.

Her only hope was in keeping her distance from this man before it was too late.

Fat chance, she thought. It was already too late. Because she wanted him to make love to her. Wanted to make love with him.

A tiny wail suddenly penetrated the fiery wall of desire around her, saving her before she wound up doing something that would haunt her for the rest of her life.

With an effort, Tina pulled back, her hands on his arms to steady herself. "Um, I believe your daughter wants to say hi."

He was already releasing her, glancing up the stairs. "I think I'm going to have to tell her to work on her timing."

"I think her timing is excellent," Tina contradicted, leading the way upstairs. But the funny thing was, she wasn't completely convinced herself.

As she marked down the inning's outcome, Tina straightened up from the chain-link fence she'd been leaning against and glanced carelessly toward the lawn chairs and blankets spread out over the grassy field. Since Michael had taken over coaching, she'd noticed that attendance had more than tripled.

No doubt about it, she couldn't recall ever seeing so many parents involved in their children's extracurricular activities. She'd been the team mom last year. Then, as well as the first week of practice this season, many of the mothers would drop off their kids as if she, the coach and any freelance assistants who hung around were nothing more than volunteer baby-sitters, there to entertain their children for two and a half hours, at the end of which the kids would be rounded up again and taken home.

It was different now. Parents remained to watch the game. Especially the mothers.

Tina smiled to herself. Most especially the mothers. She didn't remember seeing this many mothers on the field before Michael had taken over. And they weren't really watching the kids play so much as they were watching the kids being coached. Mostly, she thought, they were watching Michael and Alex.

Especially Michael.

She couldn't say she blamed them. Michael certainly did cut a mouth-watering figure with his formfitting jeans and his polo shirts. Unlike a lot of men past the age of twenty-eight, he didn't wear baggy jeans in order to hide a myriad of sins caused by long nights spent in front of the television set with a bag of junk food and a six-pack of beer. On the contrary, his almost-tight jeans showed off a body that was nothing if not athletic. A body that Tina was certain, judging by their rapt expressions, almost every woman on the field would have given anything to have in her trophy room.

So what was wrong with her? It wasn't as if Michael hadn't shown interest in her. Why wasn't she dating him, or even seeing him without a gaggle of children between them?

Maybe it was because she couldn't shake the feeling that the price of a trophy like that eventually meant hours of self-doubt and loneliness and insecurity. She sighed, tucking away the pencil she'd been using into a loop above the pad.

That had been her, insecure and alone, until she'd taken herself to task and given herself a good talking to. It wasn't she who'd had the problem, it had been Larry. Larry was the one who was married to his career rather than committed to his family. Larry who preferred the high of a rising stock to the high gotten from seeing his son's eyes light up when he walked into the house from a business trip.

The way Robby's had when Michael had come back from his trip several weeks ago. Robby was getting too close to Michael, too wrapped up in him.

Something deep and protective rose again in her breast as she watched Michael stop to show one of the boys how to choke up on his bat. She looked over to where Robby was sitting on the bench, waiting his turn. He was watching Michael with the other boy. The expression on his young face didn't reveal jealousy because Michael's attention was focused elsewhere, but pride—the kind of pride a kid took in the accomplishments of a parent. His beaming face seemed to fairly shout, "Look, everybody, he's mine."

*But he's not, Robby. He's not yours. Or mine. He's Hannah's.*

Tina bit her lip, aching for her son and the inevitable realization that lay ahead of him. The longer it took to arrive, the harder it would be for him to handle.

Why didn't she have the courage to just put a stop to all this? To separate herself from the games, the man, his daughter and just turn her back on everything, taking Robby with her?

Because Robby was having fun again and she just couldn't find it in her heart to stop it now. It would stop soon enough.

Sighing, she looked away, dragging her hand through her hair.

"Why the long face?" Michael asked, coming up behind her. "We're winning."

She hadn't realized he was so close. That was what she got for letting her mind wander. She glanced down at the score she'd been keeping mechanically. They were ahead by five runs.

"Yes, we are."

Michael raised her chin with his hand, as if to examine her face more closely. "So, I repeat, why the long face?"

She shrugged carelessly, wishing he wouldn't touch her like that. Every gesture felt so intimate, so stirring. It was just making things worse for her. "I'm just thinking."

"About?" He kept his eyes on the field. Two of the team were on base and they only had one out. His eyes shifted to Tina. "You know, for a bouncy lady, you can be awfully closemouthed at times."

She grasped at the first thing she could think of. "I was just thinking about the championship game."

"Worried already, huh?" He was beginning to read her like a book. A well-loved book. He kind of liked that. "No reason to. The team's a cinch to get in the series." There was pride in his voice.

The championship game was all Robby and Kent had talked about these last few days. They were in a euphoric state about the possibility of being in it. "I know. It's been a great nine weeks, thanks to you."

He wasn't the kind who needed to take credit. "They had the potential, they just needed someone to bring it out of them."

Even as she was trying to distance herself from him, there was something seductive about his voice. About just being around him. She could see how he'd captivate anyone from age five to ninety-five. "I meant thanks for giving up your time like that. I know you're busy."

He laughed. "Noah, collecting two of everything for the ark, was busy. I'm beyond busy." He gave a thumbs-up to the boy who slid into third base, stealing it. "Way to go!" he called out before turning to Tina again. "But things have managed to rearrange themselves."

Not without a huge effort on his part, he added silently, but it had been worth it. He felt fulfilled doing this, not to mention the pleasure he took from the expression in Tina's eyes when she looked at him, unaware that he was looking her way. The woman was having a tremendous impact on his life without even trying. Since he promised not to rush her, he was just biding his time before he let her know that. But it sure wasn't easy.

"I'm glad," she told him, "because the kids are counting on you being there for the final game. They can't win it without you."

He nodded, turning to adjust Hannah's baseball cap. The team had adopted her as a mascot and took turns keeping her entertained. They'd all signed the cap she wore askew on her head.

"That's next Saturday, right?" he asked absently.

"No, it's a week from Wednesday."

He looked up at her sharply, his mind clicking into gear, visualizing the oversize calendar on his desk. "Are you sure?"

Tina had a sinking feeling that the inevitable snake had just slithered into Paradise as she nodded her head. "Positive."

*Chapter 9*

Seeing the expression on his face, she waited for him to say that he wasn't going to be able to be here for the game.

When he said nothing, she pressed the issue, though part of her really didn't want to. Didn't want to hear the words that would destroy this fantasy world she'd found herself slipping into.

"Why?"

Leaving Alex to watch Hannah, Michael moved to the other end of the bench, close to the batter's box. *Damn.* The word ricocheted around in his head fiercely.

"No reason," he told her cheerfully. "I just

thought that the big game was Saturday, when most parents could see it.''

He was lying, she thought. She could feel it. Feel the huge letdown that was in the making for her son and his friends.

''The park's being used for an outdoor wedding, so the game was rescheduled for Wednesday at six.'' She studied his expression as she spoke. ''I guess they thought most parents could make it at that time.''

''Seems reasonable.'' He pointed to the next batter in the lineup. The boy scrambled from the bench, grabbing a bat. Michael stopped and chose a lighter one for him. ''Try this.''

The boy took a practice swing, beamed and ran off to await his turn.

With her back to the team so they couldn't see her lips, she lowered her voice, pushing the envelope further. ''You can't make it, can you?''

His eyes met hers for a moment. His gave nothing away. She got the sense that he was extremely good at poker. ''There's a conflict, yes.''

''And?''

He gestured toward the field. ''Let's concentrate on the game we're playing right now. Otherwise the point is moot.''

*No,* she thought, watching him walk onto the field to take his turn at pitching to his team, *the point's not moot at all. The point is whether or not business comes before personal promises and kids who are depending on you.* She had a feeling she knew what the outcome of that tug-of-war would be and she didn't like it.

She supposed, if the boys lost, she wouldn't have to find out and be disappointed in the man that she, almost completely against her will, had come to put her faith in.

But that was only putting off the inevitable. There would be another time, and then she would know. Know that at bottom, Michael was just like Larry. Business would come first. It was only logical.

Except that she wasn't dealing with "logical." She was dealing with feelings, and that was a whole other ball game.

"C'mon, Adam, you can hit it," Tina cheered a particularly short boy on as he took his turn at bat. She was vaguely aware that Alex had come up behind the boy to help him bat. Her mind was elsewhere.

They won.

"This means we get to play the champions, right, Mike?" Robby cried eagerly, hurrying over to him as the rest of his teammates whooped and yelled, hugging each other.

Feeling an incredible sense of triumph that, for

now, superseded the conflicted feelings he'd been dealing with, Michael nodded his head. ''Yes, it does.''

Michael was smiling, Tina noted, but she could swear he also looked worried. Worried because he knew he couldn't be there to coach the boys on what they probably felt was the most important day of their young lives.

Well, at least that was something, she supposed. Larry had never felt guilty about disappointing Robby. Still, in the long run, what ultimately would count for the boys would be that he was there. And he wouldn't be. Without Michael, who had become their magic good luck charm along with everything else, they would feel like losers before they ever took the field.

Not if she could help it, she thought. She might not be as adroit as Michael was at getting the best and then some out of the kids, or at pitching for that matter—somehow he'd managed to get at least one hit out of every child each game no matter how bad they seemed to be—but they'd put on a decent show. They weren't going to go out as losers, but as contenders who'd almost made it.

Who knew? They might even win. That would show him, she thought, slanting a look at him. He looked up to see the look in her eyes and froze.

The boys were spraying each other with shaken-up carbonated soda, the way they'd seen the big leaguers do on television with champagne after a divisional victory. With a gleeful laugh, they suddenly all converged on Michael and Tina, surrounding them. And, as one, they aimed what was left in their cans at the couple in their center.

Caught off guard, Tina squealed as she swung away from the line of fire. Directly into Michael.

Laughing, Michael swung her behind him, trying to shield her with his body, but it was impossible. The squad of players surrounded them, giving no quarter until the last of the soda was gone. Still laughing, the kids toppled on the ground like small dominoes at the feet of their coach.

Dripping, one arm comfortably around Tina's shoulders, Michael looked around at the team members sprawled out around him in a circle. "Just what I've always wanted—my own adoring subjects."

He wasn't far from wrong, Tina thought.

Taking off his shirt, he wrung it out and then used it to wipe his face. He didn't notice the look that came into Tina's eyes until he turned around.

Coming to, Tina tried to collect herself. She knew her mouth had dropped open in pure admiration. She'd expected him to be well built because of the way his clothes fit him. She hadn't expected him to have a body that looked as if Michelangelo had sculpted him after he'd learned from his mistakes when he'd created the statue of David.

Several of the mothers who'd come to gather up their collapsed, wet sons stopped dead. There was envy written all over their features as they glanced in her direction before looking back at their sons' gorgeous coach.

*Nope, you're wrong. Not mine,* Tina thought in silent answer to the looks the women had given her. There was a very real, very sharp stab of disappointment as she made the admission.

Seeing her expression, Michael grinned. "Maybe I'd better put this back on."

"Maybe." She couldn't draw her eyes away from the way his muscles moved as he dragged the wet shirt back on. "That is, if you don't want to be attacked by a squadron of women."

He didn't even bother looking behind him. "Their husbands are here."

As if that mattered. The man truly was innocent in some ways, wasn't he? "I don't think they're aware of that right now."

He glanced over his shoulder toward Alex, who was in the middle of handing out the victory candy bars he'd made a habit of bringing with him.

Shirt back on, Michael looked at Tina. "Maybe

you and I could go out somewhere and celebrate later tonight," he suggested.

*Bad idea.* She was having enough trouble trying to separate herself from him. This was not going to help. "No, I don't have a baby-sitter for Robby."

He ran a hand through his damp hair, moving it out of his eyes. "Alex can stay with him. Kent can come over. They'll have a ball."

She felt herself weakening. "Think Alex can handle two boys and Hannah?"

Michael laughed. "He's a natural. Alex is a football player." His brother could probably get them interested in that. He began to wonder if there was an official football league organized for the boys.

Self-conscious, she realized that her wet T-shirt was sticking to her chest. And that he was looking at the way it adhered to her.

And that she liked the look she saw in his eyes.

Tina cleared her throat. "And what, he'll toss Hannah at them and yell, 'Go deep'?"

He laughed, enjoying the image. Enjoying the woman who'd created it. Michael raised his eyes to her face. "Not quite." He cocked his head and looked at her, lowering his voice. "Please?"

She knew she should say no. For her own safety. But his laugh undid her and the single-word entreaty sealed the deal. She sighed, knowing she was being dumb. "All right, but I can't stay out too long."

"Tomorrow isn't a school night," he reminded her with a wink. Moving past her, he called for the team's attention. "Okay, men—and ladies— let's go to the Pizza Barn. We've got some serious celebrating to do. Pizzas are on me," he declared loud enough for the parents to hear.

Tina stepped back for a moment, giving the sudden stampede of small boys and Meghan room as they followed Michael off the field, cheering. It was like watching the Pied Piper leading the children off to the promised playland.

She was nervous.

More nervous than she'd been the first time she had gone out to dinner with him. Because then it had just been with a man she didn't know, a man she had found attractive, but nothing more.

Now there was more. Now she'd allowed herself to like him, to think about him.

To kiss him.

There were a thousand reasons for her not to go out with him tonight. A thousand reasons for her not to allow herself to feel this way. She couldn't grasp hold of even one of them long enough to make herself refuse the invitation.

Alex had come over early, bringing Hannah and taking charge of the boys. He'd said that Michael had sent him over so she could have time to get ready in peace if she wanted to.

The man thought of everything.

He'd probably thought of a good excuse for next Wednesday, too.

That thought didn't stop her from going, either. So she went, her stomach tied in such a knot she could almost feel it against her spine.

"Sorry, baby," she murmured, looking down at her waist just after she'd zipped up her dress. "Not leaving you much space lately, am I? But this'll be over soon," she promised, slipping on her shoes. "The game's on Wednesday and he's not going to be able to come. After that, things'll be different."

She knew that as well as she knew her own name. They'd be different because as entitled to his own life as Michael certainly was, there would always be Robby's hurt face between them, and she knew she couldn't put that behind her, even if she wanted to.

The doorbell rang. As she took the stairs, she couldn't help feeling that it was the bell going off for their final round in the ring.

She told herself to make the most of it.

# Chapter 10

He'd been trying to figure out how to break it to her all evening. After the game, he'd gone to his office, done exhaustive checking, made a few calls. All for naught. There was no way out of this. He wasn't going to be able to attend the last game.

"Exactly how fixed is the schedule for the last game?"

She raised her eyes from her dessert to look at him. To look at his eyes. The question came out of the blue, after a pregnant pause following an anecdote about Alex and a game he'd played last fall. Up to this point, they'd been making small talk until it had turned out to be almost an art form, keeping the inevitable moment at bay.

She didn't have to ask if he was talking about "the" game. She knew.

"Very." She put down her spoon. The vanilla sundae was melted and soupy. She'd been toying with it for a while now. "Unless we move it to a month away." Which wasn't an option. "The field's booked up. All the open school grounds in Bedford are," she added, anticipating his next question. Her mouth curved sadly. "We're a very competitive sports town. You'd be surprised at the number of different sports and teams that flourish here."

*Damn you, Michael Whittaker, damn you for breaking my son's heart. And mine.*

She took a deep breath, trying to compose herself for what she knew was coming. *Be reasonable. They're not his kids—any of them. He has a right to put his own life first.*

"Apparently." Michael sighed, thinking. "Maybe we could have the game somewhere else?" He knew just the right place. It could be done. "I know these people in Newport—"

But Tina shook her head. Anticipating this, she'd already looked into the official handbook and made an appeal to the committee this afternoon. No dice. "Not for the game to be official.

Rules.'' She pressed her lips together, then added, ''I checked.''

His eyes met hers. ''Because you had a feeling.'' It wasn't a question.

She nodded. ''Because I had a feeling,'' she echoed. Tina damned herself for asking, for pleading, but even as she did, she heard herself asking, ''There's no chance at all—?''

He hated the look he saw in her eyes, hated the one he imagined, over and over again, in the eyes of the boys who'd looked up at him with admiration and joy just this afternoon.

Michael shook his head. ''I tried.''

Tina fisted her hands in her lap. What she was thinking wasn't fair, or what she was feeling, for that matter. Michael was nothing like Larry. He'd proven that. He'd tried, putting himself out for almost nine weeks when he really didn't have to. He'd made a real difference in the children's lives.

Maybe that was the problem. He'd made a difference and now that difference was going to be the reason they were so terribly disappointed. If he'd never begun this, they wouldn't be in this position.

The higher you rose, the farther you fell, she thought in exasperation.

Wasn't that her problem, too?

Yes, it was her problem. All of this was her problem, of her own making. She'd been the one who'd allowed this to happen, allowed Michael to come into her son's life and into the lives of his friends.

And into her life.

Maybe what she was feeling wasn't fair, this huge, engulfing disappointment, but that didn't make it go away, didn't make it any less soul-wrenching to bear.

The words just seemed to come out of their own volition. "Maybe you didn't try hard enough."

Beneath the anger, he saw the disappointment, and that got to him even more than her accusation. His ability to talk the gods down from Mt. Olympus suddenly failed him. "Tina, I understand how you must feel, but it is, after all, just a game."

He was belittling something that was important to a group of children just to excuse his own actions. Suddenly she was back in her own living room, arguing with her husband. The memory stung.

Tina drew herself up. "Yes, it's just a game, and Robby is just a boy. And in a hundred years, none of this will matter. But right now it does, to him. To the other children. And to me." She threw the napkin on the table, fire in her eyes. She was so disappointed in him, she couldn't see straight. "Look, this isn't fair to you, I know, but I can't help it. I should never have let this get out of hand—"

Where was she going with this? "Out of hand? What are you talking about?"

"Nothing. You wouldn't understand." She looked around for her purse. Finding it, she grabbed it. "Go to your meeting, your trip, your whatever it is that is going to keep you away Wednesday evening." Fighting back tears that suddenly insisted on forming, she rose to her feet. "You've more than done your community service. You've more than repaid Robby for finding your daughter." She had to get out of here before she started crying, she thought. She wasn't about to give him that satisfaction. "I'm sorry if we've inconvenienced you. You've been a prince."

On his feet, he tried to reach for her hand, but she pulled away. "Tina—"

"I can find my own way home," she told him. "Thank you for a lovely evening. You'll have to excuse me. We pregnant women tend to be overly emotional."

With that, she fled the restaurant, leaving Michael staring after her, numb.

Maybe it *had* been hormones, Tina thought, that had pushed her over the edge. God knows she hadn't felt rational when she'd confronted Michael in the restaurant Saturday night.

But though he'd called after her, he hadn't followed her. She'd had the valet hail a cab at the corner and she'd sped away. If Michael had come after her, she wouldn't have known it, she told herself.

But he hadn't come over, hadn't called, hadn't tried to get in contact with her in any way since then. That told her that he didn't care, that what she'd said hadn't mattered and, at bottom, he was probably relieved to be off the hook—about everything. Robby, the game, her, everything.

She bit back a sigh as she looked out on the field. The boys from both teams were still arriving. Everyone kept asking her where Michael was. As if she was his keeper. She'd gotten tired of saying that she didn't know, wanting to add that she didn't care.

Except that she did.

But that was her problem. She just hoped that Robby could get over his disappointment without any permanent scars.

As if reading her mind, Robby looked up at her. "He's gonna come, Mom."

They'd been over and over this. She'd tried to prepare him as best she could, starting out with a "what if?" scenario and then working her way into the truth. But Robby refused to accept it.

She caught herself before she slipped an arm around his slim shoulders. He didn't want to be known as a Mama's boy. "Robby, I told you, Michael has to be out of town—"

Robby looked at her stubbornly, as if she was just trying to torment him. That hurt, too. "He was out of town before."

Wearily she took the bats out of the carrier she'd lugged from the car. "He had to go again."

Robby began to help automatically, lining up the bats, aware that this was a job Michael usually did. "But he came back for the game then," Robby insisted. "He took the pink-eye."

"Red-eye," she corrected mechanically. She emptied out the last bat and threw aside the bag. Robby was just going to have to face reality. The man wasn't coming. "And I'm afraid that—"

But Robby wasn't looking at her. He was pointing excitedly toward the parking lot. "Look, Mom, look! Mike's here! I told you he'd come, I told you he'd come!"

Dropping the bat he was holding, Robby nearly tripped over his own feet as he ran toward Michael. The latter, followed by Alex, was still dressed in his suit. Robby fairly jumped up and down in front of him. "Boy, you sure cut it close.

Mom said you wouldn't be here, but I said you would.''

By now, the other players were swarming around him, shouting greetings, asking questions. Nervous about the game to be played. Michael grinned, nodding at them, then caught Tina's eye as he looked up. ''Your mother was almost right.''

Kent tugged on his jacket until he got his attention. ''Why are you in a suit?''

''Long story.'' Quickly he shed his jacket, slinging it over the bench. He began to roll up his sleeves. ''Everybody ready?'' A cheer went up in response. ''Okay, then, let's play some ball.''

She waited for two whole innings before she approached him, busying herself with the team, the score and anything else she could find until she thought she'd burst. Finally she couldn't stand it anymore.

Crossing to him after he'd sent another batter up to face Alex's pitching, she said, ''I thought you said you couldn't get out of the meeting.''

He'd wondered how long it would take her to ask. He was disappointed she'd held out this long. Michael ran his fingers over the box in his pocket before answering her. ''I couldn't.''

She didn't understand. ''But you're here.''

He turned to face her. God, but he had missed her these last few days. He'd given her her space, tried to reassess his life and had arrived at the only conclusion he could. "Yeah, I am."

The words just hung there for a moment, without any further explanation. He knew he was driving her crazy, she thought. She wanted to beat on him. "You don't expect me to leave it at that, do you? What happened?"

What happened was that he'd rearranged his priorities. "I told the client I couldn't stay past Wednesday morning. He said he'd go with another company. I said that was his prerogative."

He said it so matter-of-factly, as if this didn't change everything. Tina held her breath, watching his expression. "And?"

"And he decided maybe he could reschedule at that. Especially when I told him that it was for a T-ball team I was coaching and a little boy I didn't want to disappoint." Michael smiled. Funny how things worked themselves out. Because he'd put Robby and Tina first, he'd actually gotten on a better footing with the client. "He told me he wished his father had thought that way, and he wished the team well."

He eyed the field. The bases were loaded. It looked promising. "Now I've got a question of my own." He looked at her. "Did you miss me?"

She knew she should just shrug this off. It wouldn't do to look too eager. "Yes."

He took the box out of his pocket, popped the lid and held it out to her. "Will you marry me?"

Her mouth dropped open. When she finally found her tongue, it felt as if it was made of lead. "That's two questions."

He laughed. "Cut me some slack. It's been a long day." Taking the ring out of the box, he slipped it on her finger.

She watched the setting sun shoot blue and white beams through the marquis-cut ring. She could barely tear her eyes away. "Isn't this rather sudden?"

He took her hand in his. "No, I think we've both seen this coming for a very long time. Nine weeks to be exact." Michael smiled at her. "I felt we connected the first time I saw you."

She'd had the same feeling. But not in a million years had she seen this coming, especially not in her condition. A condition she was sure he must have forgotten. "Michael, I'm pregnant."

Did she think that could possibly deter him from making one of the best decisions of his life? He slipped his hands around the waist that had grown a little thicker since he'd met her. "In case you haven't noticed, I like kids."

She didn't want him to say this and then take

it back. She couldn't bear that. She wanted him to be very, very sure. "But—"

"There is no 'but.' There's either yes, or no." Oblivious to the fact that they were drawing more attention than the game, he lightly caressed her cheek. "Personally, I'm rooting for yes."

Despite the ring and the magic of the moment, she was having trouble getting herself to believe this was really happening. "And if it's no?"

"Then I'll stick around for another season and see if it's yes then. You said you had feelings for me, feelings you didn't want to have—"

"Yes…"

The grin nearly split his face. "See, the word isn't hard to say."

She was afraid, so afraid of making a mistake. Of following her heart only to regret it. "I meant yes I had feelings—"

"Good, the groundwork is there. All I have to do is fill in the spaces. And I intend to." He looked into her eyes. "I intend to fill in all your spaces, Tina, until you can't think of anything without thinking of me."

Oh, what the hell, she did love him. And he was so good to Robby. Tina threaded her arms around his neck. "Too late. It's already happened. I love you, Michael."

"Good, because I love you."

"Time out!" Alex called as he saw the temporary coach kissing the team mom. "And it's about time," he added.

But neither Tina nor Michael heard him. Nor the cheer the team sent up. They were both too busy.

# Epilogue

Placing his hand on Robby's shoulder, Michael ushered the small boy forward toward the hospital bed where Tina was lying, holding the newest member of the Whittaker family: Michael Ethan Whittaker.

"So," he asked, "what do you think of him?"

Robby looked intently at the sleeping face. "He's kind of small."

"Yeah," Michael agreed, "but they grow if you water them daily."

Robby giggled as he looked up at his new father. "Like a plant?"

Michael pretended to think the question over

seriously. He winked at Tina. "More like a weed. He'll be big enough to play baseball in no time."

"Okay," Robby said magnanimously, stepping back, "I guess we'll keep him."

Biting back a laugh, Michael gave the boy's shoulder an affectionate, approving squeeze. "Good man."

Robby beamed up at him in response. Michael wondered if there was such a thing as too much happiness, because if there was, he was pretty near that point. So much had happened in the last few months. The team he'd coached had won the championship, he'd won the girl and they'd gotten married. He'd begun adoption proceedings for Robby at the same time. He intended to adopt the baby who had arrived just a few hours ago, as well. The delivery had gone so smoothly, he couldn't believe it.

As Tina's time to give birth had grown near, he'd found himself growing more and more afraid. It wasn't anything he'd discuss with Tina, but in his heart he'd lived in fear that history would repeat itself. That he would lose her the way he'd lost Rachel.

But Tina had come through with flying colors and looked no more tired than if she'd played a couple of sets of tennis.

He felt more blessed than a man had a right to be.

Tina reached for his hand, knowing exactly what he was thinking. She'd had five months to get in tune to his every thought. It had been a nice task.

"Have I told you that I love you?"

He squeezed her hand, smiling down at her, his heart full. "Not today."

Robby frowned. "Yuck, mushy stuff." Stepping forward, he leaned over the baby. "They get like that sometimes. Don't listen, Mikey."

The familiar nickname made him laugh. Michael ruffled his son's hair. "Give it time, partner. You'll like that mushy stuff yourself some day."

"Never happen," Robby said with feeling.

"We'll see, Robby. We'll see." Michael leaned over and pressed a kiss to Tina's forehead. "Good job, 'Mom.' He's beautiful."

Tina reached for Michael's hand again and curled her fingers around it. She hadn't believed it was humanly possible to be this happy and live.

But it was.

Dear Reader,

I was delighted to take part in this special anthology featuring mothers-to-be, since it's my opinion that some of the greatest she-roes in the world are moms! The idea for "The Monarch and the Mom" hit me as I was driving from my home in Virginia down to Research Triangle Park, North Carolina. I started thinking about all the research that goes on in this fabulous area, and my mind turned to fertility and genetic studies. Here's where being a random thinker comes in handy. What if a man's sperm had been collected for a genetic study? What if it was mistakenly used for in vitro fertilization? What if the man...was a prince? The first line popped inside my head: "The royal sperm is missing." Then came a man and a woman with fears and dreams, a story with heartache and laughter. I'm pleased to present the story of Prince Alexander Dumont and she-ro mom-to-be Sophie Hartman. With the way my mind works, you may see more of the Dumonts in the future. Enjoy.....

All the best,

*Leanne Banks*

# THE MONARCH AND THE MOM

## Leanne Banks

This book is dedicated to my twin in mind and spirit:
Donna Beard.
Thank you for your friendship.

# Prologue

"...The royal sperm is missing," Jean Robert said.

Prince Alexander Dumont caught the last few words of the royal family's official confidential assistant and felt a sinking sensation. Glancing up from the beautiful view of Laguna Beach outside his lush oceanside condo, Prince Alex narrowed his eyes at the short, dapper man who was frequently the bearer of family news, edicts and perpetual nagging from his mother concerning his marital state. "Whose sperm?" he asked, because Jean Robert could have easily been referring to one of his four brothers.

Jean Robert cleared his throat. "Your sperm, Your Highness." He stretched his neck against his white collar. "And it's, uh, technically not missing."

Confused as hell, Alex shook his head. "Does this have something to do with those damned sperm deposits Mother required all of us to make?"

Jean Robert dipped his head and adjusted his suit jacket. "As a matter of fact, sir, yes it does. As you know the queen required you and your brothers to make royal, uh, deposits of your sperm on your eighteenth and twenty-fifth birthdays and—"

Alex waved his hand impatiently. He well remembered his mother's demand for the deposits for the sake of the line should he and his brothers suddenly croak. "Cut to the chase."

Jean Robert's left eye twitched. That was a very bad sign, Alex thought, his sense of foreboding deepening. Jean Robert had served the family since his mother had been a teenager and very little fazed the man.

"As you know, the queen is the most progressive ruler the island of Marceau has ever had," Jean Robert said with pride.

Alex stifled a sigh. "You're not making a PR

speech to the media, JR. We're talking about my mother. I'm her son. Get to the point.''

"Yes, of course,'' Jean Robert said. ''You have a distant cousin in North Carolina who is conducting genetic research. He invited the queen to provide genetic material from the royal family for his research.''

Alex flipped through his memory bank. ''Ralph,'' he said, remembering a man with thick glasses and a perpetual absentminded air. He was the cousin of a cousin.

''Dr. Ralph Edwards. Exactly. Your sperm was sent to his facility.''

Alex knew his sperm would have been selected because of the joyous fact that all four brothers and their male children had to die before he would get within spitting distance of the throne. Alex had delighted in this fact all of his adult life. His older two brothers bore the weight of the impending throne with all the lack of freedom and privacy. There had once been six Dumont brothers, but his youngest brother, Jacques, had died in a drowning accident. After all these years, Jacques's loss was a hole the family hadn't filled, although his firebrand sister, Michelina, tried her damnedest. Through the luck of his birth order, Alex had been able to pursue his business interests and maintain his bachelor status with a minimum of interference.

"So, Ralph has lost my sperm?"

Jean Robert's eye twitched again. "I'm afraid it's more serious than that." He paused and took a breath. "It appears your sperm was mistakenly used in an in vitro-fertilization procedure."

Alex's heart stopped. He stared at Jean Robert. It couldn't be true. "My sperm was used for what?" he roared.

Jean Robert didn't flinch. He was accustomed to dealing with royal tempers. "Your sperm was mistakenly used in an in vitro-fertilization procedure. The good news is that the woman is healthy, unmarried and thirty years old, and the pregnancy is progressing normally."

Alex turned his back on Jean Robert and headed for the bar. He reached for the bottle of Scotch and poured two fingers into a shot glass. He swallowed and the drink burned down his throat like fire. His life passed before his eyes. He'd always been so damn careful about contraception. After watching his brother, Prince Michel, and his struggles, he'd never wanted to be forced into a marriage or a career for any reason.

Now he was going to be a father due to his mother's *progressive interference*. The notion clanged inside him like a discordant bell. "How far along is she?" he asked.

"Twelve weeks, sir."

"What do you know about her?" he asked, pouring more Scotch.

"I have a dossier," Jean Robert said, pulling a file from his leather portfolio. "Sophie Hartman, thirty years old, never married, blond hair, blue eyes, a master's degree in computer programming—"

Alex downed the Scotch. "A computer geek," he muttered. "The mother of my child is a computer geek. Does she know I'm the father?"

"Not yet," Jean Robert said. "But Dr. Edwards feels a deep responsibility to inform her—"

"Ralphie should be feeling a deep fear of getting his tongue wrapped around his throat. Ralphie," Alex said, invoking a tone as uncompromising as iron, "will keep his mouth shut until I figure out what to do."

Silence followed. "Is there any question what you will do, Your Highness?" Jean Robert asked.

Duty swelled inside him. Duty. The bitter taste of it filled his mouth. He downed another shot of Scotch. "Take a chill pill, JR. There is no question that I will marry Sophie Hartman. That choice has been taken from me."

# Chapter 1

This was her favorite time of the day in Cary, North Carolina, Sophie Hartman thought as she wandered away from a small cluster of people at Dr. Ralph Edwards's cocktail party. Between 5:00 and 7:00 p.m. was the most blissful two-hour time period in the world...when she wasn't nauseated.

She'd consented to attend because of the hour and because Dr. Edwards had seemed so endearingly edgy around her lately. As soon as he'd learned of her pregnancy, he'd stopped by her office at the research center even though his office was on a different floor.

"A virgin frozen peach daiquiri," she told the bartender as she slid onto the bar stool. "No alcohol," she emphasized, absently pressing her hand to her still-flat abdomen. Sometimes she still couldn't believe she was pregnant, especially between 5:00 and 7:00 p.m. when she wasn't tossing her cookies.

"You like peaches," a deep masculine voice with the barest trace of an accent said from behind her.

Sophie glanced over her shoulder and gazed up the length of a man with a lean, muscular frame, tanned skin, aquiline features and observant eyes. Her heart skipped in confusion. His cream-colored pullover shirt had the look of silk knit and his slacks were exquisitely tailored. This was not the kind of man who often approached her. She would bet he didn't have a gun rack on his vehicle and his name wasn't Billy Bob. She pushed her glasses up on her nose and shoved her curly blond hair behind her ear. "Guilty," she said. "I crave peaches."

"Alex Dumont," he said, offering his hand.

She extended hers and noticed the warmth and strength of his grip. "Sophie Hartman. You know Dr. Edwards?"

"We're related," he said, taking the stool beside her. "Scotch," he said to the bartender.

"Really," she said, trying not quite successfully to keep the disbelief from her voice. "You don't resemble each other."

Alex's mouth twitched. "Thank you," he said with a magnetic glint in his eyes. "We're distantly related. I'm here for a visit. What do you do in North Carolina?"

She took a sip of the drink placed in front of her. "It depends on your interests. You can visit the Butterfly Center, go to a concert, attend a baseball game or drive to the beach."

"What do *you* do?"

Confused that such an attractive man would approach her, she bit her lip. She may as well send him on his way, she decided. "I work as a computer specialist, garden, read, eat peaches between 5:00 and 7:00 p.m. and wait for my morning sickness to pass."

His eyes widened slightly. "You're pregnant?"

"Yes," she said, taking another sip. She fully intended to enjoy every bit of her drink even though this man was incredibly distracting.

"Your husband…"

She shook her head. "Don't have one. Artificial insemination," she said. "The right man might not have come along, but that doesn't mean I can't have a baby." She smiled. "You don't have to hang around. There's a very pretty brunette across the room who has been watching you.''

Alex looked into her guileless blue eyes and felt the pleasure of her directness down to his bones. In his world, her direct, nothing-to-hide attitude was rarer than diamonds. ''And if I'd rather share a drink with a pregnant blonde?'' He reached for the glass the bartender had handed him.

She gave a skeptical shrug and glanced at her watch. ''Suit yourself. I'm good for another hour or so. Then I have an appointment with the morning-sickness goddess who seems a bit confused about the time.''

''That bad,'' he mused.

''Yes,'' she said, her directness appealing to him again. ''But I'm told it passes.'' She smiled, and her expression softened. ''And Peaches is worth it.''

He tilted his head to one side. ''Peaches?'' he echoed.

''I've craved peaches so much, I gave the baby that nickname.''

He took a swig of Scotch. ''And if the baby becomes a three-hundred-pound linebacker?''

She leaned closer and lowered her voice. ''Then I guess I'll just have to whisper it when I call him Peaches.''

Her drawl was both sexy and endearing. The tenderness he saw just beneath the surface made him think of the sweet innocence of his childhood. His and his brothers' childhoods had been so short. Alex wondered how his mother would react to having her royal grandchild referred to as Prince or Princess Peaches. The notion gave him a rebellious sense of satisfaction.

"Are you married?" Sophie asked, interrupting his reverie.

"No," he said.

She frowned slightly.

"Why do you ask?"

"It just doesn't make sense that at a party with plenty of attractive single nongestating women, you would choose to talk to a pregnant lady."

"You don't believe I could be attracted to you," he said.

Her gaze locked with his for three electric seconds that surprised the hell out of him, then she shook her head. "I don't want to be presumptuous, but I would bet I'm not your usual type."

"Perhaps my usual type has never really been my type at all."

She met his gaze again and he saw a glint of unnecessary sympathy. "Hmm. Or perhaps even a very handsome man can get hurt in romantic games." She smiled wryly. "And I'm safe."

"Or fascinating," he countered, recalling that he was supposed to be wooing her.

Sophie snorted in disbelief and laughed. "Thank you for that. It truly was kind, but I hardly think a single pregnant woman fixated on peaches is fascinating. Very nice, but not necessary."

She clearly had no illusions about her attractiveness to men, Alex realized. In fact, she underestimated her appeal. Sure, she didn't look at all like the model he'd been seeing until recently, but if a man bothered to take the time, there was something about Sophie that could pique his interest. If a man could get past her bluntness.

Flattery would not work with her. She wasn't superficial enough to fall for it. He would have to take another route to get to her. "You're very perceptive," he said, swallowing his distaste over his temporary deceit. "I'm recovering from a—"

"—love affair gone wrong," she finished, and sympathetically patted his hand. "It happens to most everyone. You'll recover. And if you need a nonthreatening friend while you're far from home, I'm here," she said, then added with a wan grin, "at least between the hours of five and seven."

Accessibility gained, he thought. One hurdle passed, though not the way he'd originally planned. "Thank you. I'll take you up on your offer. Do you have a card with your phone number?"

He was the kind of man who could rock a woman's world, Sophie thought as she walked through the door of the white frame house she'd turned into a home. Well, rock another woman's world, she added wryly. The only rocking she would be doing involved a rocking chair and her baby, and that was fine with her.

Still, she thought, the timing was odd. An incredible man walks into her life immediately after she's given up on romantic love and gotten pregnant. Sophie chuckled. Go figure.

She smoothed her hand over the quilt on the back of the sofa and wandered toward the room that would be the nursery. When she entered the nearly empty nursery, she felt an impossible combination of excitement and calm.

Sophie had crossed her fingers and toes until she passed the three-month mark before purchasing anything. Now she could start decorating and planning. She'd been dreaming a long time.

Although her father had left when Sophie was three, Sophie's mother had nurtured and loved her into adulthood. The memory of her mother's love had been partly responsible for giving Sophie the confidence that she, too, could be a single parent.

It hadn't been first choice. Sophie felt as if she'd kept her eyes open for the right man. He just hadn't shown up, and she longed to be a mother. She might have a passel of doubts about her feminine appeal, but she had no doubt that she possessed enough love for this baby.

She walked to the single wooden dresser and turned the tiny crank of the music box sitting atop it. Gershwin's "Someone To Watch Over Me" played. Her mind drifted to Alex Dumont. Behind the adventurous glint in his eye, there was a strength about him. He gave the impression he could handle just about anything. A different woman might be seduced by that combination, but Sophie knew better.

Her life had taken a turn. There was no one to watch over her anymore. Instead, she would be the someone to watch over her baby, and that was okay.

Alex Dumont was a temporary ship on her horizon. He would be history before she was taking her Lamaze classes.

On the other side of town, Alex played back the messages on his cell phone voice mail as he continued to develop his strategy to give him and

Sophie some time to get acquainted before he revealed the truth and they got married. The notion of marriage still brought a bitter taste to his mouth, but Alex was resigning himself to the duty he must perform.

A reminder of the benefits of his bachelor status washed over him as Tatiana's sexy breathless message played. "I'm crushed by your sudden goodbye, darling. I don't know what I did wrong, but I'd love the opportunity to make it up to you. Let me know if you change your mind."

Alex groaned. Tatiana knew how to use her spectacular body to make a man forget about everything. An image of the lovely, though slightly spacey model, flitted through his head.

"Duty," he muttered to himself at the same time the phone in his luxury penthouse suite rang.

"Yes," he answered.

"Hold for the queen please, Your Highness," his mother's assistant said.

Alex rolled his eyes, knowing what was coming. He wondered if he could manage a disconnection.

"Alexander," his mother said. "How are you?"

"Fine, and you?"

"Very well, thank you. I'll be much better

when you have performed your paternal duty and married the American."

Alex stifled a sigh. "I've begun," he told her. "I met her tonight."

"What is she like?"

"Intelligent, kind, unassuming, very forthright," he said.

"Not at all your type," his mother mused.

"True, but that doesn't matter, does it?" he asked rhetorically. "Because the choice was taken from me."

"Oh, here we go again. Many choices are taken from us. You have had more choices than your brothers. This woman sounds as if her character stands head and shoulders above any of your previous associations."

"Mother, character isn't always the first thing a man looks for in a woman."

"Well, at your age perhaps it should be. As you said, it doesn't matter because the choice has been taken from you. In your case, perhaps that was for the best," she said in a crisp superior tone that stretched his nerves and reminded him why he preferred living in America. "Don't dawdle. I don't wish to intervene."

"Don't meddle," he said, and didn't bother to keep the dark warning note from his voice. "I'm handling this my way."

Silence followed. "Are you giving me an order?"

He rolled his eyes again at her imperious attitude. "You accept orders from no one," he recanted her familiar quote. "I don't take orders well, either. It's an inherited trait."

His mother sighed. "Do you find her at all attractive?"

He could have tormented her by inferring that he was doomed to live the rest of his life with a woman who did nothing for him. Although it wasn't far from the truth, he thought about her question and decided to answer it honestly. "She is more cute than beautiful. She wears no makeup and appears to make no efforts to tame her hair. She probably doesn't know what a beauty spa is. But there is something beneath the surface. I don't know if it's intelligence, or warmth or that damn character line you keep cramming down my throat, but she has a certain appeal."

"From your description, I like her. Don't mess it up, dear. Godspeed."

Alex ground his teeth and hung up the phone. His mother, God bless her, still had the ability to make him want to chew glass. Although he loved and respected her, he was too independent to accept her regal attitude when she directed it at him. He was happier and more productive when he was miles away from her. She left him alone because his ventures had benefited Marceau with a booming sailboat and yacht-building business along with attention from the press.

Alex enjoyed every angle of the business, from the manufacturing to the marketing. He never felt more free or at peace than when he was sailing on the water with the wind in his face. He thought of Sophie and leaned his head back against the sofa. What he wouldn't give to be on the water right now.

Sophie was scrutinizing the computer simulation program she was developing, when her phone rang. The program still needed a bit of refining, she thought. "Good morning. Sophie Hartman," she automatically said, still intent on her computer screen.

"It's no longer morning," a rich, masculine voice she immediately recognized as Alex Dumont's said. "Join me for lunch."

She smiled at his slight accent. "No," she said regretfully. "I can't. No time today. Thank you for asking."

A brief silence followed. "Pregnant women shouldn't skip meals."

"True," she said, thinking he sounded as if he weren't accustomed to a woman telling him no.

"I won't skip the meal completely. I'll just take a sandwich here at my desk."

"Then I'll take you to dinner," he said.

She noticed he didn't ask. "I never asked you about your accent."

"I was educated in England and spent some time in Europe. Five-thirty tonight. Is there anything you crave besides peaches?"

Her stomach took a dip at his use of the word *crave*. The notion struck her that many women would crave him. She quickly dismissed that thought and moved on. "A question at last."

"Pardon?"

She laughed. "I noticed you don't ask when you make arrangements."

"Family quirk," he muttered with a touch of irony. "Would you join me for dinner?"

His deep voice made her stomach flutter. Sophie quickly reined in the sensation, reminding herself why she was attractive to Alex. She was safe. "That would be nice. If you don't have a car, I can—"

"I have one," he assured her. "Shall I pick you up at work or home?"

"Five-thirty at home. I can give you directions—" she began.

"Not necessary," he interjected. "I can find you."

She felt another flutter at his intensity and took a quick breath. "Okay. I know a little place in Cary called Serendipity. It's casual, but nice."

"Five-thirty, then. And Sophie..." he said.

"Yes?"

"Eat lunch," he said, then hung up.

Sophie slowly returned the receiver to the cradle. There was something odd about Alex. His persistence was a little unnerving. He almost seemed purposeful about seeing her. She made a sound of frustration and shook her head. Alex was recovering from a broken heart and though his cousin Ralph was kind, Alex was clearly desperate for dinner conversation that didn't entail genetic research.

Later that day Sophie fussed over her choice of dress for several minutes before she remembered this technically wasn't a date. Despite that fact, she grabbed a sundress she wouldn't be able to wear in a couple of months. No need to go to the muumuu stage before it was necessary. Due to the humidity, her hair was more wild than usual, so she pulled it back with several clips. She splashed her face with cool water and smudged on some lip gloss just as the doorbell rang. Her heart tripped and she frowned at the response. She glanced at the clock. Five-thirty sharp.

Reminding herself she was safe, she swung

open the door. Alex stood on her front porch wearing crisp black slacks and a black silk knit pullover that emphasized his lean muscular frame. Dark wire-rimmed glasses covered his eyes, but she felt him looking at her from head to toe. The knowledge made her feel strange. Somehow she knew she'd come up wanting. In black he seemed mysterious, and a thousand questions bounced inside Sophie's head.

"You don't look pregnant," he said. "In that sundress and with your hair pulled back, you look like a teenager."

"Thank you, I think," she said. "You don't look pregnant, either. But you definitely don't look like a teenager."

His lips tilted in a mocking half grin. "Thank you, I think."

Sophie had never been one for half-truths. "Okay," she said, bowing to her penchant for honesty. "I'm probably the gazillionth woman to tell you this, and I must wonder if the gazillion who came before me might have inflated your ego, which makes me reluctant to say it, but even though the dark glasses are annoying, you look darn good." She took a microbreath but quickly walked past him toward his car. "Do you like gazpacho? This place has excellent—" She did a double take at his car. "A Jaguar? You rented a Jaguar?"

He shrugged. "Not my first choice, either, but I didn't want a Lincoln or a Cadillac. No real use for an SUV for the limited time I'm here."

He opened the passenger door and Sophie slid into the leather cream-colored bucket seat. She inhaled the scent of new car leather and told herself not to get used to this. "Actually I'm not much of a car person," she told him as he got in on the driver's side, "but I don't have any objections to a Jaguar."

He turned the ignition and the car purred to life. Grasping the gearshift with one strong hand, he slid the other over the steering wheel. Sophie couldn't help wondering how a woman would feel being touched by his hands. The notion mesmerized her for a full moment before she realized he had paused and was looking down at her. She quickly glanced up.

"Thank you," he said.

"For what?"

"For the compliment."

"Which compliment?" she asked, distracted by his closeness. She glanced away to focus. "Oh, when I said you looked darn good. I'm sure it's not the first time you've heard that."

"First time from you," he said in a deep voice

that made her breath catch and gave her the oddest feeling that her inconsequential compliment could matter a little bit to him after all.

That would be very foolish.

# Chapter 2

"Do you have sensitive eyes?" Sophie asked after the waiter had delivered their order.

"No," he said, lifting a spoonful of gazpacho to his lips.

"Are you a fugitive on the FBI's Most Wanted list or a movie star who is hiding from the press?"

Alex's lips twitched and he pulled off his sunglasses and met her gaze. "No. Do you always ask this many questions?"

"Just when I'm curious."

"And you're curious about me," he concluded, his deep tone making something inside her dip and sway.

"Yes." She made the confession quickly, getting it out of the way. "What do you do professionally?"

"Sailboat and yacht manufacturing," he said. "Most of my business has been conducted in Europe and on the West Coast of the United States. I'm looking into expanding to the East Coast."

"I used to love being on the water," Sophie said, recalling the sensation of the wind on her face and the sight of the sunlight sparkling on the ocean.

"Used to?"

"Before I got pregnant," she said with a wry smile. "I'm sure I'll enjoy it again after the morning sickness goddess decides I've had enough. I felt much better today, so I'm hoping this will become a trend. I have a doctor's appointment tomorrow. I love hearing the baby's heartbeat so much, I'm tempted to buy a stethoscope and amplifier," she said sheepishly, then wondered why she'd shared such a thing with him.

He shook his head in confusion. "Amplifier?"

"It's a little device the doctor uses to amplify the sound of the baby's heartbeat. I heard it during my last visit. It's a fast, swishing sound and it just seemed to fill the examination room. I was so excited—" She realized she was going on about the baby and Alex probably wasn't interested.

Alex looked at her for a long moment. "You've already heard the heartbeat?"

She nodded. "Yes, and I'll get to hear it again tomorrow. I won't have the ultrasound for a few months, but I'm told I can get a video and photos. And I will," she assured him. "It'll be fun showing Peaches these pictures later."

Sophie had heard his child's heartbeat. His head reeled with the knowledge. His chest tightened with an odd sensation. "Do you ever think about the father?"

Sophie paused for a moment and shook her head. "Not much except for health issues. My requests were good health, intelligence and average appearance. I was fortunate it worked the first time. It's not an inexpensive procedure, but I got a professional discount because I work at the research center."

*Professional discount.* Her words clanged inside him. His sperm had been sold at discount. It was bad enough there'd been a mix-up and he was going to be a father, but knowing his seed had been sold at discount brought him to a new low. Alex had the unsettling sensation of being a bluelight special.

Sophie looked at him with concern. "You don't look like you feel well. Is the gazpacho disagreeing with you?"

"No," he said. The entire situation was disagreeing with him.

They finished the meal with a sprinkling of conversation. Alex seemed distracted. He drove Sophie home in silence and walked her to the door.

Sophie looked up at him and sighed. "You must be thinking about her," she said.

His brow wrinkled in confusion. "Who?"

"The woman who hurt you," she said.

"Oh," he murmured, and ran his hand through his hair.

The easiness between them had evaporated like dew on a hot summer day and Sophie struggled with a ridiculous pinch of disappointment. "I should let you go. You could probably use some time alone. It might be best," she said, and turned to unlock and open her door.

"No," he said, his hand sliding past her to keep the door closed.

Her heart tripped faster. "No?"

"No," he repeated, and guided her back around with one gentle, but sure hand on her shoulder.

She slowly met his gaze. His eyes were dark and tempestuous with emotions she couldn't name, yet somehow felt.

"Being with you makes it easier."

Sophie held her breath. "I can't understand how—"

He touched her lips with a fingertip. "You don't have to understand. Just believe."

Looking into his eyes, she felt something inside her shift. If she didn't know better, she'd say she saw a war between honor and frustration. How could she make anything easier for this man? He was clearly a man of the world and she was not a worldly woman. Something still and quiet inside her whispered yes when her brain yelled no. There were many sound reasons for Sophie to be skeptical, but she believed.

"Invite me in," he said.

A twinge of humor eased some of her tension. "There you go ordering again. Is this a CEO thing?"

"Family trait," he muttered.

"You're all CEOs?"

"Something like that. Are you going to invite me in?" he asked.

The dare in his voice affected her breathing, but she quickly reminded herself she was the equivalent of a soft blanket to him. "Sure," she said, turning around to open the door. "I've got lemonade. If you like, we can spike yours with gin."

Sophie headed straight for the kitchen without

looking back. She suspected Alex was accustomed to a level of luxury she'd never experienced. She didn't want to make excuses for her home when she was actually proud of it. She'd made her home a comfortable haven.

Grabbing a fistful of ice cubes, she spilled them into two glasses. She poured lemonade into both, then reached in a cupboard for gin and splashed some into his drink. She glanced sideways to make sure he wasn't watching and pressed her glass to her forehead. She wasn't certain a man this hot had ever walked into her life, let alone her home. She couldn't be turned on by him. Women in early pregnancy didn't get turned on. Maybe if she kept telling herself that, she would believe it.

She walked back into the den and handed him his drink. "Lemonade with a kick."

"And yours is—"

"—kickless," she said with a grin.

He studied her carefully. "Why aren't you married?"

She shrugged. "The right guy didn't come along."

"But you're eminently marriageable. You're intelligent, reasonable and—" He seemed to search for the right word. "Presentable," he said.

Sophie blinked. Although she didn't need to be reminded, his description reminded her that he was clearly not romantically interested in her.

"Your home is so—"

"—comfortable, domestic," Sophie said.

"But more." He took a drink and narrowed his eyes. "It's strange. When I entered this room, I felt relieved. Welcomed in a quiet way."

"Safe," she said with a whisper of a smile. "That's me. I chose the furnishings and colors, even the scent of the candles, to evoke comfort and tranquillity. No harshness is allowed." She rubbed the rounded corner of table. "No sharp edges on the furniture. No scratchy fabrics."

"I don't understand why you're not married."

"Beats the heck out of me, too," she said, and sank down on the sofa, "but it's not on my list of top ten things to think about anymore."

"Would you like to be married?"

"To the right person. At the right time." She glanced up at him. "Why? Do you know someone who's dying to marry a pregnant woman?" she asked dryly.

He looked at her in exasperation. "When you put it that way—"

"That's the way it is," she said. "But enough about me. Tell me about her."

Alex's face turned blank. "Her, who?"

"Her," she said. "The woman who hurt you."

"Oh, her," Alex said, taking a long drink from his glass and looking away. "I don't like talking about it."

"I think it might help you."

"No."

"Really," she said earnestly. "Keeping the hurt bottled up just makes you feel worse. I know," she admitted.

He quickly searched her face. "A man hurt you?"

"I've been hurt before by a man, but I think what I'm talking about is loss. I know what it's like to experience loss. My father left us when I was very young, and my mother died three years ago."

"No brothers or sisters?"

She shook her head. "And you?"

"Four older brothers, one younger sister. She's a terror," he said with a half grin.

"I always wanted brothers and sisters," Sophie said.

He looked at her thoughtfully. "Maybe one day you will have them."

Sophie had no idea how that would happen, but she did know the conversation had gotten off track. "And the woman who hurt you," she ventured.

He sighed and sat down beside her on the sofa. "She never looked beyond the surface. She was interested in me for my image. I never felt she wanted to know me as a man."

The need behind his words touched a chord inside her. "Would you have let her know you?"

He glanced at her. "You're very perceptive."

She smiled. "And you didn't answer the question."

Uncomfortable with the deception, Alex also knew there was an element of truth in his words. Talking with Sophie made Alex feel all his relationships with women had been shallow. She made him want something deeper. "I'm not sure. Allowing someone to know you involves risk and trust. In the beginning everyone wears a mask. After a while, the mask slips and a beautiful, enchanting woman can turn into a witch."

"And an intelligent, fascinating man can turn into a real P.I.T.A.," Sophie said with a nod.

"Pita?" he echoed.

"It's an acronym. Pain in the..." She paused. "Asterisk."

He looked into her wide blue eyes and smiled. "I've never heard that before."

''Feel free to use it,'' she said. ''I think I know what part of your problem is.''

Alex blinked. No one except a member of his family had ever possessed the nerve to even suggest he had a problem. He bit his tongue for a full moment. ''What would that be?'' he managed in an even voice.

''It's proven that when you share a confidence with someone, it makes you feel closer to them even more so than the person with whom you've shared the confidence.''

''And your point is,'' he said.

''If you want to feel closer to a woman, you need to share more of your real self with her.''

''I'll bear that in mind,'' he said. ''Have you figured out your problem?''

She looked at him blankly. ''I don't have a problem.''

''You're not married, you don't have any prospects and you don't have a lover.''

''It doesn't bother me,'' she said. ''I'd rather be alone than be with a P.I.T.A.''

''I think I know what part of your problem is. You're so brutally honest right from the start that you scare men off.''

She slit her eyes at him in a surprisingly sexy

expression. "Then they can't be real men, can they?"

"It's a test," he said, realization hitting him. "You deliberately take a man's breath away with your brutal honesty and if he can't survive—"

"Then he's history. But I don't think of it as a test. I just don't wear the mask. What you see is what you get," she said with a boldness that stirred something inside him.

"We all wear masks," he said. "If not a mask, then we do things to keep people at a comfortable distance. You like to be in control, don't you?"

"I suspect no more than you," she said.

He leaned closer to her, looking into her wide blue eyes for answers. "You're an interesting woman," Alex said.

"Safe," she corrected.

"That could be a mask," he murmured, his gaze dropping to her lips. "I wonder what's behind the mask."

She bit her lip. "Nothing interesting."

Following an instinct, he lowered his mouth to hers.

"What are you doing?" she asked breathlessly.

"Kissing you," he said, brushing his lips back and forth against hers.

"You're not supposed to do that," she said, but didn't move back.

"Why?"

"Because you like me because I'm safe, not because you're attracted to me."

Alex swallowed her protests by taking her mouth with his. She tasted sweet with a hint of spice and her lips were as soft as velvet. A lick of arousal ran through him, surprising him. He slid his tongue past her velvet lips and the little breath she took shimmied down his nerve endings like a satin sheet.

He tugged gently on her bottom lip and tasted her with his tongue again, inviting her response. She twined her tongue with his and sucked him into the shallow recesses of her mouth. Her tongue cupped his the same way he knew her body would cup him intimately.

Alex grew hard. He slid his fingers through her curly hair and tilted her head to give him better access. He glanced down and saw the small mounds of her breasts beneath her sundress. He wondered how responsive her nipples would be to his hands and mouth.

He felt her grow warm and restless. She opened her mouth and arched against him. The sensual invitation cranked his arousal another notch. He dropped his hand to her shoulder and slid the tiny strap downward, then skimmed his fingers over the soft skin of her chest to her breast. He found her nipple already taut and rubbed it with his thumb and forefinger.

She gave a soft, gratifying moan, then pulled away and brushed aside his hand. She shook her head and adjusted her dress. "It's going to be difficult for us to be friends if you're going to play games with me."

She looked up at him with pink cheeks, swollen lips and eyes dark with arousal and accusation. Alex had the overwhelming urge to do a hell of a lot more than kiss her.

"Have you forgotten I'm pregnant?" she demanded, and stood.

"Have you forgotten you're a woman?" he returned, rising beside her.

She blinked. "No, but it's not your job to remind me. You're supposed to be heartbroken, in need of a friend."

Alex shrugged. "You cured me."

She threw him a dark glance. "You are so full of it. I really don't like lines."

"How do you know it's a line?" he asked. Alex knew he wasn't in love with Sophie, but the woman had damn well managed to make an impression on him during the short time he'd known her.

Sophie groaned and headed for the door. "It's time for you to go. Thank you for dinner."

Alex stood there in surprise. No one had ever thrown him out before. He deliberately left his sunglasses on the arm of the sofa. "You didn't answer my question. How do you know it's a line?"

"Because I'm smart," she said impatiently. "I may not be one-tenth as experienced as you, but I'm not a dummy. I know I'm not the kind of woman you usually look twice at, and I'm not the kind to change your world."

"Perhaps," he said, moving toward her. "But you could provide perspective. Being with you might make me see how shallow my choice in women has been. You may not consider yourself experienced, but you kiss like a courtesan. When you kiss, you make a man think of sex."

She hesitated a whole beat, then took a breath and lifted her chin. "Considering the fact that the average male thinks about sex once every two minutes, this is hardly groundbreaking."

Alex felt a scratchy impatience along the nape of his neck. He wasn't accustomed to impertinence. The women he dated might be spoiled and shallow, but at least they were agreeable. He leaned toward her and dipped his mouth just inches from hers. ''Okay, then it should come as no surprise to you that right now I'm imagining taking you out of that sundress and getting to know every inch of you from the top of your head down to your toes, and making you like every minute of it.''

# Chapter 3

Sophie had never felt such a strong desire to club a man. "It's time for you to go."

"What's wrong?" he asked in a silky voice that affected her in all her secret places as he stepped onto her porch. "Afraid of losing control?"

"Actually I am. It's called assault and battery," she said and closed the door in his face.

Her heart pounding a mile a minute, she paced the length of her den and drew deep mind-clearing breaths. She scowled. Why was Alex acting this way? Surely he could see that the route of friendship would be best for both of them. Besides he couldn't truly be attracted to her. She was pregnant for heaven's sake. That should be enough to squelch most men's desires immediately.

Still pacing, she couldn't decide if it was a plus or minus that Alex had come on to her knowing she was pregnant. Her ruthless honesty reared its head. If she were perfectly honest, she would have to admit that what bothered her far more than Alex's kiss was her reaction to it.

"Please hold for Her Royal Highness," the voice on the other end of the line said.

Alex was sorely tempted to hang up and blame it on a bad connection. It was a major pain when a man's mother was also his ruler.

"Alexander, I'm calling to check on your progress," his mother said.

"I took Sophie to dinner tonight," he told her.

"That's wonderful, and you're using her first name. Does she like you?"

"I think it's safe to say I inspire powerful emotions in her," he said, thinking of her comments just before she kicked him out of her house.

"That's wonderful news. I must say I'm surprised and delighted, Alex. You don't usually choose intelligent women, so I wasn't sure you would know how to treat one. I almost thought I should send an emissary on your behalf. Do you plan to tell her that you are her baby's father soon?''

"No rushing. Four weeks," he reminded. "You agreed."

"Yes, but I believe this should be taken care of as expediently as possible."

"And it will be," he told her firmly. "On my terms. You gave me your word."

She gave a long-suffering sigh. "As long as the press is kept at bay," she warned him. "The minute the media steps in, I will, too."

Not if he could help it, Alex thought.

On Saturday morning, Sophie reclined on her sofa with orange juice, and a plate with a croissant and a sliced peach. The sunlight shone cheerily through her window. Still dressed in her shorty pajamas, she savored the security and peace of the moment as she enjoyed the private pleasure of listening to her baby's heartbeat on tape.

Her doctor had chuckled at her request to tape the magnified sound of the life inside her. Even now, the sound made her smile and filled her with a sense of peace and rightness.

A knock sounded on her door and she frowned at the interruption. Using the stereo remote control, she turned down the volume and set her plate and glass on the end table. She walked to the door, looked through the peephole and scowled. Alex Dumont. What did he want?

She glanced down at her pj's and decided she wasn't indecent. Cracking the door open, she poked her head through. "Hello?"

"I came to get my sunglasses," he said, meeting her gaze. "And to offer an apology."

"Just a second," she said, and closed the door to collect his sunglasses. Returning, she cracked open the door again, slid her hand through the narrow space and offered the sunglasses. "Here they are."

He lifted a dark eyebrow. "No comment on the apology."

"Apology accepted, thank you. I need to go."

"I'd like to come in."

"I'm not dressed."

"At all?"

"Well, not appropriately—"

"Grab a robe. I have a proposition."

Sophie lifted her chin. "I think I've had enough of those from you."

"This one is harmless."

Sophie took in his dark hair, dangerous eyes and sensual mouth and knew nothing about this man could be harmless.

"C'mon, Sophie. All I want is for you to take a ride with me to the shore."

He'd found her weakness. She was always game for some time at the beach. "Which shore?"

"St. Patricia's Island."

Not touristy, she thought, her reluctance transforming into interest. "You have to have a special pass. They don't let everyone on the island," she told him.

"They'll let me," he said with a quiet confidence that made her curious.

She waffled. "No hanky-panky?" she asked.

He shrugged his broad shoulders, momentarily distracting her. "Not from me."

Her back stiffened slightly. "Nor from me. A day trip?"

He nodded. "That's why we need to get going. Do you want me to wait on the porch or in your den?" he asked archly.

The porch, she thought, but reluctantly relented for the sake of manners. She opened the door. "You can come inside. It won't take me long."

Grabbing her plate and juice, she headed for the hallway. "Have a seat."

Alex took in the sight of her slim legs and shapely backside as she retreated. Her house had the same soothing effect on him. In the background he heard a rhythmic swishing sound. "What is that noise?"

Sophie stopped midstep and glanced over her shoulder. Her smile combined self-consciousness and a contagious joy. "The baby's heartbeat. I taped it yesterday in the doctor's office. Turn it off if it annoys you," she said, and disappeared around the corner.

Alex's breath stopped. He stood in the center of her den and listened to the fast swishing heartbeat. The sound shook his foundations. He walked closer to the speaker to listen. This was the sound of life, a life partly formed by him. His knowledge or lack of it was unimportant.

The heartbeat continued. His child. He listened to the tape and heard the shared laughter of Sophie and the doctor. Then the sound stopped.

Alex glanced at the sound system and punched the button for rewind. He listened to the heartbeat again and let the sound emanate inside him. His child.

"I'm ready," Sophie said as she entered the room.

Alex glanced at her at the same time he heard the baby's heartbeat. His child. Her child.

She locked gazes with him for a long moment, then glanced down at her shirt. "You're staring. What's wrong? Do I have a stain?" She lifted her hand to her cheek. "A smudge?"

He shook his head. "I like your hair," he said.
So far, he liked her heart, he thought.

She absently patted her tousled curls. "Thank
you," she said with a cautious grin. "I think."

He extended his hand, but she gazed at him
warily. "I'm harmless," he said. "Remember?"

She gingerly took his hand. "So you say."

"You don't believe me," he said. "Then why
are you coming?"

"I rarely turn down an offer to visit the ocean.
I love the water," she said.

Good, he thought. A selling point, he thought
wryly. She may not like him, but his country was
surrounded by water.


It was a hot, golden summer day and Alex was
a gentleman. Sophie was relieved. At least, she
kept telling herself she was relieved. It was good
that he didn't try to kiss her or touch her. It was
good that he wasn't trying to seduce her, she told
herself, but wondered why she felt seduced anyway. He moved with athletic grace, and when he
introduced himself and her to the marina owner,
he exhibited confidence and an aura of power
she'd never seen before.

She sensed something brimming beneath the
surface of his gaze. She caught him looking at her
at odd moments and her stomach dipped with an

odd feeling of foreboding. It wasn't dangerous, just mysterious, she thought.

Or maybe she was just nuts.

She watched him staring out at the ocean as they stood on the beach. She wondered if he was thinking of the woman who hurt him. "You look like your mind is far away."

He nodded. "I'm thinking of an island I know off the coast of France, where the sand is like sugar and the water is the color of—" he turned toward her "—your eyes."

"Nice place, huh?" she asked.

He nodded. "At times a little small for my taste, but for the most part it's very nice."

"Do you go there often?"

"For business. My yachts are manufactured there. Have you traveled much?"

"I haven't had much of an opportunity," she said. "I have worked a lot of hours at the research center, so I spent most of my extra time fixing up my home. I'll probably be a homebody for a while with the baby coming."

He glanced at her intensely. "It's not safe for you to travel?"

She shook her head. "Oh, no, I'm past the first three months. The doctor told me I can do just about anything."

"Good," he said, and glanced at his watch.

"We should leave if we want to get back at a decent hour."

"Why did you say 'good'?" she asked, too curious to let his comment pass.

"It's good that you'll have the freedom to do what you want," he said with an enigmatic grin. "Who knows? Someone might come along and whisk you off to an island."

She walked with him toward the Jaguar. "I haven't had anything like that happen to me during the first thirty years of my life, so I don't think there's any cause for concern now."

Alex opened the passenger car door for her. "You didn't know me then."

She shot him a sideways glance. "I'll worry about that some other time. Soon enough, I won't be able to fit into my bathing suit."

Alex got into the car and slid a jazz CD from his small travel case into the player. Despite the fact that he had an unsettling effect on her, Sophie gradually relaxed during the return drive to Raleigh. Along the way she saw small roadside stands with tomatoes, corn, cucumbers and more. At one such stand, she saw a small collection of wooden furniture.

"Oh, look. Rocking chairs," she murmured.

"What?" Alex asked, slowing as they passed.

"Nothing," she said. "I just noticed that vegetable vendor also sells rocking chairs. I want to buy one sometime during the next few months.''

''I can turn around,'' he offered, slowing.

''No, it's not nece—'' She stopped when Alex turned around despite her protests. ''You didn't have to do that,'' she said as he pulled to a stop.

''It's no problem.'' He got out of the car and extended his hand to hers. ''Come along. You should choose only the very best,'' he told her.

''I fully intend to,'' she told him, ''since I'll be spending a lot of time in that chair. I hope this baby will be a rocker instead of a walker.''

''Rocker instead of walker?''

''Some babies prefer to be walked around rather than rocked, and I think that could get exhausting in the middle of the night.''

She sat down in one rocker, leaned back and began to rock. She felt Alex studying her face.

''Verdict?'' he asked.

She made a face and stood. ''The back hurts.''

''That's why we sell cushions, too,'' a woman at the vegetable stand said as she walked toward them carrying a selection of cushions. ''Hi, I'm Gladys Miller. See any of these you like?''

Sophie looked through the fabric colors and patterns. ''I hadn't totally decided on the nursery color.''

Gladys smiled. "Baby on the way. Congratulations to both of you."

"Oh, no," Sophie began. Horrified at the woman's assumption, she glanced at Alex for help, but he didn't look distressed.

"You're keeping it a secret a little longer," Gladys said. "That's okay. Your secret's safe with me. You're always safe going with white for the cushion color. White's okay for a boy or girl."

Confused by Alex's lack of reaction, she glanced from Alex to Gladys. "White shows dirt more easily."

"That's true," Gladys said, placing a cushion in the chair. "But these are one hundred percent washable. You can throw them in the dryer, too. Here. Take a seat and try it now."

Sophie sank into the chair and leaned back.

"Better?" Alex asked.

"Much," she said, wondering why he cared.

"What color finish do you like? My husband makes the chairs by hand and I make the cushions," she said proudly. "Do you like the pecan finish or the walnut? Or do you like this painted one? I like the stencil work on it. I always thought the dark mahogany was a bit heavy for a baby, but everyone's got their own tastes."

"I like the lighter pecan," Sophie said, rubbing

her fingers over the smooth wooden arms. She liked that the chair had been handmade. "The cutwork on it is beautiful."

"You can take it today," Gladys said. "I wonder if there's some way we can strap it to your car."

"Oh no." Sophie shook her head and smiled. The woman's sales tactics were friendly yet pushy. "I hadn't planned on buying today. And I don't think it would be a good idea to strap the chair to a Jaguar."

A moment of silence passed.

"If we pay you today, can you store it until we arrange to have it picked up?" Alex asked.

Sophie gaped at him. She opened her mouth in surprise.

"Of course," Gladys said, clearly pleased as punch to have made the sale.

"I didn't bring my checkbook," Sophie said.

Alex shrugged. "That's okay. I have cash."

She stood, wondering how this had gotten beyond her control in the blink of an eye. "But—"

Gladys patted her on the shoulder. "Let him fuss over you. You've got hard work ahead of you. I'll be back in a minute with a written receipt for you."

By the time she and Alex got back in the car,

Sophie's head was still spinning. "You must let me reimburse you."

"No," he said in an implacable voice.

She looked at him in confusion. "Why? I never would have said anything if I'd dreamed you would insist on buying a rocking chair for me. For goodness' sake, it's not as if you'll be using it."

She watched his jaw twitch slightly. "Consider it a gift."

"But—"

"Sophie, did you never learn the proper way to accept a gift?" he asked in a steel and velvet voice.

She was still confused. This made no sense to her, but if the man wanted to buy her a rocking chair, maybe she should just chill out. It wasn't as if he were offering her jewelry in exchange for sexual favors. She took a deep breath. "Thank you very much."

"You're welcome," he said and slipped another CD into the player, conveying without words that he didn't want to talk.

All Sophie could do was wonder what was ticking inside him, because his tension was so strong she was breathing it. As they drew closer to her house and the sun fell behind the horizon, she gazed at him surreptitiously in the darkness.

"Did you and your girlfriend have a disagreement over children?"

He shot her a quick glance of surprised bafflement. "Hell, no. What makes you ask that?"

She lifted her shoulders as he turned onto her street. "Well, you just seem different than most men about my pregnancy. I don't—"

Alex pulled to an abrupt stop and swore.

"What?" she asked. "Was there a dog or cat in the road?"

He stared into the distance at her house. "No, more like a rat."

She glanced at her house and saw several vehicles parked in her driveway and in front of her house. She frowned. "Who are they?"

"The press," he muttered, backing up and turning around. "Damn."

Her stomach took a dip of apprehension. "I'm boring. Why would the press be in my driveway?"

"Because you've been seen with me. I've got to get you away from here."

Her heart started to pound. "Alex, you're making me very nervous."

"Don't worry. I'll protect you. I'll take you somewhere they won't find you."

Alarm charged through her. "I just want to go home."

"Later," he assured her. "I'd never forgive myself if I let them near you."

She swallowed hard as he pulled onto the freeway. "I think you better tell me why the press is so interested in you."

"In just a minute," he said, punching out a number on his cell phone. "Jean Robert, the media has arrived. I need a jet and necessary transit papers in forty-five minutes. Raleigh-Durham Airport."

"Alex!"

He sighed, and she felt the silence with every beat of her heart. "I have a title that makes the press interested in me."

"And that title is?" Sophie asked, wishing her voice didn't sound so high. She just hoped his title wasn't escaped serial killer or dangerous lunatic.

"God, I hate this," he said. "My title is Prince."

# Chapter 4

*Dangerous lunatic,* Sophie concluded, and she began to perspire. She swallowed. "How long have you had this title?" she asked, her voice still much higher pitched than she preferred.

Alex shot her a quick glance as if she were dense. "I'm a prince, dammit. I've been one since I was born."

"If you don't mind my asking, from which country?"

"The island country of Marceau."

"I've never heard of it," Sophie said.

"It's off the coast of France."

"Oh," she said, wondering how she could

most expediently get out of this car. "You know, Alex, one of the wonderful things about the Raleigh-Durham area is that we have terrific medical facilities. Mental health facilities."

He glanced at her in astonishment and started to laugh. "You don't believe me. You think I'm nuts."

"Well, Alex," she said as patiently as she could, "just because someone suffers from delusions doesn't mean they can't be—"

"Delusions!" He roared with laughter.

She stiffened. "I've never heard of Marceau, and to be perfectly honest, I would like you to take me home."

He shook his head. "I'm not letting the press loose on you."

"I'm a grown woman. I'm perfectly capable of telling them to leave me alone."

He gave her a pitying glance. "You have no idea what you're in for. They're scavengers, probably going through your trash as we speak."

Sophie's stomach twisted in distaste. "Then I'll call the police."

"The police can't protect you, but I can," Alex said. He shifted slightly, withdrew a slim leather wallet and held it out for her. "Take a look at the card in the inner pocket."

Sophie opened the wallet and read the card with

the raised seal. "Alexander Claude Dumont, His Royal Highness. Marceau." It looked official, but she still didn't believe him. "I don't want to offend you, but documents can be falsified. I was serious when I told you we have some wonderful mental health facilities."

He shook his head and chuckled to himself. "And I was serious when I told you I was a prince. I've spent my life trying to keep that information secret, and the one time I need someone to believe it, she thinks I'm a nutcase."

"I didn't say you were a nutcase," she said, even though she'd thought it. He seemed so convincing. She wondered if most delusional people were this convincing. "I've just never heard of Marceau or you."

"What magazines do you read on a regular basis?" Alex asked.

"*The Journal of Computer Scientists, Research Laboratory Computing, State of the Art Simulation Studies for Advanced Computer Professionals.* I occasionally read the newspaper and novels by Janet Evanovich."

"But you don't read the celebrity or entertainment magazines, the ones at your checkout counter at the grocery store," he said.

"I can't say that I do," she admitted. "I did

pick up a parenting magazine at the doctor's office the other day, but—"

"You may stay current on periodicals related to your career, but you wouldn't win any trivia contests on public or entertainment figures."

Sophie felt a sinking sensation in her stomach. "I wouldn't," she admitted. "Would I have been likely to find references to your country and family in those publications?"

He gave her an unsmile. "Much more likely than finding us in computer journals."

"Oh." Sophie allowed the possibility that he was truly a prince to sink in for the first time. *Wow.* "I don't know what to say. I'm stunned. I've never met a—" She broke off when he took the exit for the airport. "I can just get a taxi home when we stop at the airport."

He shook his head. "No."

Sophie's stomach twisted. "No?"

"I told you I can't leave you to face the press. Especially in your condition. I'm taking you away from here."

"Absolutely not," she said, her heart hammering against her ribcage. "My home is here. My job is here."

"I can take care of all of that," he said, with the ease of a man who was accustomed to moving mountains with a few orders.

"I'm not getting in a plane with you. I don't have a passport. This is total insanity and unnecessary, and I'm still not totally convinced you're a prince," she said, although she was beginning to deeply suspect he was telling the truth. His slight foreign accent, his international education, his wealth, his aura of quiet command. Sophie began to perspire again. "I'm not getting on a plane with you."

"No need to worry. I may have my pilot's license, but I leave the big jobs to the professionals. I won't be flying the plane."

"I'm not getting on a plane with you."

Thirty minutes into the flight, Sophie stared at a tray of cheese, crackers and herbal tea. It would be a long time before she felt like eating. She was so upset she could spit.

A short, portly man named Jean Robert watched her as if he were certain she would leap out of the plane at any moment. She conceded the validity for his concern given the fact that he and Alex had practically dragged her onto the jet. She still didn't know how they had gotten her past customs with no papers, and she damn well wanted to know. "The least you can do is tell me how you managed to kidnap me from my own country's airport onto this plane," she told him.

He shifted slightly in his seat and tugged at his shirt collar. "We did what was necessary to protect you and the child."

"But I had no passport," she told him, wondering how he knew about her pregnancy.

"We were able to provide appropriate paperwork."

She narrowed her eyes at him. "What paperwork?"

He cleared his throat. "Appropriate paperwork."

She stood. "You owe me the truth," she demanded.

He also stood. "Please don't get upset. You shouldn't get upset," he pleaded with her.

Sophie's heart continued to hammer in her chest. At this rate she didn't know when she would calm down. Maybe in a month or two. "If you don't want me to be upset, then tell me the truth."

He swallowed audibly. "I'm not sure that will help."

"I can guarantee you that my blood pressure is higher than it has ever been. If you want to lower it, you'll tell me the truth."

Mopping his brow with a handkerchief, he gestured for her to sit down. "I will tell you what I can. As soon as His Royal Highness called me to arrange transport, I produced several documents that would ease the departure process.''

''Those documents were?''

''A marriage certificate authorized by the government of Marceau, additional Marceau citizenship records and as a last resort, a power of attorney transfer due to temporary mental incompetence.''

Just as Alex was wrapping up his discussion with the captain, he heard a scream from the cabin. The pilot's eyes widened. ''Your wife sounds upset.''

''Yes, she's a totally different person on the right medication. I'd better go.''

Alex walked through the living area of the luxury jet to the cabin in the back. He opened the door and a silver tray flew in his direction. Her eyes blazing like blue fire, Sophie continued to scream at the top of her lungs. Deflecting the tray, Alex glanced quickly at Jean Robert whose shirt appeared stained from tea.

''*Mon Dieu!* She told me she would calm down if I told her the truth.''

''How much of the truth?'' Alex yelled, dodging a cracker.

Jean Robert shook his head. ''I left the best for you.''

"You may leave."

The little man scurried out the door. "God bless."

"Let me out of here, you kidnapper!"

"We're at thirty thousand feet," Alex said. "I can't let you out."

"I want to talk to the captain. I want to tell him you are guilty of forgery and kidnapping and using false documents."

"The captain won't believe you. He thinks you're my temporarily mentally incompetent wife."

The fire in her eyes blazed hotter. "I want to talk to air traffic control."

"It won't make any difference. No one will believe you right now."

"They would if you told them the truth," she told him.

"I can't do that right now. I would not have handled the situation this way, but I cannot change the plan until we arrive in Marceau."

Tears filled her eyes and she shook her head helplessly. "You can't do this to me. It's not right. It's against the law, and morally—" She broke off and swallowed a sob. "I don't know how this happened to me. My life was fine, even wonderful, before you crashed into it. I wish I'd never met you. All I want is to go home and forget you exist."

The hopelessness in her voice tore at him. She looked up at him. "Are you some kind of monster? Why are you doing this to me?"

Alex felt his gut churn with turmoil. "I had to protect you and the baby from the press."

"The press would've been cake compared to this," Sophie insisted. "They would have eventually gone away after you did."

"No, they wouldn't have. You don't know everything."

"What else could there possibly be to know?"

"Sit down, please," he said as gently as he could.

"I don't want—"

"Sit down so you won't fall down when I tell you," he said, invoking an authority he rarely used.

Her eyes mutinous, she sank into the seat.

"I didn't want to tell you this way—" he began, and looked away from her. "The reason the press would never have left you alone is because the father of your child is a Dumont. The father of your child is me."

The plane felt as if it were tilting. Sophie grew light-headed. "Is there turbulence?" she heard herself ask as if she were speaking from a deep tunnel.

"No," Alex said, his face close to hers.

He looked worried, she thought. She felt his hands on her shoulders.

"Why is it so cold?"

"It isn't," he said, his face wavering in front of hers. "Don't faint, *ma chère.*"

She closed her eyes against the spiraling sensation, against him. She felt him gently shake her shoulders.

"You must not faint. You must be strong for yourself and the baby. You must—"

If he gave her one more *you must* she was going to club him. Sophie opened her eyes to slits. "You are a major P.I.T.A." she said, then closed her eyes again. "I'd like a few moments alone to digest this."

She felt his continued tense presence. "You won't hurt yourself, will you?"

"No. If I were going to hurt someone, it would be you or that short guy who falsified paperwork declaring me mentally incompetent."

"Temporarily mentally incompetent," Alex corrected.

The injustice sent her temperature through the roof again. Counting to ten, she opened her eyes and glared at him. "How long have you had to adjust to this information?" she demanded.

"Weeks," he admitted.

"Then I don't think fifteen minutes is asking too much, do you?"

He rose and looked down at her. "No. I'll check in later."

"Destroy the mental incompetency papers," Alex said to Jean Robert.

A mixture of alarm and protest crossed Jean Robert's face. "But what if she—"

"This plan has offended and upset the woman who is carrying my child."

"But she would not have come willingly," Jean Robert said, wearing a respectfully disagreeable expression.

"She's here now. The necessity for such a device is over."

"But she may try to leave the country."

"She has that right," Alex said, coming to terms with the knowledge that he and he alone would have to be protector and buffer for Sophie. "Do you like being forced, manipulated or tricked?"

"No," he admitted.

"Miss Hartman didn't choose this situation. Our objective is to show her the positive changes that my and my family's association with her will bring to both her and the baby.''

"Such as the wealth,'' Jean Robert said.

Alex thought about Sophie and what he'd learned of her priorities about life. She wasn't driven by wealth. "Perhaps not wealth,'' Alex said.

"Then power,'' Jean Robert suggested.

Alex sighed. Sophie struck him as a woman who was much more interested in having power over her own circumstances than having power over other peoples' lives. He shook his head. "Not power.''

"Fame? Ancestry?''

Alex bit back a grimace. Sophie wasn't the least bit interested in fame. "I'll let you know. In the meantime, destroy the false documents.''

He checked his watch and saw that he still had ten minutes to kill, so he gave Jean Robert instructions on preparations for his and Sophie's arrival. Alex was determined to keep their entrance low-key.

At exactly fifteen minutes since he'd last seen her, Alex entered the cabin fully prepared to dodge a barrage of questions along with another silver tray. Instead, he found her curled up on the couch sleeping.

Stepping closer, he studied her cramped, uncomfortable position. She looked as if she had fought her drowsiness, but the day had been too much and she had surrendered to temporarily resting her eyes. There was a lack of commitment to sleep in the way her fingers clutched her eyeglasses, the absence of a pillow for her head, and the lamp burning brightly down on her. Her only concession to comfort was her hand covering her face to shield her eyes.

A trickle of tenderness took him by surprise. Alex gingerly pried the glasses from her hand and placed them on the table beside her. He slid a pillow beneath her head and watched her shift into a more comfortable position. He pulled a blanket over her, cut the light and took a seat in the recliner facing her. The questions would come later.

Hours later he awakened to the scent of coffee and the sight of Sophie staring at him. She gave him approximately three seconds to gather his wits.

"How in the world did I end up with your sperm?" she asked.

Alex told her the entire story beginning with his mother's requirement of him and his brothers to make a deposit.

"Why did you lie to me about who you were?" she asked, her blue eyes laser sharp.

"I didn't lie. I just didn't reveal everything because I wanted us to get to know each other without the clutter of my unusual family situation."

"But you knew everything about me, didn't you?"

"I knew a lot," he conceded, "but—"

"So you had all the cards in the card game, all the control. I bet you weren't even suffering from a broken heart. Everything you told me was a lie."

"That's wrong," he said. "Neither of us holds all the cards in this game. You didn't request sperm from a royal family."

"No, I specifically requested high intelligence and average appearance, and I got you instead," she said in a disgusted voice.

Despite the gravity of the situation, he couldn't help wondering if he'd just been insulted or complimented. "Are you complaining about my appearance or intelligence?"

"Both," she said, returning to her characteristic frankness. "I'm sure I'm not the first to tell you that you are much more attractive than the average man. As far as intelligence is concerned, you need to remember I'm accustomed to dealing with research scientists, not yacht tycoons, not that there's anything wrong with yacht tycoons," she quickly added as if to soften the jab.

"I never would have taken you for a snob," he told her.

Her eyes grew wide with disbelief. "Me? A snob?"

He nodded. "A snob about intellect. It's important to you for your child to get the same genes as a geek, yet have a shortage of practicality and common sense to help him in this world."

"I didn't say I don't want my child to have common sense. I just wanted Peaches to have the benefit of high intelligence. But that's not the point," she said. "The point is you misrepresented yourself to me."

Alex ground his teeth. "So we could get to know each other without the complication of my family's position."

"So you could get to know me without me knowing who you really were."

The truth stung again. "You'll have plenty of time to get to know me now."

She paused and met his gaze with defiant blue eyes. "I'm not sure I'm interested."

# Chapter 5

After the jet landed in Marceau, Sophie and Alex remained silent as the chauffeur drove them down a curving road. Sophie took in the sights of the charming Mediterranean village. It was morning and shopkeepers were opening the windows to their stores and setting up carts on street corners. The vegetation was lush and green, the flowers vivid. As the chauffeur pulled to a stop beside a villa, she craned her neck for a peek at the ocean.

"You'll get a better view if you look between those trees once you get out of the car," Alex said. "According to my mother, this is the 'other side of the island.' Less populated, less tourists, less shops, and she refers to my house as a cabin,'' he said with a dry grin. ''The yacht-making business is here. I prefer it over the palace.''

''You like a little distance from the family politics, too,'' Sophie mused.

He shrugged. ''A continent and ocean are even better.'' He took her arm and led her to a clearing so she could see the ocean.

''It's so blue,'' she said, taking in the sunlit beauty.

''The color of your eyes,'' he murmured. ''Remember?''

Sophie thought back to the moment they'd shared on St. Patricia's Island just over a day ago. It seemed so long ago. Despite the fact that she still felt incredibly manipulated, the warmth of his hand on her arm was comforting.

''Come inside the cabin,'' he told her. ''You'll have plenty of time to sun in the yard or go to the beach later.''

Her hackles raised, she looked at him sideways. ''I won't be staying long.''

''We have to plan how to handle the press,'' Alex said and led her toward the villa.

''There's also my job,'' she began.

''Which has already been handled,'' he said, opening the front door. ''Ralph is pretty much indebted to you and me for the rest of his life and that of his firstborn child, so your job is secure.''

A vision of Ralph strung up by his toes flitted through her mind. ''It occurs to me that I don't know much about the politics of your country. Do you practice capital punishment?''

''I've thought about practicing it,'' Alex said darkly. ''My mother only has one guillotine in her basement and she reserves it for rare threats against her children. Capital punishment isn't practiced. Our people are very protective of each other, so it's not necessary. I make it my business not to get involved in politics. My oldest brother is welcome to all that. I supply the jobs, the products and find the markets.''

She sensed he found his royal responsibilities a burden and wondered if he would one day feel the same way about fatherhood. The thought nudged at her as she looked at his house. Italian tile greeted them in the foyer. Dark wood lent the home a rich, intimate feel. The long windows kept dreariness at bay. The furnishings looked more comfortable than elegant, spartan rather than cluttered.

It was a man's hideaway. A fresh fruit, wine and cheese basket, and the scent of pleasant cleaning disinfectant revealed someone had made preparations for their arrival. Alex led her past the kitchen, a large living area, bathroom, then upstairs to a suite of bedrooms and baths.

"This is your room," Alex said. "I'll be down the hall. If you should need anything, you can—"

"I'll be available for your service while you are in residence," Jean Robert said from behind them on the stairs.

Sophie frowned. "How did he get here?" she muttered.

"He was in the vehicle behind us," Alex said. "I'm not usually chaperoned when I stay here."

"So why now?" she asked.

His gaze fell over her, causing a surprising warm rush. "Because of me?" she asked.

Jean Robert joined them with an official air. "At your service."

"It occurs to me that I don't have any clothing, not that I'm going to need very much since I won't be here long," she quickly added.

*"Au contraire, mademoiselle,"* Jean Robert said, stepping to the dresser and opening a drawer to display its contents.

Sophie stared in surprise at the array of silk lingerie, shorts and tops, and bathing suits. "Who did this?"

"His Royal Highness contacted one of his staff from the airplane."

"But how did you know my size?" she asked, sifting through the clothes.

"I have an excellent eye," Alex said.

The sensual undertone in his voice made her heart go bump. "Well, thank you, I think."

He dipped his head. "If you need anything at all, don't hesitate to ask Jean Robert or me. Excuse me while I pay a visit to my workers."

She watched him leave and felt a strange tug in her heart. He wasn't what she'd thought. He was more than an idle rich boy, unimpressed by his title, eager to make his own mark. His discomfort in his own homeland bothered her. For some reason, she wished she could help with that. Some crazy reason, she thought, and shook off her thoughts.

"I'm curious, Jean Robert. What is your position with the royal family?"

He lifted his chin proudly. "I am the official royal confidential assistant."

"Then why are you baby-sitting me?"

He looked nonplussed. "Because you are—" He glanced down at her stomach and stumbled. "You are special to the royal family. You require special treatment."

Sophie translated his vague explanation. "I'm trouble."

"I didn't say that."

"Is it that unusual for Alex to have a woman here?" she asked, sinking down on the bed.

"His Royal Highness has never had a female visitor here. These are his very private quarters. It is his wish to protect you from anyone who might upset you."

"Then he needs to protect me from himself," she muttered. "I'd like the use of a computer."

"One has already been ordered and will be delivered this afternoon."

She paused in surprise, then decided she should stop being surprised. "I'll take a walk to the beach, then."

"I will escort you."

Sophie sighed. "I'll be frank. I haven't decided if I like you or not since you produced false documents declaring me mentally incompetent. Besides, I haven't had a baby-sitter in years."

"You have not been pregnant with a child of royalty, either, have you?"

The truth irritated her. "Okay, you show me around this time. Next time I'm on my own."

"But what if you should fall?"

"I'll do what I've always done," she told him. "I'll get back up."

The little man appeared dissatisfied, but he didn't argue. With a courtly air, he guided Sophie around the villa's small, but beautiful grounds,

then down the stone steps to the private beach.
She enjoyed an impertinent moment of satisfaction when he muttered something about sand in
his shoes. She took a long walk on the beach and
when they rounded a curve, the private beach became public. Sophie noticed with dismay that
most of the women wore only half of their bathing
suits. It was a topless beach. Although she knew
she could never do it, the freedom of the partial
nudity fascinated her.

"Just ahead is one of the yacht-building areas.
When he visits, His Royal Highness frequently
works alongside the workers. He has created
many jobs for our citizens, and they have great
respect for him."

"Does he visit often?"

"Three times per year," Jean Robert said. "He
seems always eager to leave. His mother is proud,
but misses him."

Sophie could imagine the woman's desire to
see more of her son. She might well be in the
same position when her child grew up. "Same
struggle whether you're royal or not. A mother
wants her children close by. A man wants to make
his own mark."

"He serves his country without surrendering
himself."

Tricky, Sophie thought, and spotted Alex sawing a piece of wood. Shirtless, he moved in a rhythmic motion, his muscles clenching, his skin tanned from the sun, glistening under the sheen of his perspiration. For just a moment, the murky image of him as her lover flitted through her mind. Her heart jolted, and she shook her head.

"Too warm?" Jean Robert clucked. "We must get you out of the sun. Something cool to drink and some rest after your long trip. I insist," he said when she started to protest.

Over the following days, Sophie developed a routine of taking a long walk on the beach at dawn and sometimes at dusk. In between, she worked on her simulation project with material sent her via e-mail. After a week, she craved more human companionship. During one of her walks, she stopped to watch two men play a game of chess. When one of the men had to leave, she offered to finish the game.

Her older competitor spoke more French than English, but she soon lost herself in the game.

"It's dark," Alex said, breaking her concentration. "We've been worried."

Sophie's heart picked up at the sound of his voice. She looked up and saw that fire lamps had been lit. "I forgot," she said, laughing with pleasure at how the game had distracted her.

*"Merci,"* she said to her competitor. "You're an excellent opponent."

The man rose and took her hand. "And you, mademoiselle. We play again?"

"I'd like that," she said. "Alex, this is Martin. He took pity on me and allowed me to finish a game of chess."

He nodded, studying the man intently. *"Bonsoir."*

The two men exchanged a few words in French, then Alex escorted Sophie toward the villa. "How long have you played chess?" he asked.

"Since freshman year in college. I even played on our college team for a year, but once I began working, I let it slip. Do you play?"

"A little," he said. "Perhaps we can start a game after dinner tomorrow night."

"You haven't been at the villa for dinner the last few nights," she said.

"No. I've been working on a new design for a yacht."

Surprised, she studied the planes of his face in the moonlight. "Really? Will you show it to me?"

He met her gaze. "Are you interested?"

She stopped. "Of course. Why wouldn't I be?"

"Most of the women I've known—"

"Oh, there's the first distinction. I imagine I'm definitely not like most of the women you've known."

He nodded, looking down at her. "You're more intelligent," he admitted. "Brutally honest at times. Vulnerable, but not helpless."

"I'm not vulnerable," she said.

He laughed, his teeth flashing white in the darkness. The sound zipped through her.

"Yes, you are. You're pregnant. You couldn't go into battle in your condition."

She searched his eyes. "Do I need to?"

His face grew serious. "No. I'll do that for you."

What battle? she wondered. She was unaccustomed to anyone protecting her, yet she knew that he would protect her. He would protect their child, too. The air between them grew intense with a swarm of emotion she couldn't decipher. Sophie took a shallow breath. "But we were talking about the other women you've known. I'll never be five feet eight inches tall and my face will never grace a fashion magazine cover, and that is okay with me," she added for good measure.

"And it's okay with me," he said, his expression mysterious. "Your problem is you're not shallow, vain or egocentric. It's hard enough keeping older men at the beach and delivery boys from falling for you. If we put you on the cover of a magazine with an interview, think how many hearts you'd break.''

It was the silliest backhanded compliment she'd ever received, but Sophie couldn't fight a rush of pleasure. She laughed. ''Is everyone in your family full of baloney?''

''I could take offense to that, but I won't. There are other members of my family who are dreadfully serious.''

The wind whipped through his hair and lifted his white shirt. A strange longing shot through her. He was such a compelling man. She couldn't take her eyes from him. ''I wish—'' she said, then shook her head and looked away.

He put his hands on her shoulders. ''Oh, no. Finish that.''

She looked up again. ''It doesn't matter.''

''Finish,'' he said. ''Please.''

Her lips twitched at the softening afterthought. Say what he might about disconnecting himself from his title, his royal attitude still showed itself on occasion. ''It's a silly thought, but sometimes I wish we had known each other under different circumstances.''

He nodded. ''That was why I waited to tell you who I was.''

"But that was one-sided," she said, and pulled back. She turned to climb the steps to the villa with a heavy heart and a mental overload of confusion.

The following evening after dinner, Alex invited her to his quarters. She was hesitant to join him until she saw the ivory chess set on a small table between two comfortable chairs. "It's beautiful," she said.

"My father gave it to me when I was ten," Alex said, waving his hand for her to sit. He picked up a piece and ran his fingers over it.

The movement reminded Sophie of the same caress he would use on a woman. She looked away, and her gaze encountered his large bed. She turned her visual attention to the picture on the wall behind Alex. "Did your father teach you to play?"

Alex nodded. "We spent hours playing chess. My oldest brother and I were the only two interested. I continued to play after my father died, but it's been a while since I've had a good game, so I may be a bit rusty."

Jolted by the new information, she looked at Alex. "I didn't know your father was dead."

Alex nodded. "When I was twelve. It was a huge loss for all of us. It changed my mother. She

lost her softness and became more intrusive. With
six children and a kingdom to manage, there was
little room for flexibility.'' As if he wanted to
reveal no more on the subject, he nodded toward
the board. ''Your move.''

And so the seduction began. Only, Sophie
didn't truly understand the seductive nature of
their chess game until their first game dragged on
for three nights and she finally won. He insisted
on a rematch. It was only fair, he said.

Chess became the great equalizer. When they
played, he wasn't a prince and she wasn't the
mother-to-be of his child. Along the way, she
learned bits and pieces about him that made her
want to know more. Every once in a while, he
touched her hand or arm and distracted the living
daylights out of her.

It surprised her, but despite all the manipulation
and the insanity of their situation, she liked him.
She liked the way his laughter rippled through
her. She liked the way he listened. She liked the
excitement in his voice when he showed her his
new yacht design. She enjoyed his interest in her
computer simulation studies.

Secretly she liked the way he relaxed around
her. Sometimes, though, the intensity in his eyes
took her breath.

Tonight he was winning, but Sophie was still

determined to win despite the fact that she hadn't been able to concentrate well all evening. As she studied the board, he twined his fingers through hers, further distracting her.

"Where are you, *chère?* You seem far away tonight."

The fact that he'd noticed made her weak. Sophie closed her eyes, enjoying the sensation of his warm hand and fingers enclosing and mingling with hers. She closed her eyes. "Let me finish this move." She reluctantly disengaged her hand from his and studied the board again. She made her move, and immediately realized her error.

So did Alex. As any true victor should, he took full advantage. "Checkmate," he said. "Now tell me what has been on your mind."

She held her breath and met his gaze. "I felt the baby move today," she said.

His eyes widened in surprise and he moved toward her, putting his hands on her abdomen as if it were instinctual. "So soon? Are you sure?"

She nodded, overwhelmed by an array of emotions about the baby and Alex. "At first I thought it might be indigestion, but my stomach wasn't upset at all. It happened several times throughout the day." Her heart swelled in her chest. "Peaches is getting bigger," she whispered.

In his eyes, she saw a mixture of the same wonder and joy she felt. He smoothed his hand over her stomach. "I want to feel it."

She swallowed a laugh at the demand in his voice. "I don't think you can yet."

"Why not?" he asked, the imperious note increasing.

She shrugged. "I don't think the movements are strong enough yet. Probably in a few weeks," she said, then felt a tinge of sadness. "If I'm still here."

His expression grew serious and he slowly withdrew his hands.

The magic of the moment disappeared like a vapor, and Sophie felt its loss. "Is your family pressuring you to take care of me?"

"My family pressures me about many things. My mother has threatened to disinherit me more than once, so this sure as hell isn't the first time," he said with wry laughter as he rubbed the back of his neck. "But I've always wanted to keep this between you and me as much as possible. This is too important not to listen to the voice inside me."

Sophie's admiration for him grew. "Sounds like your mom has some control issues," she muttered.

"Probably," he said. "Being queen has exacerbated them."

She smiled. "How hard is it to be you?"

"The responsibility of my legacy makes it more challenging. If I were to turn my back on my family, I would succeed and I would have more freedom, but in my way, I love my family and my country. In my way, I must contribute."

At that moment, Sophie felt her heart began to slide toward him.

The following day, Jean Robert took the day off and Alex was working with the yacht builders. She piddled with her computer work for a while, but her mind kept wandering to Alex, so she put it away. The sun shone brightly and with her baby-sitter gone, freedom beckoned. Sophie pictured the public beach with all the barely clad sunbathers. She would never be able to sunbathe topless, she told herself.

Well, she would never be able to sunbathe topless in front of other people. She gazed longingly at the private courtyard. Glancing down at her blossoming belly, she wondered if she had the nerve.

Sophie glanced through the drawer that held a bikini. A ridiculous prospect for a pregnant woman, she thought, as she lifted the two scraps of material. Despite all her sensible arguments to the contrary, she pulled on the bathing suit, grabbed a towel and lotion and walked down to the courtyard.

She settled into a chaise longue with a book and a CD boom box playing softly in the background. After looking approximately a dozen times from side to side for any signs of humans, she loosened the ties of her bikini top. She took a deep breath, then dropped the bikini top to the ground beside her.

## Chapter 6

Alex watched Sophie from the path leading to the beach. Shielded by trees, he stood perfectly still while he watched her battle her modesty, then bare her breasts to the sun.

The tiny bikini revealed the way her body was ripening from her pregnancy. Her abdomen swelled gently with their child, and her breasts were plump, her nipples like lush berries. An insidious, insistent desire twisted through him. He was familiar with the sensation. It had increased during their games of chess. Alex had never imagined a woman's intelligence and curiosity could be such an aphrodisiac. He never would have thought chess could feel like fore-play.

She poured sun tan lotion into her palm and worked it over her full abdomen. The movement of her hands made him grow hard. When she began to touch her breasts with the same caressing motion, his mouth went dry.

Heaven help him, he wanted her.

He'd never wanted a woman this way, this much. Before, it had been easy to take what was offered to him, because he hadn't been required to give much of himself. Sophie, however, wouldn't be satisfied with just his body. She would have to know his mind and soul, too. That knowledge both pleased and disturbed him. Without trying, she had changed his point of view. A part of him trusted her. She would never be careless with him. But he also knew that by virtue of his family, he threatened her autonomy, her control over her life and the baby's life.

Torturing himself a little longer, he watched her finish applying the lotion, then lean back in the lounge. Her skin gleamed from the lotion. Even from this distance, he could see her nipples were erect. It was ironic as hell that the woman he wanted was carrying his child, but he'd never made love to her. In his mind, he caressed her body with his hands and mouth. He suckled her nipples and made love to her. He slid between her legs and made her his. How much longer before his thoughts became real?

That night after Sophie and Alex ate sandwiches for dinner and she joined him for the continuation of their latest chess match, she sneaked a quick glance at the pink skin of her chest and grimaced.

"Too much sun?" Alex asked in a mild voice.

"I guess. I used sunscreen," she murmured.

"Did you apply it before you went outside?"

"No," she admitted.

"Ah," he said. "I have aloe."

"Okay," she said, thinking she would take the bottle and apply it in the privacy of her room later.

Alex pulled the bottle from a cabinet. "Loosen your blouse and I'll put it on your back."

Sophie's stomach tightened. "Uh, that's okay. I can do it."

"Nonsense. You can't reach back there."

"I—uh, I'm not sure the burn is on my back."

"Really?"

"No."

"Then where do you think it is?"

"On my front," she said cheerfully, and extended her hand for the bottle.

Alex moved the bottle out of reach. "Where?"

Embarrassed, she bit her lip. "I thought it might be kinda nice to sun so I don't have strap marks."

Alex set the bottle down and began to unbutton her blouse.

She covered his hands with hers. "No, I—"

"Do you trust me?"

The expression in his eyes made her mouth dry. She opened her mouth, but nothing came out. "Uh, kinda," she finally managed.

She allowed him to continue to unbutton her blouse. Holding her breath because she knew she wasn't wearing a bra, she could feel his gaze on her breasts.

"Ouch," he murmured. "You should take better care, *chère.*" He guided her to sit on his bed and began to apply the aloe to her chest. With gentle strokes, he slid the cool lotion over her. She closed her eyes as her nipples stiffened. She felt a pleasurable twist of sexual tension between her thighs.

This wasn't smart, she told herself, but his hands felt warm and the lotion was soothing, and she wanted more. He lingered on her nipples more than was necessary, but with each stroke she felt a seductive tug of arousal.

"If your skin weren't so tender, I would want

to take your breasts into my mouth,'' he murmured.

She wanted him to do just that, tender or not. He made her feel incredibly sensual.

He leaned down to blow over her stiffened tips.

Sophie sucked in a quick, shallow breath. Her heart was pounding. All the games of chess and walks on the beach had forced her to learn more about him. The more she learned, the more she wanted to know. In dark moments at night, she'd remembered the time he'd kissed her at her house in Raleigh. There were many reasons she shouldn't be sitting on his bed topless, but at the moment she couldn't muster one. She only knew she wanted him to kiss her again, touch her again.

As if he read her mind, he lowered his head and tasted her mouth with his tongue, the same way she knew he would taste her entire body.

Sophie felt herself warm and blossom beneath the caress as he joined her on the bed. Ditching her inhibitions the same way she had earlier in the day, she kissed him back, responding to his seduction, drawing his tongue more deeply into her mouth.

His hand grazed her breast, then he muttered

against her mouth, "You're burned. I don't want to hurt you."

"You won't," she said, and couldn't withhold another moan when he caressed her. He touched her with tender sensuality, then lowered his hands to her shorts and pushed them down her legs.

"There's no reason for me to stop this time," he warned her, skimming his tongue down her neck.

"I know," she said, and wondered why this felt so right and scary at the same time.

"Touch me," he told her in a low, needy voice that made her heart race. "You've touched my mind. Damn if you haven't touched my heart. Now touch my body."

Part command, part plea, his words made her crazy. With hasty hands, she unbuttoned his shirt and tugged it from his shoulders. She ran her hands over his muscular chest and lower. Unfastening his shorts, she pushed them down and touched him intimately.

While his mouth took hers in a kiss that drove them both hotter and higher, she stroked his hard masculinity. One of his hands slid between her thighs, seeking and finding her moist and aroused.

"You feel so good," he told her, toying with

her, making her swell beneath him like a bud ready to bloom. Lowering his head, he dropped kisses down the front of her body until he came to her thighs. He kissed her intimately, and the wicked stroke of his tongue sent her over the edge.

Sophie gasped at the speed and force of her response. Staring into his dark gaze, she felt herself tumbling for him, toward him, unable to stop. "This has been coming since before I met you," he said, looking at her with wonder and aching desire in his eyes.

He parted her legs and entered her with a sure, but gentle thrust that took her breath. He filled her with delicious completeness. She instinctively tightened around him and he closed his eyes in pleasure, muttering something in French.

Taking a deep breath, he opened his eyes and looked at her. Lifting her palm to his mouth, he kissed it, then entwined his fingers through hers. She felt him inside her, all around her, and that last gesture stole another piece of her heart.

"You are so beautiful," he said. "So incredibly beautiful."

Sophie knew there was no way she was the most beautiful woman he'd known, but his words touched a secret place inside her. He already had her. Those words hadn't been necessary, yet he'd said them. Her heart was so full, she wanted to give him everything.

She tightened around him again, and he groaned. Moving in a fluid, mind-robbing rhythm, he stretched inside her, filling her, caressing her intimately with every stroke. At the same time she saw his face tighten with pleasure, she felt herself spiral upward. One last thrust, and he climaxed, murmuring her name.

Sophie spent the night in his arms. She knew that ultimately nothing had been settled. They had yet to discuss the future, but she knew she had feelings for Alex that she'd never experienced before. When she awakened in the morning, he was gone, but he'd left a rose on his pillow. The scent reminded her of the sweetness of their lovemaking.

Excited and unsettled, she rose from his bed and showered. Distracted, she ate a small breakfast and tried to work. She made a little progress on the simulation studies, then forwarded her information to the institute via the Internet. The sound of several car engines entering the driveway interrupted her. Unable to see the cars from her window, she rose from the desk.

A knock sounded at the door followed by several voices. Before she knew it, Jean Robert met her at the top of the stairs. "Her Royal Highness, Queen Anna Catherine, is downstairs waiting to meet you."

Her stomach immediately tightened. Sophie glanced down at her casual shirt and shorts. "I'm not exactly dressed for the occasion."

"Perhaps you can change quickly," he said, guiding her back to her room. He whisked through her closet and pulled out a dress as if he'd performed the same kind of task a hundred times before. "I must warn you the queen doesn't like to be kept waiting."

"Has she heard of the telephone? Even an e-mail would have been nice," Sophie grumbled, then waved him out of the room. "I'm not prissy. I'll be down in a minute." Her stomach began to dance with more nerves. "Jean Robert, is she kind at all?"

He stopped, and she saw loyalty and honesty war on his face. "She can be quite kind. She has the heart of a lion and a lamb combined, but she is—" He groped for the best word, but couldn't seem to find it.

"Tense?" Sophie guessed.

He nodded. "Tense. Change quickly," he said, and left the room.

Sophie pulled the dress over her head and wished she had a paper bag to prevent hyperventilation. She fluffed her hair, stepped into a pair of sandals and took a breath before she descended the stairs.

Two men who resembled bodyguards stood on either side of Alex's mother along with a beautiful, much younger woman with curious eyes. "Her Royal Highness Queen Anna Catherine of Marceau and Princess Michelina, I present Miss Sophie Hartman," Jean Robert said.

Sophie had the odd sense the sound of trumpets should have followed. She managed a smile and gave a slight dip of her head. "It's a pleasure to meet you. I apologize, but I don't know the protocol for meeting royalty. I think I may need to take Bow and Curtsy 101."

Michelina giggled in approval. Queen Anna Catherine did not.

"Your pregnancy is showing," she said. "Has my son proposed yet?"

"Mother," Michelina said in dismay.

"You may be excused," the queen said to her bodyguards. "Jean Robert, please bring us some tea." She glanced around the room and shook her head. "Why he prefers this over the palace, I'll never know. Let's sit in the living area."

Sophie decided "tense" was an understatement when describing the queen. She took a deep breath to keep from reacting to the woman's strong aura. She also decided she was keeping her side of this conversation to a minimum.

"Please call me Michie or Michelina, whichever suits you. Alex tells us you're a computer expert," Michelina said.

Sophie was drawn to the warmth of Alex's sister. "Yes, I do computer simulation studies for the institute in Research Triangle Park in North Carolina. I've always had a knack for computers. And you?"

"Michelina just completed her studies at the Sorbonne," the queen said, "and we're still determining the best use for her talents."

"I'm interested in doing some additional studies in New York. I find your country fascinating."

"As does my son Alex," the queen said with her first touch of wry humor. "How are you feeling? Is the nausea gone?"

Disconcerted at the woman's knowledge about her, Sophie hesitated a half beat. "I'm doing great. The nausea has been gone for weeks, thank goodness. I just recently began to feel the baby move."

The queen nodded with a faint smile as Jean

Robert returned with a tray of tea. "I remember…" She seemed to catch herself and focused again on Sophie. "I've permitted Alex to handle this situation in his way until now, but I feel compelled to step in."

"Really? Why's that?" Sophie asked before she could stop herself.

The queen looked slightly affronted, as if she weren't accustomed to being questioned. "Because you have not married yet, and Alex may have experience with women, but not with women of intelligence."

He does now, Sophie thought. "Has Alex indicated that he planned to marry me?"

"Alex indicates as little to me as possible, but I believe he agrees that this child deserves a home with two parents. Don't tell me he hasn't discussed this with you? I was afraid he would mishandle this."

Sophie was torn between the idea of Alex marrying her for duty and the queen's criticism of him. "Alex hasn't handled our situation perfectly. I'm not sure anyone has, but I believe he is listening to his heart and his head."

The queen studied Sophie. "Are you in love with him?"

Sophie's heart hammered. "I'm not comfortable with your questions at this point," she confessed. "But I will tell you something I'm sure you already know. You have every reason to trust your son. You helped shape a man with heart and the kind of confidence you can't get from a title. He is his own man probably like his mother is her own woman."

The queen softened slightly and sighed. "But I do have an interest in the welfare of this child."

"I appreciate that," Sophie said. Then a terrible thought crossed her mind. "This baby wouldn't be anywhere close to inheriting the throne or anything, would—"

"Not a snowball's chance," Michelina reassured her cheerfully. "They have to go through four other brothers and their male children—when they get around to having them—unless of course," she added with a combination of sly innocence, "those sperm samples turn up somewhere else they're not supposed to."

"I told you not to refer to that again," the queen said.

"Oops. Sorry," Michelina said.

"We should leave," the queen said, rising despite the untouched tea.

She looked at Sophie again, a thousand questions in her eyes. Sophie had the strong sense that it took enormous restraint for the woman not to demand answers.

"How have you become acquainted with my son?" she finally asked as she moved toward the door.

Following them, Sophie shrugged. "We play chess."

An expression of realization crossed both her and Michelina's face. "Have you bested him?" Anna Catherine asked.

"Yes," Sophie said, and dutifully added, "He beat me, too."

"Ah," the queen said with a mysterious smile. "It was good to meet you. Take care of yourself, *chère,* and the child."

Sophie watched them leave and tried to digest the entire visit. She turned to Jean Robert. "Excuse me, but did I just tell the queen to mind her own business and I survived?"

"You did," Jean Robert said.

"And you're sure Marceau isn't into the guillotine?" she asked, still unsettled.

He waved in a dismissing gesture. "Oh, it's been centuries since the guillotine was used."

"Good," she said, "I think."

"After His Royal Highness gets over his mother completely ignoring his request to leave you alone, he'll be very impressed with the way you handled her.''

Sophie nodded, thinking. "Why did she ask about chess?''

"His Royal Highness has fond memories of playing with his father. He was so expert, he represented Marceau in a European competition and won.''

"Which royal highness?'' she asked. "Alex or his father.''

"Alex.'' He raised his eyebrow at her, revealing he knew entirely too much. "Smarter than you thought he was, isn't he?''

"Yes, he is. Much smarter,'' she said, and decided to take a long walk on the beach.

The day was beautiful, the temperature perfect, the slight breeze heavenly. Sophie barely took it in. She was so busy pondering the questions Alex's mother's visit had conjured.

*Much smarter* than she'd thought. For a few moments she wondered if he'd devised this plan to persuade her to do what he wanted. The man she'd come to know, however, wasn't that manipulative. She could see how much he resisted and resented manipulation from his own family. No, he wanted to operate from his own inner integrity. She admired him for that.

She feared he would never be able to look at her without thinking of her as his ultimate personal sacrifice. His duty. The thought sickened her. She didn't want to be that to him. He was a wonderful man. He deserved to love and be loved with passion. If she stayed with him, if she married him, she would always wonder if she was who he truly wanted and needed.

Her heart ripping, she knew what she had to do.

# *Chapter 7*

She tossed her backup zip drive, a few toiletries and a change of clothes into a plastic bag and paced the bedroom as she composed her words to Alex.

"I don't want to be an obligation or a duty," she murmured as she paced. "You deserve better. I—" She broke off when she heard him enter the villa.

Her stomach twisted in a vicious knot. She heard him climb the stairs. Unable to bear the dread a second longer, she flung open the door. "I need to talk to you," she said, her breath so tight, she could barely draw a breath.

His face tightened with concern. "*Ma chère*, you're pale. Sit down. Is it the baby?"

She wrung her hands. "No, I can't sit. No, it's not the baby. It's me and you and the baby and your mother—"

"My mother!" he thundered.

Sophie continued to wring her hands. She prayed she could say what she needed to say. She prayed she would have the strength to do the right thing. "Your mother paid a visit today, but—"

"*Today!*" he roared, his volume climbing. He rolled into a spate of French she didn't understand, but suspected it wasn't a litany of praise for his mother.

"Alex, you can scream at her later. I need to tell you why I'm leaving."

He went completely silent, his face creasing in confusion. "You're leaving?"

"I must," she said, and her heart ripped a little further. "You are a wonderful man and Peaches will be very lucky to have you for a father, but I can't marry you because I would always wonder if you married me out of obligation, and that would kill me. You deserve better than to marry me out of duty. You deserve to marry for love—" She held up her hand when he opened his mouth to interrupt.

"This is hard for me. Please let me finish," she

said, hating the crack of emotion in her voice. "You and I may have feelings for each other, but the problem is," she said, hearing her tone grow high and strained and feeling her throat tighten, "because of the way we met, I'll never know if you wanted me out of duty or if you wanted me for me. And I just can't live like that," she finished in a whisper, her eyes burning with tears.

She swallowed and closed her eyes against the waves of pain. "I need to leave. If you're worried about the press, send Jean Robert with me. He's short, but shrewd."

"I don't want you to go," Alex said.

"Yes, but you'll let me because you would want the same freedom."

He stood there, his eyes dark with pain and anger. It emanated so strongly from him it was all Sophie could do not to take back her words and hold him. But she couldn't if she was determined to give him the freedom of choice she knew he craved.

"You may go. I'll arrange the charter," he finally said.

Alex made it all happen so quickly, her head spun with the speed of it, her stomach turned with the finality of it. With Jean Robert alternately shooting her looks of disapproval and desperation, he climbed into the opposite side of the limousine.

Alex opened the door for her, but blocked her entrance. "Wherever I am, *chère,* there will be a place for you. *Au revoir.*"

Unable to speak, she got into the car and burst into tears. Jean Robert spent the entire ride to the airport trying to persuade her to stay with Alex, but Sophie was determined. Even as they waited in a private seating area, he continued to hound her.

"*Mon Dieu!* You are making a terrible mistake. You are ruining his life and yours. And what of your baby? Your baby deserves a father, *non?*"

Sophie blew her nose with the handkerchief Jean Robert had offered her. "The baby will have Alex as a father regardless of anything I do. I'm not ruining his life. Can't you see I'm giving him what he wants and needs more than anything?"

"What could that possibly be?"

"A choice."

"That is not true," Jean Robert protested. "You do not allow him to choose *you.*"

"Why would he choose me?" she argued, refusing to allow the strange expression on Jean Robert's face to distract her.

"Because you are the most passionate, intelligent and loving woman I have ever met," a voice from behind her said.

Sophie froze. She had decided she wouldn't be

hearing that voice for a long, long time. The room felt as if it were spinning. She turned around and wobbled as she looked into eyes so fierce with passion and emotion she could barely stand it. "Alex?" she whispered.

He caught her by the shoulders when she wobbled again. "I would choose you because you know me better than anyone ever has. Because you make me better than I was. I would choose you because you make me complete in a way I never thought I would be. Because I love you."

Sophie couldn't believe her ears. Her heart couldn't comprehend his words. Another stream of tears ran down her cheeks. She looked at him in confusion. "But your family," she said. "Your responsibility—"

"Losing my title matters little to me," he said, and Jean Robert murmured something desperate in French.

"Losing you would be the tragedy of my life."

As she looked into his gaze, everything clicked into place for Sophie. A sudden peace and joy overwhelmed her. She didn't know how it had happened and couldn't imagine explaining it, but fate had brought her and Alex together for more than the baby. She loved him. He loved her, and everything was going to be okay.

Swiping the wetness from her cheeks, she

sniffed. "Would you like to take a little break from island life with me and visit the States for a while?"

Comprehension dawned. Alex's face cleared and he gave a smile that would always make her heart turn over. "Yes. North Carolina?"

"I'd like to see your place in Laguna Beach, California."

"Done," he said, pulling her into his arms and holding her so tight, she could hardly breathe.

"Other than not telling me who you were from the beginning and letting Jean Robert claim I was mentally incompetent, you only did one thing wrong."

"What's that?" he asked, pulling back to look at her.

"You never asked me to marry you," she said, lifting up on tiptoe to kiss him. "But don't worry. You still have time."

# *Epilogue*

Five months later Alex and Sophie welcomed Peaches into the world at the Jules Dumont Hospital in Marceau. During the beginning stages of labor, Alex had distracted her with a game of chess, but Sophie had grown tired when the labor dragged on for eighteen hours. The doctor had mentioned the possibility of a cesarean section, but with her husband's encouragement, she had summoned the strength to finish the delivery. Tears of relief fell from Alex's eyes.

"It's a boy," the doctor said with a smile as the baby let out a lusty cry. "Great lungs."

The nurse cleaned and weighed the infant, then wrapped him in a blanket and placed him in Sophie's arms. Sophie immediately fell in love with her child. "He's beautiful," she said as her little darling let out another cry. "And he's got the Dumont temper."

Alex cupped his son's head and rubbed a tear with the back of his hand. "I hope he'll have blue eyes like yours."

Despite her exhaustion, Sophie's heart was so full she thought it might overflow. She remembered the day everything had changed and Alex had left Marceau with her. After a week in California, they'd married in a private ceremony in Marceau, then returned to the States again. The rocking chair Alex had bought her so many months ago had been delivered to her home in Cary—but she and Alex had brought it with them to Marceau. It was waiting for her back at the palace.

As a concession to her new family, Sophie decided to give birth to her baby in Marceau. Jean Robert had told her this was a gesture of peace the queen would never forget. For some reason, Alex's relationship with his mother had improved immensely. She allowed him the freedom he needed and he was supplying her with her fourth grandchild.

"I love you," Sophie said to Alex. "Thank you for giving him to me."

Alex looked into her gaze with pure devotion. "After you've rested, I'll give you more. I've always thought strip chess sounded more interesting than strip poker."

She laughed with joy. The door to the delivery room swung open and Queen Anna Catherine entered, followed by Alex's brothers and sister. His oldest brother, Prince Michel, the heir and most serious, gravely looked at the baby. One of the twins gave a thumbs-up, while the other passed a cigar to Alex. His other brother, Prince Nicolas, a medical resident, patted Alex on the back. Princess Michelina craned to get a better peek. Bringing up the rear, Jean Robert gave a wink of approval.

The queen looked down at her grandson and covered her lips with her hand. Overcome, she shook her head. "He looks just like you when you were born." She glanced from Alex to Sophie with a wistful smile. "Many people have wondered why I had so many children," she said. "The reason is because your father and I loved each other so much. I see that same love between you and Sophie. You are blessed.''

Alex squeezed Sophie's hand and she knew he felt the same way she did. The blessing of their love and life together had just begun.

\* \* \* \* \*

*If you loved the story of Sophie and Prince Alex, be sure to watch for Prince Michel, the next royal member of the Dumont family, to find true love, in*

### ROYAL DAD

*the upcoming book in Leanne Banks's exciting new miniseries*

### THE ROYAL DUMONTS.

*On sale in September 2001, from Silhouette Desire.*

# REGENCY ROMANCE

Visit the elegant English countryside,
explore the whirlwind of London Society
and meet feisty heroines who tame roguish
heroes with their wit, zest and feminine
charm in...The Regency Collection.

*Available in July 2001 at your favorite retail outlet:*

**THE LARKSWOOD LEGACY**
by Nicola Cornick

**MISS JESMOND'S HEIR**
by Paula Marshall

**A KIND AND
DECENT MAN**
by Mary Brendan

**AN INDEPENDENT LADY**
by Julia Byrne

Visit us at www.eHarlequin.com